Other Titles By

A. C. Arthur

LOVE ME CAREFULLY

OBJECT OF HIS DESIRE

OFFICE POLICY

UNCONDITIONAL

Within the Shadows

A. C. Arthur

Parker Publishing, LLC

Noire Passion is an imprint of Parker Publishing, LLC.

Copyright © 2007 by Artist C. Arthur

Published by Parker Publishing, LLC
12523 Limonite Avenue, Suite #440-245
Mira Loma, California 91752
www.parker-publishing.com

This book is a work of fiction. Characters, names, locations, events and incidents (in either a contemporary and/or historical setting) are products of the author's imagination and are being used in an imaginative manner as a part of this work of fiction. Any resemblance to actual events, locations, settings, or persons, living or dead, is entirely coincidental.

ISBN 978-1-60043-012-1

First Edition

Manufactured in the United States of America

Dedication

"Some friendships do not last, but some friends are
more loyal than brothers."
- *Proverbs 18:24*

To my friends—you know who you are—what I lack in number
is exceeded in love and support.

Acknowledgements

I would be ungrateful if I did not acknowledge my Lord and Savior for the gift He has given me and the people He has placed in my life to make sure that the gift is used.

To my Koinonia Baptist Church family: you encourage me, you frustrate me, you give me more material than I could ever use, but most of all you love me for being me. Thank you and may God continue to bless the vision.

To my Arthur family: Damon, André, Asia and Amaya. Thank you for everything, again and again…

To the extended Arthur and Moore families: It's not possible to name you all and all that you do for me (because that would be about three additional books) but know that you are all greatly appreciated.

To the ladies of Parker Publishing, LLC: I am so proud to be a part of this venture, so proud to know and love you all. Keep it moving and keep it real! ac

Prologue

D ry leaves and twigs cracked and snapped beneath booted feet. A heavy blanket of darkness surrounded them, and sounds of wilderness echoed in the distance.

Blood pumped hot and fierce through his veins as he watched her struggle. She was beautiful. She was his.

They had been the perfect couple, their future together as clear and enticing as anything he'd ever imagined.

Then she'd changed. They'd changed her.

Landy.

She was the love of his life, and they'd taken her away from him. They'd taken the one thing that he'd longed for, and he despised them for it.

Now they would pay. They would all pay for the pain they'd caused.

Tonight his quest for retribution would begin.

She watched him, her large eyes wide and focused on his every move.

Blood trickled down the right side of her face, its darkness marring her perfect honey- hued skin. He hadn't meant to hurt her, but she hadn't been acting like herself. She had been saying things to him. Mean things. Things he knew they'd put into her head. He'd tied her hands and feet to keep them still. Breasts, full and plump, strained against the material of her shirt and he licked his lips. She squirmed and a bit of her belly showed above the rim of her pants. He stiffened, heat rushing to his groin.

She was his. She would always be his. This was the only way to make sure of that.

Within the Shadows

He'd taped her mouth, which made her appear helpless, but he knew better. She knew how to hurt him. She'd done so many times before.

Tonight would be different. He was in charge, and he'd made sure she knew it. From the depths of his being he loved her and knew that she loved him back. His heart hammered mercilessly against his rib cage until the thought of it simply bursting was all too real. This had to be done. She'd left him no other choice. They'd left him no other choice.

Looking down at her, he remembered happier times. With the back of his hand, he wiped the sweat from his forehead and tried to focus. He'd loved her for so long his mind had almost become oblivious to anything else. He'd loved the sound of her voice—smooth and melodic like a Sarah Wilson classic. It didn't matter what she said; he'd been spellbound by the first syllable. Kneeling in front of her, he blinked against his own tears, needing to hear her voice just once more. With slow, deliberate motions, he pulled the duct tape from her lips.

"Please, let...me...go," she spoke immediately, panting with each word. "Let me go."

He smiled, the sound of her voice filling his head, flooding his heart with a surge of inexplicable emotion. Tears streaked her face, running alongside blood. With a trembling hand, he wiped both away.

"Please," she whispered again.

Bringing his hand to his mouth, he licked the tears and blood from his fingers, let the acrid taste linger on his tongue, and moaned in ecstasy.

Chapter 1

Ten Years Later

Turning off Main Street, Nathan Hamilton steered his silver Lexus into the visitor's parking lot of Tanner City Hospital and combed the narrow lanes for an available space. Breathing a sigh of relief when he spotted a minivan pulling out, he switched his left turn signal on before cautiously turning into the opening.

He was back in Tanner. After ten years, he'd finally come home. *Home.* The word sounded foreign to him. He'd been away so long, he'd forgotten what a real home was. The small town looked the same. He'd noted that on the drive from the airport.

Nothing had changed, and yet everything seemed different.

Stepping out of the car, he inhaled the sweet smell of spring in Maine. The air was still a bit brisk, but it was April; things would warm up soon. New York never smelled like this, never sounded like this. The quiet alone should have been enough to bring him back.

Walking toward the entrance of the hospital, he tried to focus on the reason for his return. He had a job to do. Eli wanted to leave the hospital for private practice and needed him to take over the growing maternity wing. It was that simple.

Who was he kidding? It wasn't that simple. The letter. It had come via FedEx. Someone had wanted to be sure he received it. The words written on plain white paper had scared him, opening wounds he'd tried to tuck away, making him remember what was probably best forgotten.

But those things had not been all that brought him back. Like metal to a magnet, he'd been steadily drawn toward Tanner, making his way back to the town he'd left and to the girl who'd turned him away.

The electronic doors opened as they sensed his presence, and he stepped into the busy foyer of the hospital's main floor. He felt a little out of sorts. Would anybody recognize him? Would they whisper behind his back as they had done in the days before he left?

"Good morning." A smiling elderly woman wearing a green and white volunteer badge greeted him.

She didn't look familiar to him. And apparently, he didn't look familiar to her either. For the moment he was relieved.

"Good morning, I'm Dr. Hamilton. I have an appointment with Dr. Grant."

"Oh, yes sir, it's right here in the log. You'll want to take the east elevators to the sixth floor. Dr. Grant's office is immediately to your right."

"Thanks," Nathan leaned over the counter to get a closer look at her badge, "Earline."

Earline smiled brightly. "You're very welcome."

He walked down the hall, his Kenneth Cole tie-ups clicking against the buffed floors. He made a right turn beneath a sign that pointed towards the east elevators and followed the hallway until he spotted them. Pressing the button, he waited for the elevator doors to open. Out of nervousness, he straightened his tie and cleared his throat. This was a big step for him, one that he knew would either make or break him.

When the elevator arrived, Nathan stepped inside, and two nurses boarded with him. He stood in the corner, holding the handle of his briefcase in a death grip. His heart thumped in his chest as he wondered if they would notice him. They didn't.

Stepping off the elevator, he admonished himself, turned to the right and walked until he saw the black sign, *Dr. Elias P. Grant, Head of Obstetrics*.

He knocked only once before the door was pulled open.

"Nate! How are you? I've been waiting for you!"

Elias Grant, tall and graying at the temples, held out his hand in greeting.

"Mornin', Eli." Nathan gave his old classmate a tense smile as he shook his hand. Although he'd talked to Eli a few times since his departure, he still wasn't sure how Eli felt about what had happened that night.

"Have a seat." Eli motioned to Nate before going around the desk and sliding into his own chair. "It's good to see you. What's it been? Six, seven years?"

Nathan's palms were sweating. He rubbed them against his thighs and kept his eyes focused on the man he'd once called friend. "It's been ten years since I left Tanner and seven since I saw you in New York at the convention."

"Yeah, seven long years that I've been workin' my butt off trying to get you to come back. Now you're finally here. I can't believe it."

"I can hardly believe it myself," Nathan muttered. Eli didn't respond. Nathan used those few minutes of silence to take in Eli's office.

His certificates of qualification hung on the wall in sleek black frames, and silver ornaments adorned the credenza and glass-topped desk. A plant housed on the windowsill looked to be about on its last leg.

Nathan suppressed a grin. Eli had done everything he'd said he would. Nathan wondered why, if that assumption were true, his friend looked so stressed and why he was so willing to leave it all behind.

"You thinkin' about seeing the gang again?"

Eli's question shouldn't have startled him. They'd always been a part of the gang—the invincible group of six African Americans on their way to ruling the world.

His stomach shouldn't have clenched at the mere memory. But then there were so many things that should never have happened.

"I'm thinking about getting to work." Nathan purposely kept his face blank. He had reason to believe that something was going on in Tanner, something that had begun that warm summer night ten years ago. Something he had every intention of uncovering. But he needed to do that alone. Nobody could be trusted. Not even the gang.

Especially not the gang.

Eli rested against his elbows on the desk. "You know you're going to have to face them sooner or later. This town's too small to avoid it."

Nathan's hands stilled on his thighs. He'd known he'd have to see them. In fact, he was counting on it. "I'll deal with that when the time comes. Right now, I'd like to see what I've gotten myself into by agreeing to take over your position."

Eli paused, his dark eyes studying Nate. He'd changed a lot since college, since that night. He looked stronger, more stable than he had back in school, if that were possible. Nate had been the most intellectual and the most attractive guy in the gang. Eli frowned because it appeared that hadn't changed.

"So, you want to show me your floor?" Nathan asked, a bit concerned by Eli's intense gaze.

Eli chuckled. "Well, it's *your* floor now, or it will be when I give my notice, but I guess it'd be a good idea to show you around." He rose from his chair and crossed the room to face Nathan, who had stood as well. Clapping the slightly taller man on the back, Eli gave him a sincere smile. "It's good to have you home, man. Things will be different this time."

For a split second Nathan wondered what Eli meant by that. "I'm sure they will," he finally mumbled.

Tenile Barnes had just assisted in the delivery of her next-to-last patient. It was a quarter after five in the morning, and she had been on duty since eleven the previous morning. Her feet hurt, her back hurt, and now, courtesy of Mary Kaler, her right arm, wrist and hand hurt. The woman had tried to wrench Tenile's arm out of its socket each time a contraction hit, and by the time she was ready to push, Tenile's arm was completely numb. That numbness had disappeared as she watched Mary nurse her newborn son. The magical sight of new motherhood always touched her heart.

Her final patient, Darcy Bloom, had only dilated four centimeters in the last nine hours. Although Darcy's cervix was steadily thinning, it was her first baby, so she was bound to labor a little longer. Tenile was fairly sure she had time for a little nap.

The staff lounge, decorated in warm hues of brown and red, was reasonably quiet. The television was on but turned down so low that only the intern sitting in one of the deep cushioned chairs directly below it could hear. Casting a tired glance toward the coffee machine, Tenile decided to forego the caffeine and fell down stomach first onto one of the four couches that filled the room.

Exhaustion enveloped her, and before she could slip off her other shoe, she was sound asleep.

⟷

"This is the lounge," Eli told Nathan as they entered. This was only about the twentieth room Eli had shown him. By now, Nathan was tired of the tour.

Labor and Delivery consisted of eleven birthing rooms, two of which contained large whirlpool tubs. NICU, which was located two floors down, had a twenty-bed capacity with all the latest equipment and medications, along with a highly skilled staff. Four procedure rooms, two operating rooms and a host of other rooms made up the unit. Nathan had stopped trying to remember all the places and routes to get there, deciding he'd simply have to go on trial and error for the next few weeks.

"The couches roll out into beds, and a fridge, microwave and all sorts of stuff are over there. I'll get you a key to one of the lockers, but you'll probably use your office for your personal stuff anyway."

Nathan nodded in agreement just as Eli's beeper went off.

Pulling the small instrument off his hip, Eli examined the numbers and frowned. "I've got to go take care of this," he said. "You can just hang around in here until I get back. Then we'll go and make the big announcement."

Eli was out the door before Nathan could tell him that a simple memo would announce his arrival just fine. There was really no need to draw a lot of attention. He moaned inwardly. His return would draw interest; raise questions and speculation all over again. He'd known that the moment he determined he was coming back but felt ready for it.

Eli had been badgering him for years to come back to Tanner, and now that Eli was going to open his own private practice shortly, the ideal position had opened up for him. For years obstetrics had been the main focus of his life. He'd dedicated time, energy and a good portion of his own money into research regarding premature birth. Tanner City Hospital would give him the opportunity to put some of his theories to the test. Despite the less glorious other reasons for his return, the medical prospects excited him.

A rumbling noise jarred Nathan from his reverie, and he turned in the direction of the sound. A small body lay slumped on a couch across the room. One arm hung down over the side, a delicate hand scraping the chocolate brown carpet. One bare foot was propped up on the armrest while the other, still clad in a white nursing clog, was buried in the seam. A small head was completely covered with silky dark hair. Another grumble erupted from the body and Nathan suppressed a grin.

Poor girl, she must be dead tired. A sense of familiarity tugged at him. Nurses sometimes worked long shifts and in labor and delivery did as much work with the patients as the doctor, if not more. He crossed the room to get a closer view. The closer he got, the more insistent the tugging became. Helpless to resist, Nathan bent forward and, with the lightest touch he could manage with his large hands, smoothed several strands of hair from her face, exposing a chubby cheek, pouting lips and closed eyes with long lashes that fanned against smooth, clear skin. Something stirred deep inside him, something he hadn't felt for a long time.

He continued to stare at the woman while she slept, mesmerized. As if she finally sensed him hovering above her, her eyes shot open in alarm.

Nathan took a hasty step back, embarrassed at being caught admiring her.

"Is she ready to be checked again?" Tenile shuffled about until she sat upright on the sofa and looked at him with hazel-streaked eyes.

Nathan stared in awe. It was Tenile, the one person who'd ever possessed a part of him, the one person he'd trusted implicitly. His heart stopped, thudded loudly then slowly regained its rhythm. "Huh?" Entranced, he fought valiantly for control.

"Ms. Bloom? Do I need to check her progress?" Rubbing her eyes and slipping one foot into the clog that had been lying on the floor where she'd kicked it in an exhausted stupor, she continued talking. Bending to put her shoe on, she tilted her head to the side and squinted up at him. "You don't work here, do you?" Tenile stood, then felt her world tilt on its axis when she took in the six foot-plus man with cocoa-colored skin, broad shoulders and an intoxicating smell.

It was Nathan. The man she'd loved with all her heart. The one she'd trusted. The one who had betrayed her.

"Hello, Tenile." What else could he say? He hadn't seen her since that morning at the police station—since her eyes had told him she didn't believe his story.

Tenile took a slow step backward. "Nathan? What are you doing here?" Damn it, she was trembling. She straightened her back and tried again.

Waves of emotion washed over her as she stood not a foot away from the man she'd loved then had sworn to hate forever. He'd said he loved her, promised they'd be together forever. Then when she'd needed him most, he'd deserted her, taking with him all of her hopes and dreams.

"I just drove in this morning." He stared at her, unable to believe the subtle changes yet marveling at the awareness still thick between them. "I see you followed your dream to work in medicine." He used that as an excuse to boldly rake his eyes over her body. If the quickening of his pulse were any indication, beneath her baggy scrubs was the same curvaceous body that had kept him awake for endless nights back in college.

Tenile's entire body warmed, then chilled in rebellion. No, he was not looking her over as if she were a succulent piece of meat and he a starving animal. She rolled her eyes and stepped around him. "My life didn't stop because you decided to leave, Nathan." She was halfway to the door when his words halted her.

9

"I didn't presume it would." Nathan waited a moment before turning to face her. He'd needed that time to adjust to her tone, to remember that he probably deserved it.

Tenile looked back at him, daring her body to react to his dynamic good looks, the familiar warmth of his presence. She was courageous—her grandmother had always said so—and she was strong. Time had proven that. But she didn't think she would ever be immune to Nathan Hamilton or get over the havoc he'd wreaked on her. She wasn't about to forget it—no matter how tempting he looked.

"You didn't care either way." She didn't wait for a response, couldn't chance that he'd come closer or maybe even touch her. That's the way Nathan was, physical and overpowering, and she'd loved every minute of it. Tired legs took her out of the room, putting distance between them yet failing to remove his image from her mind.

Not until she was locked in a stall in the women's bathroom did she let her head fall back against the icy blue surface of the door and will herself not to cry.

Nathan was back.

Eli stood at the nurses' station with as much of the night and morning shift around him as could be spared. Their eyes were fixed on the stranger who stood to Eli's left.

But Nathan's thoughts drifted to the dimly lit room he'd just left. To the beautiful woman who'd just walked away from him. In all his time away, he'd never forgotten her, never lost the mental picture of her face. Her hair had grown, hanging well past her shoulders now, but its dark tint was still intriguing, enticing. Her eyes still grew dark and mysterious when she was angry, and she still possessed whatever it was that turned his mind into mush in seconds.

She was still the woman he'd fallen in love with so long ago. But in the depths of her eyes and the tinted edges of her voice, he realized she'd become so much more.

Tenile had gathered her things so she could go home. It was after seven, and the morning shift had already come in and was on the floor. She was back on duty at seven tonight, so she desperately needed to get some rest in her own bed. Ms. Bloom was still at four centimeters the last time she'd checked, and Tenile was sure that by the time she returned this evening the woman would have undergone a cesarean section and be well on her way to recovery.

Her mind was more than a little blurred, a mixture of exhaustion and the run-in with her past she'd had earlier, so her usually quick stride was slowed a bit. When she passed the nurses' station the crowd of people standing around barely aroused her curiosity—until she heard his name. *Nathan Hamilton.*

The sounds of clapping and talking registered somewhere in the back of her brain, but loud and clear and above anything else, she heard his name. *Nathan Hamilton.*

Visions of the tall, attractive young student flashed through her mind as the wide shouldered, brown-skinned man came into view.

Nathan shook hands and tried to match names with faces as the staff, *his* staff, greeted him. His stomach churned as he continued to search the crowd for her. He didn't see her. He wanted to see her again, wanted to be close to her again. It had been ten years, but the spark was still there. *She* was still there.

Tenile stood behind the long line of people, debating if she should move closer, if she should chance being close to him again. She remembered with picture perfect clarity the last time they'd faced each other ten years earlier—the razor-sharp pain searing her very soul. In that instant she knew she had to get away. She had to get far away.

Her eyes locked with his in a silent plea for mercy. She didn't want to relive that night nor the weeks that had followed. But with Nathan's return, she wasn't sure how she could avoid it.

Nathan wanted to go to her, to pull her into his arms and apologize for all the pain he saw so clearly in her eyes. But the crowd around him and the tension he saw in her stopped him.

Tenile broke the connection, intense emotion fueling her stride toward the elevator.

Helpless, Nathan let her go. He'd come back to find Landy's killer and put to rest the suspicion that had always surrounded his name.

But as he watched her lithe form enter the elevator, above all else he realized he'd come back for her.

Chapter 2

Tenile spent her drive home remembering their college years, the nights they'd all shared in the huge colonial house they rented. They'd grown thick as thieves in those years, sharing everything from bathrooms to secrets.

Eli had been cool, his average looks and good humor adding a sense of lightheartedness to their ensemble. Nicole had been the superstar—a beautifully toned body, pretty face and sultry singing voice, with college only a pit stop for her. Kareem had been the quiet one, spending most of his time reading or at his father's office learning the business he would one day inherit. And then there had been Landy.

Tenile's hands gripped the steering wheel tightly.

Landy had been the strong one, the thread holding them together. Her energy seemed to breathe life into the group, always restoring their loyalty to one another. She was pretty and intelligent and had been a pre-law student when she was brutally murdered.

The police said it must have been someone she knew because there were no signs of a struggle. Landy knew everybody, and she loved everyone she knew. That made the crime more senseless, more hateful. The fact that Tenile's boyfriend, Nathan, was the last person to be seen with her made it unbearable.

Now he was back. Nathan was back. The thought churned over and over in her mind.

As she climbed out of her car, she tried to figure out why he'd returned. Why, after all these years, had he decided to come back to Tanner? To the town where they'd fallen in love—the town where Landy had died and he'd….

About three steps away from the door to her apartment building, she heard steps behind her. She stopped. Turned. There was no one there.

Deciding she was imagining things, she proceeded to the door, punching her code into the keypad. The door buzzed and she pulled it open, but a sense that she was not alone kept her from entering. Turning again, she scanned the parking lot, her hip holding the door ajar: familiar cars, shrubbery surrounding the six-story building, shimmering rays of gold and orange breaking through the horizon. Other than that, she was alone. There was no one else there, yet she felt… a presence.

A breeze lifted the hair from her neck. She smelled jasmine. Faint yet undeniable, the scent was there and she cringed.

Landy had always smelled like jasmine.

◈◈◈

Nathan spent the next hour acquainting himself with the floor and the schedules of the staff working the floor. A quick visit to the GYN clinic gave him a good idea of how the process worked at Tanner City. Patients visited the clinic for routine pre-natal care before coming to maternity to deliver. The top obstetricians in the hospital handled high-risk pregnancies on Mondays and Tuesdays. The doctors attended normal pregnancies during the rest of the week with Fridays reserved for elective procedures such as tubal ligation and fertility sessions.

Overall, it was a good program, but he'd done his research early, so he already knew that. His work on preterm labor and premature birth would go a long way here since the clinic's statistics for saving the lives of premature infants were rather low compared to larger, big city hospitals. He hoped to change that. He grabbed the files filled with grant information, intending to go over them later today after he had a chance to finish unpacking and get his house in some semblance of order.

When he'd decided he was returning to Tanner, he quickly called a real estate agent and put him on notice that he would need to purchase a home. He was back in Tanner to stay, and he was tired of living in apartments and condos as he'd done in New York. He wanted something more stable. He wanted a place to start a family.

It was time, he had decided. Just a few months ago his mother had sold their family home and moved to Florida with her only sister. Other than the two of them, Nathan didn't have any relatives, any connections. He'd realized he wanted connections. He wanted a place he belonged and people that belonged with him.

Tossing the folders into his trunk, he quickly got into the car and placed his doctor's sticker in the front window. Tomorrow, he'd park in the reserved section and avoid what seemed a half-mile walk from the visitors' parking to the front door.

Nathan turned out onto the road, staring at landmarks that had been there when he was younger and reminiscing about a time when he'd believed himself invincible. He passed the coffee and donut shop where he and his friends had always met after classes. The six of them, *The Mod Squad*, they'd called themselves. They were the people he'd been closest to, people he'd trusted with his life.

On impulse, he made a U-turn and pulled into the parking lot. The old sign was still hanging, but the u and s in Donuts had long since blinked out. He sat behind the wheel, wondering if he should go in.

The afternoon before, he swallowed the lump that had formed in his throat, before Landy's death, they'd been there. Nicole and Eli had left a message at the house for them all to come immediately after their last classes. Since this wasn't unusual, they'd all filed in for role call, he and Landy arriving last, together.

He remembered her infectious laughter, the tight jeans and bright yellow shirt she'd worn that day. The conversation had been melancholy with everyone discussing their plans for after graduation.

He was headed to New York for med school. Landy was headed to law school in L.A., along with Nicole, who was going to find stardom. Kareem was headed into the shipping business with his father, and Eli was going to med school in Connecticut. Tenile was going to New York with him.

The gang would be split up, and none of them really knew how to handle that. Coffee had grown cold and donuts had been left uneaten as they'd tried to fill the intervals of silence with light banter.

Landy had received a page on her beeper and announced that she needed to leave. "Cheer up guys, this isn't the last time we'll ever see each other." She'd smiled and walked quickly out of the shop.

None of them had ever imagined that would be the last time they'd see her alive. But sometime between then and the next morning, Landy's bright beautiful smile and vivacious spirit had been cut down, taken away from the world well before her time.

And he had been blamed.

⬥

"So you finally got him to come back." Nicole crossed her long mocha-colored legs and sat back against the plush burgundy sofa.

Eli passed her a glass of wine before taking a seat beside her. "That's right. Now we're all where we belong." He took a sip of the cool dark liquid.

"Says who?" An elegantly arched eyebrow lifted as she turned to face him.

"Says me. We were all a lot better together, as a group. After what happened, we were never the same. It's time for that to come to an end."

Nicole pouted. "Togetherness isn't all it's cracked up to be."

Eli emptied his glass and set it on the table in front of them. He moved a hand to her bare knee. Nicole wore the shortest skirts, her legs advertising what an appealing package she was. He let his fingers glide along the smooth dark skin. "Now there are some aspects of togetherness I know you used to enjoy." He paused at her upper thigh, just inches away from her heat. "And some I know you still do." With his free hand, he grasped her breast.

Nicole smiled above the rim of her glass. Eli knew her well, maybe a bit too well, she surmised, taking another drink. His eyes devoured her as his hands gripped and stroked. Her mind filled with the heady sensation of power and lust. She uncrossed her legs, allowing him full access, and leaned forward to place her glass on the table. "Be careful, darling. Nathan never could be controlled." She knew that for a fact.

Eli captured her bottom lip between his teeth. "I don't want to control him." He nipped again, stroked his tongue over the moistened spot. "I just want to contain what he knows."

❧

It didn't take long for Nathan to find the house. It still sat in the same spot—back from the narrow road, a hop, skip and a jump from the deep wooded area. To the west, trees deepened and stretched to the sky. To the east, a small dock led the way to the river where gulls circled collecting their breakfast.

The structure looked the same, white siding with black shutters—a smiley face of sorts. He stepped onto the porch, a loose board creaking beneath his feet. His pulse beat strong and thick as he approached the door. A screen had been added—he made a mental note to remove it. He liked the white door with its paned center and wanted it to be seen clearly.

Forgetting all foolish reservations, he slipped the key into the lock and stepped inside. The floor in the entryway was bare, the wood a little worn. He dropped his bags and walked into the living room. It was just as he remembered, spacious and homey with its large fireplace and bay windows.

A memory of evenings spent there entered his mind: Kareem in the recliner with an economics book in his lap; Nicole on the couch polishing her nails or something else ultra feminine; he and Tenile by the fire, cuddling yet pretending to study. That seemed a lifetime ago.

Nathan continued walking through the house until he reached the kitchen where dull yellow walls greeted him. He looked around, wondering what he could do to brighten the desolate space. Landy's laughter echoed in the air, catching him off guard. Nathan turned with a start, his eyes searching the room for a visitor. But he was alone. His imagination? It must have been. Memories were bound to haunt him. He'd known that the moment he purchased the house.

But memories were a good thing, at least they would be as soon as he pieced enough of them together to find Landy's killer. He looked at his watch and realized he was running late. He had a very important appointment he needed to keep.

On his way back into town, Nathan thought of Tenile. Seeing her again so soon had been a shock to his system, but he'd never been more sure of the fact that he still wanted her as he was now. He knew his coming back to Tanner shifted things, would make people think of a time they'd all rather forget. But whether she was ready to admit it or not, they had unfinished business.

Even though he was already running late, he made the left turn and maneuvered his way through the cemetery. He got out and walked the short distance to Landy's grave. Daisies would bloom in the summer, but for now, irises brightened the ground. There was a small bench adjacent to the plot. A stone statue of a dove about to fly marked the grave. Tenile had picked that out, saying Landy's spirit would always be free to soar.

Nathan closed his eyes. He'd lied to Tenile and to the police. He knew who had paged Landy that afternoon and had a pretty good idea where she'd run off to, but he'd never told. He'd never said a word to anyone because Landy had begged him to keep her secret.

A secret he now knew might have caused her death.

～∞～

Tossing and turning in her bed did not constitute rest by a long shot. Tenile couldn't sleep, and she knew why.

Nathan.

He was back and his image haunted her as if he'd never left. Dropping an arm over her eyes, she sighed.

"Nathan." His name was a whisper on her lips.

They'd fallen in love the summer of '92, a year after they'd all agreed to be roommates. His room, the one he shared with Eli, was down the hall from hers. Each morning they'd time themselves just right so that they got dressed and down to the kitchen before anyone else.

Raisin Bran with big glasses of orange juice was their favorite breakfast. They shared it at the old wooden table they'd found at a yard sale. They'd learned a lot about each other in that kitchen and made a lot of plans.

Plans that had never come to fruition.

The ringing phone jarred her from her memories, and she leapt from the bed to retrieve it.

"Hello?"

"Tee? Wake up. I've got some news I know you want to hear." Her mother, Oneil Barnes, was on the gossiping committee of Tanner, so she always had news for Tenile. Usually, it didn't bother Tenile since she had inherited her mother's genes and was as nosy as the next person. But today, she sensed she didn't want to hear the headlines fresh from Tanner's rumor mill.

"Yes, Mama. But can it wait? I'm trying to get some sleep. I have to work again tonight."

"Nonsense. You work too much. You need to find yourself a good man and settle down. Then you won't be so concerned about work and money."

Oh Lord, Tenile groaned inwardly. Which was worse—her mother's speech about her snagging a good man and settling down or hearing the gossip?

Gossip, hands down!

"What's the news, Mama?" Tenile interrupted her just as she was about to go into the type of man Tenile needed to marry.

"Oh yeah, I almost forgot why I called." Oneil chuckled. "You are never going to guess who had the nerve to waltz back into Tanner."

Tenile bet she could guess, but that would undoubtedly steal her mother's thunder, so she refrained. "Who?"

"Nathan Hamilton. You remember him. He went to school with you, just before he got thrown in jail."

"I'm sure you remember how well I knew Nathan, Mama. Just as I'm sure you remember that he was never put in jail."

"That's because his father bought him a get-out-of-jail-free card before they could formally charge him."

Tenile stifled a grin at her mother's corny reference to the board game. "We don't know that he was going to be charged." They didn't know, but the thought had crossed everyone's mind.

"Anyway, he's back and I reckon he's going to stay a while."

Tenile's chest tightened. "What makes you say that?"

"He bought that old house y'all stayed in when you were in school. Looks to me like he's planting roots."

For the second time today, Tenile felt herself gasping because of Nathan. Why would he buy *that* house? Tanner wasn't huge, but it had other houses available for sale. She hadn't set foot in that house since the day Nathan left. How could he simply waltz back into town and go back there as if nothing had ever happened?

"Tee? You listening to me? I said it seems he's fixin' to stay a while. Have you heard from him?"

Oneil had liked Nathan once, before that night. "I'm listening, Mama." She was also climbing out of bed, preparing to get a shower. She was going back to the old house. Back to find out what Nathan Hamilton wanted and if it had anything to do with her. She'd thought to just stay away from him, to hide, so to speak. But she'd never run from anything in her life, and she'd be damned if she'd start now.

Chapter 3

Nathan was on his way home. That sounded good to him—home. He was just about to pull into his driveway when a dark blue car came speeding out. He swerved and barely missed hitting it.

The other driver slammed on the brakes before jumping out of the vehicle. Initially stunned from the near miss, his confusion continued when he realized the woman heading directly for him was Tenile.

Hands fisted at her sides, she stopped a few inches from his car. "I would think that since you spent a small fortune on this car you'd drive with a little more care."

Hair pulled back into a ponytail, face free of any makeup, her huge expressive eyes made it clear that he'd managed to tick her off again. Nathan stepped out of the car slowly, as was his way. He rarely rushed, patience being a virtue he was blessed with. He closed the door and leaned against it, casually folding his arms over his chest to keep from reaching for her. "Were you coming to see me?"

"I was…" she stuttered. She was getting damned tired of reacting to him that way. "I was coming to discuss something with you." She paused, rethinking her rashness in coming here to find out why he'd returned and to let him know how she felt about it. Then she remembered the phone call. "But now I have to go." Turning, she was about to walk to her car when his hand on her elbow stopped her.

More than a shiver, more than an electric jolt, the feeling rushing through her arm and spreading like wildfire through the rest of her body was both foreign and familiar. She hadn't felt it in…in ten years.

"Don't go. I'd like to talk to you." He spoke quietly, praying she'd stay.

Tenile turned to look at him. She wanted to touch him, run her hand along the strong jaw that shaped his face, over the lumpy bend of his nose where it had been broken in a basketball game. "I have to go." She swallowed hard. "It's an emergency. My brother's girlfriend may be in premature labor, and she's alone in her apartment." She clamped her mouth shut in disgust. She'd stopped stuttering, but babbling wasn't an acceptable option.

Nathan's medical training kicked in, and he didn't waste anytime deciding what would happen next. "Come on, I'll take you and you can tell me everything on the way."

Before Tenile could protest, he was pulling her towards his car, opening the door for her. When he reached across her to fasten the seatbelt, she inhaled his scent. She shouldn't be in his car—shouldn't be with him. But there was no time to argue. Tracy's call had been frantic; she needed to get to her as quickly as possible.

In seconds he was pulling off and asking for directions. "Now tell me about Tracy. How far along is she?"

"Um, I think she's about twelve or thirteen weeks. Last week she went to the doctor because she was cramping. He told her to rest, stay off her feet, you know the drill. Well, she did that and the cramping seemed to subside a bit, but yesterday, it started again and it was more painful. She called the doctor and he told her that, at this point, if she were going to miscarry, there wasn't much he could do about it. Jerk!" Tenile exclaimed and Nathan agreed.

"She used a heating pad and tried to rest through the night, but she called and said the pain was getting worse. She's scared and she's all alone. This is her first baby."

"Where's Aaron?" he asked, remembering her older brother as he turned the corner nearing the apartment complex. He was driving so fast and trying to listen to Tenile at the same time that he almost jumped the curb. He held the steering wheel tighter, trying to concentrate on his driving.

"He's in the navy and his ship's out at sea. Her mom lives in Bar Harbor, but she doesn't want to call her until it's absolutely necessary. Right here, it's that one there." She motioned toward Tracy's unit.

He pulled into the first available spot, and they both jumped out, Tenile running to the door and Nathan stopping to grab his bag before following her.

She banged on the door marked 3A. "Tracy, it's me, Tenile. Open the door."

Shuffling sounds came through the door before it opened. A tall woman with sienna skin and flaming red hair stood crookedly before doubling over in pain. Nathan pushed past Tenile and guided Tracy to the sofa. Laying her down, he began to check her vitals, one hand on her wrist and the other rummaging through his bag for a thermometer, which he stuck into Tracy's mouth.

Tracy looked from the man to Tenile in question.

"Oh, this is Dr. Hamilton. He's the new head of the maternity ward at Tanner City. Just relax, it's okay. I told him everything that's been going on." Patting her hand, Tenile consoled the panic-stricken Tracy. When she seemed to relax, Tenile moved closer to help Nathan.

Taking the thermometer from Tracy's mouth, she announced, "Normal. I'll get her pressure." Without another thought, she reached into his bag, removed the cuff and began taking Tracy's blood pressure.

"Tell me where it hurts, Tracy," Nathan said as he pulled her dress up to gently poke her stomach.

She winced. "Mostly in my back, but it's starting to hurt in my stomach too. Yeah, right there," she told him when he pushed just above the line of her pubic hair.

"What does it feel like?" Nathan pushed there a little longer, feeling for the embryo.

Tracy tried to breathe normally beneath the pain and discomfort of his exam. "Cramps, horrible menstrual cramps."

"Get me the gloves," Nathan directed Tenile.

Not hesitating, Tenile pulled the gloves from his bag and found a tube of lubricating jelly. Pulling off the cap, she squirted it onto his now-gloved hand. As Nathan smoothed the cool substance on his fingers, Tenile moved around Nathan, rubbing Tracy's legs for comfort. "He's going to examine you now. Just try and relax, okay?"

Tracy nodded while Tenile pulled her panties down and pushed her thighs slightly apart. Nathan took one leg under his arm, holding Tracy's knee securely before inserting two of his fingers and using the other hand to press against her abdomen.

Tracy hissed, closed her eyes. Tenile rubbed her other leg and crooned, "It's okay. Just relax. That's it, relax." At her words, the muscles in Tracy's leg tightened and retracted.

"She's dilating; we need to get to the hospital right away!" Nathan exclaimed, pulling his hand abruptly from her and standing. Ripping the gloves off, he asked, "Where's the phone so I can call and tell them we're on our way?"

Tracy pointed and Nathan dropped the gloves into a nearby trashcan as he crossed the room to the phone.

"Oh God, Tee, I can't lose my baby," Tracy whimpered.

"You're not going to lose the baby. Come on, let's get you up. Nathan knows what he's doing. He'll take care of you and the baby." Tenile was pulling Tracy's panties up, helping her into a sitting position. She had no idea why she was so sure that Nathan knew what he was doing except for the fact that he wouldn't be the head of the ward if he didn't. Still, she'd felt comfortable in her reassurance to Tracy that he would take care of everything.

"Okay, they're expecting us. We have to move quickly. You ready?" he asked Tracy.

"Yeah, I guess so. What's going on?" she asked when he wrapped his arm around her waist. From where she stood behind him, Tenile could see the broad muscles of Nathan's back as he bent and scooped Tracy up. His dress shirt stretching over the broad expanse rendered her throat dry. He'd definitely seen the inside of a gym on more than one occasion, she thought breathlessly. *Stop looking!* she scolded herself. *That's over and done with.*

Tenile moved to open the door, trying to keep her mind on the situation at hand.

Nathan was informing Tracy of his diagnosis. "It feels like your cervix is already beginning to open, and if it continues, you'll lose the baby. We have to get you to the hospital to get a better look at what's really going on. Then we can decide our next move." He explained while walking rapidly to the car; Tenile right behind him.

Tracy began to cry. Tenile slid into the back seat beside her. "Oh no, you don't. You can't cry and get all upset because then the baby will sense something's wrong and get upset too. You have to stay as calm as possible so we can save this pregnancy. Do you understand me? You have to stay calm."

Tracy nodded her head in agreement, and Nathan pulled out of the parking lot.

All the way to the hospital, he listened to Tenile soothing and calming her friend—her patient—through this frightening time. She was a good nurse, he thought. She had really good people skills; she was blunt yet caring, compassionate and optimistic. All these characteristics reminded him of the girl he'd fallen in love with. The girl he'd willingly, stupidly left behind.

Putting his new sticker to good use, he pulled into one of the reserved doctor spots and snatched his keys from the ignition. As he helped Tracy out of the car, he noticed the weary look on Tenile's face. "You need to go home and get some rest," he told her. "You've been up all night."

A little startled by the frown on his face, Tenile blinked before responding. "I'm fine. I won't rest until I know she's okay, so I'll go home then."

His mouth clamped tight, he fought the urge to touch the smooth skin of her cheek and instead continued through the front doors of the hospital. Tenile had never been a person to argue with, her stubbornness rivaling only his own. Besides, he couldn't help enjoying her closeness.

A nurse spotted them as soon as they walked through the doors and quickly pushed a wheelchair to them. When Tracy was seated, Nathan informed the nurse that they were going to labor and delivery. There was silence on the elevator as they rode up to the sixth floor. As Tenile held Tracy's hand, Nathan tried not to think of the soft skin beneath Tenile's right ear and how sensitive it had always been. He could touch her now

25

if he reached out his hand. The longing burned deep inside him, but he turned away. Now was not the time.

Stepping off the elevator and moving to the nurses' station, Nathan barked more orders. "Find Dr. Grant and get the patient set up for an ultrasound now! And get one of the operating rooms ready. I'll need it in about twenty minutes!"

Myla, who was clearly experienced and respected by the other nurses, took the lead. "Right away, Doctor. I'll take her with me. Michelle, have Dr. Grant paged and then prep OR2 for Dr. Hamilton." The woman was brisk as she came from around the counter to push the wheelchair.

Before her feet were run over, Tenile released Tracy's hand but kept eye contact with her. "It's going to be alright. I'll be there in a minute," she reassured her.

"Okay," Tracy nodded.

As Myla pushed Tracy down the hall, Nathan's voice sounded from behind.

"She's good," he surmised with a nod in Myla's direction.

Tenile faced him, trying like hell not to see him as a man but to concentrate on him as a colleague. "Yeah, she's the head nurse. She trained me. What do you need me to do?" she asked when Nathan turned away from her.

Nathan wasn't sure if he could stand being this close to her. He needed to touch her, to hold her. He'd thought of little else in the last ten years, and now that they were face-to-face, the urge was all too real. He promised himself he'd be professional. He was the doctor and she was the nurse. They could work side by side; there was no reason why they couldn't. Besides, they didn't have a choice; it was their job.

"Get her chart and meet me in the exam room." He didn't give her a chance to respond before walking away. If he was going to have her at his heels for the next two or so hours, he needed a breather first.

On the way to Tracy's house, he'd noticed there was no ring on Tenile's left hand. She wasn't married. He'd wanted to shout with joy but wisely restrained himself. So far, his return to Tanner was turning out to be the best decision he'd ever made.

Myla had already removed all of Tracy's clothing and pulled a gown around her when Tenile walked in.

"Where's the doctor?" Tracy asked when she was on the examining table.

"He's coming, just relax." Tenile took her hand, stroking it gently in an effort to stop the incessant shaking.

"Tell me again who he is and how you found him so fast," Tracy said.

Tenile waited for Myla's retreat. When the door closed, her eyes returned to Tracy's. "He's actually the new chief of obstetrics here, and he's an old classmate who just happened to be in the neighborhood when I left to come and get you." Tracy didn't need to know the truth. She didn't need to know what Nathan had once meant to her. And Tenile didn't need to remind herself.

The technician came and went, leaving Tracy with even more questions.

"Trace, relax," Tenile said while re-adjusting the covers on the bed.

"How can I relax? She didn't tell me anything!" she practically screeched.

"She's just doing her job; you know that. It's not up to us to discuss medical diagnoses with the patient. Nathan will come in, and he'll answer all your questions."

"Nathan? You mean the doctor? How well do you know this guy?" The mention of Nathan seemed to effectively take Tracy's attention away from her anger toward the technician.

Tenile frowned at her slip. She would have to remember not to call him that at work; she didn't want to start any rumors. Tongues would already be wagging about the new doctor, the fresh meat available.

Pulling the thin white sheet higher over Tracy's belly, Tenile avoided her quizzical stare. "I told you we went to school together."

When Tracy would have persisted, the door opened. Nathan came in with Eli right behind him. He didn't miss a beat, simply came in taking command, giving his diagnosis. He had that type of presence—one that could take a woman's breath away in an instant.

"Your cervix has already started to open."

Tracy gasped. Tenile gripped her hand tighter.

Nathan took Tracy's free hand. "There are two things we can do," he spoke in a soothing tone.

Eli moved to the foot of the bed, more comfortable with Tracy than Nathan because he'd known her a few years. Glancing at Nathan, Eli turned back to Tracy and spoke calmly. "You can either go on strict bed rest for the duration of the pregnancy and hope that the cervix stops opening or…" Eli hesitated, looking grimly at Nathan.

"Or you can have a cervical cerclage to tie the cervix and keep it from opening further," Nathan finished. Eli was wasting time. As they'd discussed in his office just a few minutes ago, this was Tracy's only real option. Bed rest guaranteed nothing. At least with a cerclage, combined with bed rest, she stood a better chance of the baby surviving. Eli thought it was hopeless since she was well into her second trimester already, but Nathan had seen it help before and was determined to save this baby.

Tracy looked from one doctor to the next before turning to Tenile in question.

"It's for the best," Tenile told her. She knew the look on Eli's face well, and even though she hadn't seen Nathan in ten years, she read him easily. Tracy's baby would not survive without their intervention.

"How soon can it be done and how long will the stitches stay in?" she asked.

"The OR's ready now, and I'd like to keep the stitches in place until around thirty-seven weeks. You're seventeen weeks now." Nathan noticed the panic creeping back into her eyes. Tenile stood across from him, still clutching Tracy's other hand, her concern masked with professionalism. Nathan now felt compelled to console both women.

Wishing he could hold Tenile, he focused on Tracy, looking directly into her eyes. "This is your only chance to save your baby's life. Your cervix has opened about one and half centimeters already, and it's softening. I know you know what that means. In all likelihood bed rest alone is not going to stop it. This is the best option we have to give your baby a chance." He spoke quietly and directly to Tracy, as if no one else was in the room but aware that Tenile was listening, absorbing his words as well.

Touching her hand and initiating eye contact had sealed the human bond between Nathan and Tracy, making him more than just her doctor, making him a person who actually cared about her and about the health of her unborn child. Tracy nodded in agreement.

"I'll get the forms," Tenile said as flutters quickened in her stomach. Watching Nathan for these last few moments had been nothing short of amazing. This was not the boy she'd known in college. Basically, he was the same, yet everything about him seemed different, if that made any sense. She couldn't pinpoint it, rather she chose not to, yet it was there, daring her to look closer, to get closer to the man he'd become. But there was no way in hell she was doing that. They had a past. So what? It was over and done with. The present was all that mattered now; she would not regress. Still, she breathed a sigh of relief when she was out of the room, away from him.

"Tee?"

His voice startled her so that she nearly jumped through the wall.

"Sorry. I didn't mean to startle you." He lifted his hands to steady her, then thought better of it and let his arms fall to his sides. "I was going to see if you wanted to assist." She wasn't on duty, he knew, but he wanted her with him. Then, because she looked tired, worried and confused all at once, he ignored the warning in his brain and touched her, his hands moving up and down her arms. Even through the material of her shirt, her arms felt soft beneath his hands. His eyes dropped to the hollow of her neck, lingering over the creamy skin. He ached to touch her there.

His touch was disconcerting, but she'd never admit it. "Um, yeah…I can do that," she answered after several steadying breaths that hadn't seemed to do one bit of good.

"Okay, OR2 in about fifteen minutes. Have her sign the papers. Anesthesia is on the way," he told her, her voice drawing his eyes back to her mouth.

They stood like that for a moment, neither one of them moving, neither one speaking. It had sometimes been that way between them. Words weren't always necessary. "Ah, Nathan?"

"Yes?" he answered, breathless from the way she looked, winded from the jump in his heart rate initiated by her intense gaze.

"I can't move until you let me go," she told him.

Time was of the essence for his patient, yet he wanted to linger with Tenile. "I should have never let you go," he whispered.

Like a vice, his words gripped her heart, threatening to weaken her stance. "Don't," was all she could manage.

"Don't what?" One hand moved to cup her face, his thumb moving closer to her lips. "Don't admit I was wrong? Or don't remind you of what we shared?"

She closed her eyes and searched for strength, found a tidbit, then slipped out of his reach.

"Either," she said finally. Looking at him again, mainly to prove to herself that she could, she squared her shoulders. "This is not the time or the place."

Nathan nodded his agreement, slipping his hands in his pockets. That was the only place they would be safe. "Then tell me when and where, and I'll start over."

"It's too late. It's over."

"No. It's just beginning."

Chapter 4

After the surgery was over and Tracy rested quietly in her room being monitored for any contractions or other complications, Tenile wondered how she was going to get home. She was preparing to call her mother when Nathan came up behind her.

"You ready to go?"

"Go?"

"Yeah, go home. You didn't drive, remember?" He smiled lazily.

"Yes, I remember but you don't have to go to all that trouble. I'll just call my mother and she'll come to get me and take me to my car." The thought of being alone with him both terrified and excited her.

"Nonsense. Your car is at my house." He was still smiling, his eyes liquid and dark.

"Your house? You actually bought the house?" She searched his face for some semblance of reason. She needed to know why he'd done it. Why he was back. Not that she could say at this very moment that she was sorry to be standing next to him.

He felt a tingle of guilt trickle down his spine. He hadn't considered her reaction to his purchase. In fact, he hadn't thought she'd care. But from the way she was looking at him, he'd definitely been wrong. "Does that bother you?"

She blinked and looked away before finding his eyes again. "No. I mean, yes." She paused, took a deep breath. "I guess I just don't understand."

The urge was too strong, her eyes too alluring. His arm reached out, and he smoothed a strand of hair from her cheek. Soft, just like he remembered. "If you let me take you to your car, I can try to explain."

She needed answers; that was the only reason she was agreeing. That, and not liking the prospect of riding in a car with her mother to Nathan's newly purchased house and having to explain the events of the last few hours. "I'll meet you in the parking lot."

Another nurse walked by, and Nathan jerked his hand away from her face. "I'll be waiting."

He walked away and Tenile wondered if that's what they'd both been doing all these years. Waiting.

Fastened again in the passenger seat of Nathan's Lexus, Tenile was a little uncomfortable. There was a time when they had been almost one and the same, when his thoughts coincided directly with her own. Now her mind ran in several different directions, all beginning and ending with him.

Nathan glanced at her. She was quiet. They'd been driving for about ten minutes. He was supposed to be explaining why he'd bought the house, but he really wanted to hear about everything that had gone on in her life since he left.

One step at a time. Though the way she was huddled as close to the door as possible with her arms folded tightly over her chest said she was more than a little nervous. He was going to have to give it his best shot.

"The house is really special to me."

She didn't move but he knew she listened.

"While I was away, I thought about our time there. The good memories seemed to outweigh the bad. When the realtor said it was on the market, I jumped at the opportunity."

The flurry of thoughts in her mind softened such that they now spilled over each other like a gentle snowfall. "I haven't been there since you left."

"It must have been hard for you." He knew because it had been hard for him too.

"I couldn't believe she was gone." She stared out the window, watching the houses whiz by. "I couldn't believe *you* were gone."

There it was, the hurt and confusion he knew he'd caused. At that very moment, he wished he were Superman, able to turn back time with repeated laps around the earth. "I'm sorry. I shouldn't have left." His voice was quiet, in the tone a man used to seal his seduction or soothe the injured.

Her heart stumbled and she chanced a look at him. "Why did you leave?"

He stopped at a red light, letting his hands rest on the wheel as he looked at her. He wouldn't touch her. Instinct told him she'd bolt if he did. "It was easy."

Her gaze locked with his. "You were never a coward before."

The light changed and he proceeded through the intersection. "The sound you hear is my ego deflating."

She chuckled. Nathan had always been able to make her laugh. "I just meant that taking the easy road wasn't like you."

"Did you think I was strong?"

She didn't hesitate. "Strong enough for both of us."

He didn't answer.

"That's why it hurt so much when you left."

They were at the driveway, and there was her car.

"You thought I was involved," he said when he turned off the ignition.

She sat perfectly still, digesting his words, searching for a denial. She couldn't find one, even now. Her hand found the handle, and she let herself out of the car. Walking briskly to her own vehicle, she was a little shocked when his arm circled her waist, pulling her against him.

"Why didn't you believe in me? I needed you."

His chin rested atop her head, and for a moment she wanted to apologize, to turn to him and tell him she was sorry for not sticking up for him. But how could she when she wasn't sure what she believed then, or now for that matter? "I needed my boyfriend. You know, the person I trusted not to cheat on me. Not to lie to me." She struggled free of his grasp.

His fists flexed at his sides as he remembered Nicole misrepresenting the night he'd spent with Landy.

"It wasn't like that," he began.

She cut him off with a hand in the air. "Spare me the details."

She took another step away, creating more distance between them because that was the only way she would survive—and she'd sworn the day he left that she would definitely survive. "I came here earlier to ask about the house and tell you how I felt about your return."

Nathan's jaw clenched. She'd shifted. Right before his eyes, she'd closed the shutters tightly over her emotions. He couldn't talk to her now, let alone touch her. It would be a futile effort. "And?"

"And it doesn't even matter. You don't matter." She took a deep breath and straightened her spine for confidence. "I appreciate everything you did for Tracy, but that's where our connection ends."

"Our connection will never end." He knew that as surely as he knew his name.

Inside, Tenile seethed with anger, but she wasn't sure it was all aimed at Nathan. Her emotions were threatening to betray her. He watched her with that lazy patience he had a knack for, and she felt herself weaken.

"The day you left, it ended. I've moved on and I suggest you do the same." She found her keys in her purse and moved to open the car door.

"You never married." It was more a statement than a question.

She paused. "Don't you dare presume that my single status is because of you." She spun around to face him. "I'll have you know that I'm in a very committed relationship with a man I don't have to worry about leaving town on me."

She was in the car and speeding away before he recovered from his shock. She was seeing someone. "But I can still get to you." He smiled as he walked to his door.

That fact was a good sign. It said she still felt something for him. He'd just have to peel back all her protective layers to get to it. And like reaching the center of a Tootsie Pop—it would be oh-so-sweet when he did.

Kareem Winston walked down Main Street with a deliberate glide in his stride. His father had just named him CEO of Winston Shipping. He was on cloud nine—or at least he should have been.

It all changed when his secretary, Ophelia, had come back from lunch fifteen minutes late. Ordinarily, he wouldn't have complained about Ophelia's tardiness—complaints weren't in his nature. But Ophelia had been in a state upon her return, going on and on about the handsome new doctor over at Tanner City Hospital. It seemed her niece had just given birth, and Ophelia had gone over to the hospital on her lunch hour to visit. The nurses were all abuzz with news of fresh meat in the Tanner bachelor pool, and she wanted to get a look for herself.

Kareem heard all of this through his open office door as Ophelia told Netta, another secretary in the office. He'd been about to shut the door, closing out Ophelia's boisterous gossip, when a name stopped him in his tracks.

"Nathan Hamilton, that's his name. He lived here a while back. I don't know if you remember him. But I remember a nasty scandal running him out of town. His daddy's rich, you know. Lives in New York. He came all the way up here to get his boy and take him back to the big city with him."

Ophelia's next words were blurred as Kareem remembered the name, the person it belonged to and the scandal that had changed all their lives.

Forty-five minutes after he'd confirmed that Dr. Nathan Hamilton was, in fact, his old college roommate and friend, he left his office. He needed some air, some space to stretch his long legs and think of what would undoubtedly happen next.

Memories flooded his mind: the seductive way Landy's eyes half-closed when she smiled, the sweet sound of her laughter and the pain of her broken-hearted cry. Landy had been more to him than any other woman he'd known before or after.

She'd had issues, though, problems that she wouldn't allow anyone to help her with. Her father had loved her but had been blindsided by a mean-spirited woman who'd given him a son. That son, Donovan

35

Connor, had shared his mother's hatred of Landy, only he didn't show it quite as bluntly as Miranda did.

Still, Donovan had hated her, and Kareem knew it. He remembered the feel of Donovan's pretty-boy skin beneath his hands as he barely restrained himself from choking him to death.

"If you harm her in any way, I swear I'll kill you." The words had burned in his throat as sweat beaded on his forehead. He'd been as serious as a heart attack, and Donovan knew it.

When Kareem had released him, he'd scuttled across the floor until he was close to the door before making a hasty retreat through it.

For years Kareem had closed off that memory. Losing his control like that didn't happen frequently, but when it he did, the results could be deadly, and that scared him. So he'd buried the feelings that led to his rage just as effectively as he'd seen the gravediggers bury Landy.

His mind was so filled with raw emotions and turmoil that he didn't see the two older women approaching, didn't register their faces and didn't prepare himself for their attack.

"Why Kareem, dear, it's so good to see you out and about." Oneil Barnes spoke first, pulling herself up on tiptoe and grasping him by the shoulders to plant a kiss on his cheek.

The smell of apricot and fried chicken tickled his nostrils, and the past slipped into the dark corner of his mind that was its home. "Hello, Mrs. Barnes. Mrs. Finley. It's good to see you both." He smiled at the women, wondering how long it would take for one of them to mention it.

"You're looking quite handsome today. I'm surprised some young filly hasn't snatched you up yet," Geraldine Finley added with a pat to his cheek.

Kareem smiled. He knew she was just making conversation. His six-foot-four lanky frame made him look like a giant among the rest of Tanner's citizens—especially the women. His skin, an unsavory shade of tree bark, had never been acne free, and his nondescript eyes wore a dazed expression most of the time. "I'm surprised by that fact myself, Mrs. Finley."

"Where're you off to at this time of day? Shouldn't you be down the road running your daddy's business?" This was Mrs. Barnes again. She watched him closely, suspiciously. She wanted to know what he knew of Nathan's return.

They stood in front of Darma Cooley's bakery, so a steady stream of people flowed around them. Mrs. Cooley made the best caramel cheesecake, and everyone in town tended to eat it as if it were the last delicacy on earth.

"I took the afternoon off. Figured I needed some time for myself. I can't very well find a wife if I'm cooped up in that office all the time." The two women looked at each other, then back to him. He found them amusing and decided to give them something more to gossip about over their slice of cheesecake and coffee. "How's Tenile, Mrs. Barnes? I hear she's doing very well at the hospital."

Just as he'd hoped, Mrs. Barnes' eyes narrowed and she moved closer to him. "My girl's doing just fine, son. Although I reckon that may change a bit since Nathan Hamilton's back in town."

Kareem's jaw clenched, but he doubted either woman noticed. "Is he really? I hadn't heard."

Mrs. Finley clucked. "Well, then you do need to come out of that office more often. It's been the talk of the town all morning. Didn't you two used to be close some years back?"

This question and answer session was quickly growing old. The two women knew precisely what had happened all those years ago. Especially Mrs. Barnes, since Tenile had been involved as well. He didn't care to hear their questions or summarizations any longer. He had enough to deal with before he confronted Nathan, something he planned to do as soon as possible.

"Nathan and I went to school together. I wish I had time to stand here and tell you all about our youthful escapades, but I have an appointment." He took a step to move around the women, but they both moved with him.

"Thought you were taking the afternoon off?" Mrs. Barnes gave him a sweet smile.

"You going to see anyone in particular?" Mrs. Finley asked at the same time.

Kareem's lips formed a tight line, and he sidestepped the duo once more. "Good day, ladies."

He wasn't two steps away when he heard them murmuring behind his back. Some things never changed.

And some things changed too much, he thought as he made his way towards Pine View Road—toward the high-rise condos built a few years ago and the only person he knew who could afford to live there.

Chapter 5

At ten minutes after seven, Nathan took the offered glass of brandy from Eli's hand and moved to the chair on the deck. At the same time, on the other side of town, Tenile walked into Room 310 to examine her first patient for the evening.

"It's really good to have you back, Nate. It's been a long time." Eli took a seat across from him.

Nathan studied the dark liquid before looking at his friend. "Yes, it has. Too long."

Nathan's look was somber, and Eli wondered what was going on in his mind. He had so many questions he wanted to ask but knew he had to proceed with caution. Nathan was and had always been very smart and insightful. If he asked too many questions too soon, he would surely become suspicious. "So, what do you think?" With his own glass in hand, Eli gestured around them. "Not much has changed around here, huh?"

Nathan took a sip, then set his glass down. The sun was setting, the sky brilliant hues of orange and gold. In the distance birds made their final calls of the day. Eli's house faced the park, and children chasing balls and dogs on leashes contributed to the serenity of the scene. How could such a pretty town harbor such an ugly secret?

"Some changes aren't as easy to see as others," he commented quietly.

Eli recognized the wistful expression on Nathan's face. "So you've seen her, now what?"

Nathan sighed, looked away. He and Eli had been very close. Close enough that his feelings weren't easily masked. "When you left me in the lounge this morning, she was asleep on the couch." He sat back in the chair, steepled his hands and rested his chin on his fingers. "Why didn't you tell me she worked at the hospital?"

"To be honest, I didn't think about it until the announcement was made and I noticed her boarding the elevator."

They sat in silence.

"It's still there, huh?"

"Is it that obvious?"

"Only to a person who knows you as well as I do. Did you talk to her?"

Nathan nodded. "Briefly. This morning. I took her to her car after the episode with Tracy Patterson."

"I heard she's seeing this gym teacher from the high school, Robert Gibson. Don't know if it's serious though."

Nathan let the name sink in as prickly thorns of jealously vibrated over his skin. "She told me she was seeing someone."

"You gonna stand for that?"

Eli's voice held a hint of surprise, and Nathan couldn't help grinning. He shrugged. "You know me."

"Yeah, I do." Eli chuckled. "Gibson doesn't stand a chance."

Nathan laughed, lifted his glass and waited for Eli to do the same. "To Robert Gibson."

"To his unfortunate loss," Eli added.

Their glasses clinked and the men shared a moment of closeness, a moment of contentment they both knew wouldn't last much longer.

⸗

Tenile drifted through the rooms, checking each patient, signing the strips of paper the fetal monitors spit out, documenting contractions and heart-rate activity, smiling and offering words of comfort. But her mind was elsewhere.

She wondered what Nathan had been doing all these years and who he'd been doing it with. She knew she had no right; it wasn't any of her concern. She shouldn't even care. He hadn't stayed with her—that was the point that should have permeated her mind.

However, that was in the past. Neither one of them could do anything about it now. Besides, she needed to focus on her life. The life she'd made for herself. The life she'd been forced to live without him.

At least she had Robert. Robert was stable, supportive and attentive to her every need. He wanted a home and family just as she did, and that made them a perfect match.

So what if Robert's touch didn't make her heart flutter, if his being close didn't cause her mind to void out anything else but him? He had been there for her for the past nine months, giving her the security she'd longed for.

With all that firmly set in her mind, the fact still remained that Nathan was back and they had both grown up. He was absolutely gorgeous now, right down to the confident stride and almost arrogant gaze. She was attracted to him; there was no mistake about that. She always had been. But she wasn't that naïve young adult anymore. Her life was vastly different from what it had been ten years ago. She needed more than Nathan had given her before and, most likely, more than he was prepared to give her now. Besides, there was something between them now that wouldn't allow a reconciliation. Something that was creeping up on them all like a storm brewing offshore. Something that was neither stable nor happy, things she desperately needed from a relationship.

Since this morning, she'd felt a presence with her, a heavy aura lurking nearby. She couldn't pinpoint the feeling, nor could she see anyone about, but the sense was there. The dread that had settled like a lump of coal in her chest was real. So real, in fact, Tenile was near to calling it fear.

Donovan's plane landed in Bar Harbor. His car would be waiting at the gate, and he would drive to Tanner, the town where his sister had died.

He had known the precise moment Nathan Hamilton had stepped out of his luxury car into the small town. Just as he knew the man's purpose. For years he'd kept tabs on Nathan and all the other members of his sister's college crew.

They were all together now. All in the same place where it began. Just like old times.

In a few hours he'd be there too. Then the reunion would be complete.

⸎

It was near midnight when Tenile made her way into her apartment. She didn't bother to turn on any lights, just stripped off her clothes piece by piece as her tired legs carried her into the bedroom. She wore only her bra and panties when she pulled back the covers and slipped beneath the cool linen. It would be a long time before she agreed to work a double shift again.

Though exhaustion claimed her body, her mind drifted back to that hot and sticky June before they graduated. They were twenty-one, she, Landy and Nicole, graduating in a few weeks. Landy and Tenile's friendship was special, a closeness that protected them from the world. Nicole was not a part of the connection. Landy and Tenile didn't quite understand her, but they tolerated her just the same. Everything was perfect, their plans made, their futures bright and waiting. And then everything changed. Sighing, Tenile fell into an uneasy sleep.

⸎

"Why'd you have to leave?"

"I've never really left you." Landy smiled. She wore a hot pink sundress, and her hair was pulled tight into a high ponytail that dangled between her shoulder blades. Huge pink hoops swung from her ears, and

thin pink bangles crowded her arm. She was barefoot, toes wiggling as she sat with her legs dangling off the side of the porch.

"I know. I've been wondering lately why you didn't...really leave."

Landy leaned back, her hands flat on the porch behind her, supporting her. "I have to show you something."

"Show me what?"

Landy grinned then jumped from the porch. "Things were never quite what we thought they were, Tee. He knows. He knows all about it." Her words were spoken with her soft northern lilt as she walked barefooted to the line of trees in the back yard, into the dense darkness."Landy? Don't go!" I stood, trying to stop her, fear holding my heart in a death grip.

Her head turned, her hair swishing in the sudden breeze. "He's come back for you...and for me."

"He?" Her eyes said there was no need to speak the name aloud.

❧

Tenile woke with a start, her heart playing a rapid beat within her chest. She took a deep breath to steady herself, her eyes closing then opening again. Moonlight peeked through the window, casting shadows in the room. Bringing her hands to her face, she tried to rub away the tumultuous feelings swirling inside her. She took another deep breath and shivered.

She smelled jasmine, clear and fresh in the air. She was there, in the room with her, watching and waiting.

Landy, her best friend.

No. It was a dream. Tenile sighed. But it had felt so real. Landy was exactly the same, her look, her scent, her smile. *He knows.* Tenile was confused. Who knew? She realized she still had so many questions about that night, about Landy's death and about Nathan.

Had Nathan come back to Tanner for her or for Landy? A thunderous bolt of rage scorched her senses as she struggled with that thought. *She* was supposed to have been his girlfriend. Landy was only his friend. *She* was supposed to be the one he spent his nights with, not Landy. He'd betrayed her with her best friend, and then he'd killed her.

"No!" Involuntarily, the word was wrenched from her soul. Her hands flew to her mouth. It couldn't be. She'd never really believed it, despite what was being said. Nathan couldn't have killed Landy; he just couldn't. Even if he didn't love her the way he should have, he'd loved Landy, of that Tenile had no doubt.

What was happening? What was going on? She didn't know. Nathan could help her and no doubt would if she asked, but she wouldn't. She couldn't. Having Nathan in the same town was risky enough. If she dared go to him, dared tell him about her fears, her premonitions, he'd be on her doorstep in no time. They'd be together, close, trying to figure out what had happened all those years ago. She couldn't afford to do that. She couldn't handle it.

Whatever was going on, whatever Landy was trying to tell her, she'd have to figure out alone. Nathan couldn't be involved. For her own peace of mind, he couldn't be near her. It was as simple as that.

For years she'd wanted to know who Landy's killer was and why she'd had to die. Landy's appearance, whether it be dream or hallucination, was proof that she was meant to find out. Now she knew without a doubt she'd never have closure, never be able to fully enjoy the life she'd been blessed to live, if she didn't know. Feeling that Landy was near was one thing, but *knowing* she was there and *knowing* she was there for a reason made her jittery, uncertain.

She fell back onto her pillows wondering what her next step should be.

Robert. His face came to her clearly, and she decided she'd call him first thing in the morning. He would help her find Landy's murderer. Then they could continue with their lives. Her life.

Her life without Nathan. That's the way it had to be.

Nathan sat on the back porch of his newly purchased house. He liked the back view best. The woods, a barrier to some unknown place, seemed to hold firmly to secrets.

The air was cool but he wasn't bothered. It was almost silent out tonight, a good night for thinking. He folded the piece of paper in his hand.

There's something in the dark. Landy's in the dark. That's what the note said. It had taken him only a few moments to realize that someone was trying to tell him something about the murder. Now that he was back, he could feel the growing tension around him. He'd felt it earlier this evening while sharing a drink with Eli. Felt it between old friends like a barrier blocking their paths.

He'd also felt it when he'd talked to Tenile. But with her it was different because that summer they'd lost more than just a friend. They'd lost each other.

With shocking clarity, he remembered the look on her face when they learned Landy was gone. He'd reached for her, but she'd pulled away, seeking solitude in her room. He'd wanted to go to her that night, to hold her until she knew everything would be alright. But he didn't. And now he knew that had been a mistake, the first of many he would make.

The next day she'd seemed unreachable, in some far off place that he couldn't get to. He should have tried. He should have done whatever he could to get to her, to make her understand.

Unfortunately, they couldn't go back. They could never go back.

But now, he could do something. He could make her see the truth. Propping his feet up on the thick wooden railing—which sorely needed re-painting—he remembered what she'd said. She was seeing someone. Her life hadn't stopped because he'd left. But his had, the moment he realized she was no longer by his side. She'd moved on. She'd been so much stronger than he was in that regard. There'd never been another woman in his life who could come close to what he'd felt for her.

Within the Shadows

A rabbit darted quickly from the bushes by the porch into the thick lushness of the woods. And just that fast, he realized he'd never stopped loving her, needing her, wanting her.

So she had a man. Well, they'd just have to see about that. He was a tenacious guy, used to getting what he wanted. But he wouldn't rush, wouldn't push. He'd get her back with patience and persistence. He'd win back Tenile's trust and her love.

Together they'd figure out the truth about Landy's murder. The truth that hung over Tanner like a sinister storm cloud. Together they'd avenge the death of their friend. Then they'd start their life anew, just as they'd planned to do that summer.

Chapter 6

S o your ex is back in town. Should I be jealous?" Robert stretched out his muscled legs and lounged on Tenile's couch.

Tenile had just fixed glasses of iced tea, placed them on the table and plopped down next to him. "Nathan and I are definitely over." She ignored the light tapping in the back of her mind. It *was* over. "I mentioned it because we'll be working together, and talk is bound to surface about our past."

"Man, I'm glad I'm from Philly. People in Tanner talk too much."

Tenile wasn't all that thrilled with the town gossip either, but his comment appealed to her even less. Still, she figured for someone not used to the ins and outs of small town life, it would be a bit annoying, even though it was no different than big city tabloids and gossip rags. As a matter of fact, small towns tended to be a little more honest than the media. "You get used to it," she said in a neutral tone.

Then she thought about his remark again and wondered aloud, "Why does gossip bother you so much? You have something in your past you're trying to hide?"

His fingers grazed the nape of her neck, gently pulling her closer. He smiled and she noticed there was no parade going on inside her belly, the way it had been yesterday when Nathan had pulled her close. With much effort, she pushed thoughts of Nathan and his touch into the past where they belonged and concentrated on the here and now.

She liked Robert's smile, his caramel-colored skin and his hazel eyes. He wasn't buff, but he was no small fry either. His six-foot frame and toned medium build suited his low-key personality just fine.

Thick lips grazed hers, and she snuggled closer to him. Maybe close proximity would stir something inside of her.

"You know all there is to know about me."

His voice was a soft whisper over her skin. She kissed him again before laying her head on his shoulder. "That's good because I don't like secrets."

"Why don't we go out for dinner tonight?"

The question was quick and completely unexpected. Saturday was her first day off in her tedious workweek, and she normally didn't go out that day unless absolutely necessary. Because she worked seven to eleven at night, she used her days to run errands. She and Robert spent Sundays after church and Monday evenings together, as she was off on those days too. With summer quickly approaching, she'd now be able to spend more time with Robert since school would be closed.

A million reasons she should beg off a restaurant dinner entered her mind. But one thought—the one that told her things with her and Robert needed to heat up soon or she'd be in big trouble—won out. "Sounds good."

Robert moved away slowly, so as not to jolt her, then stood and walked away. "Get dressed. Something nice," he said as he moved toward the door. "I'll be back to get you around seven.

Hmph. She was thinking more along the lines of Tanner Deli where she could wear the jeans and cotton blouse she had on. "Ah, that sounds cool." Tucking her thumbs in her belt hoops, she smiled up at him.

"Good. And wear your hair up. I like it better that way."

Tenile's hands had unconsciously moved to the long black strands hanging past her shoulders. She didn't like to wear her hair up; it made her feel like her mother. She would have contemplated this issue longer had a familiar shrill voice not demanded her attention.

"Good day. Hope I'm not interrupting." Nicole gave a flamboyant smile as she lied. She'd seen Tenile's door open with that geeky-looking Robert Gibson standing there and prayed she was interrupting, breaking up the worst match she'd ever seen, thereby saving her friend from utter boredom.

"Hi, Nicole." Robert gave Nicole a polite smile before turning his attention back to Tenile. "Seven sharp. Don't be late." The last was said as he glared at Nicole, then left.

Nicole breezed past Tenile. "Good riddance!"

She smelled like Chanel. Her black miniskirt and sheer white blouse matched perfectly with the black and white pumps Tenile knew were expensive. "Hey, Nik. What brings you by?"

Tenile tried not to frown as she surveyed her friend. Nicole's hair was impeccable, as always. Fluffy bronze curls danced seductively at her shoulders, and her flawless makeup completed the chic gorgeousness of the woman. For a split second, Tenile envied her. Then Nicole sank onto the couch and pouted.

"I need help," she whined.

This was a new one. Tenile picked up her glass and sat beside her. "*You* need help. This I've gotta hear."

Since Landy's death, Nicole and Tenile had clung to each other. An odd pair but connected by something inside them both, they'd managed to seal the friendship and support each other throughout the years.

Nicole ignored Tenile's dry humor. She toyed with one of the throw pillows on the couch. She never could be still when she was pumped up. "Have you ever wanted something really badly but couldn't quite reach it?"

Tenile thought about the question, then thought about the person asking it. As far as she knew, Nicole had always gotten exactly what she wanted, when she wanted it, so she didn't really understand her meaning. But Mama always said the best answer was the simple truth. "Yes."

Clutching the pillow to her chest, Nicole sat back on the couch, letting her head fall against the cushions. "So what do you do about it?"

Because she didn't know what Nicole was really talking about, the truthful answer needed some tweaking before she could speak it. "That depends on what you want. I mean, if it involves someone else and how that someone will react to you getting it, if you really deserve it or if it's just a whimsy. If this something that you want will inevitably cause you pain—"

Nicole stared at her in disgust. "Alright, alright. I get your drift. You don't have to go on and on about it."

Tenile shrugged. "You asked."

"That I did."

Tenile leaned over, put her glass down, and turned sideways so that she now faced Nicole. "Why don't you just tell me what it is you want that you can't get?"

Long red nails drummed over the ivory pillow. She was really nervous. This too was new for Nicole and had Tenile a little alarmed.

"I would tell you but considering your previous answer, coming here might not have been the smartest thing for me to do." With a feminine howl, she threw the pillow across the room. "I just don't know what to do."

Tenile rolled her eyes. Nicole had always had a flare for the dramatic. "You can start by not disrespecting my furniture." She stood, crossed the room, reclaimed the pillow, puffed it a bit, then tossed it back at her houseguest. "Now, whatever it is, it can't possibly be that bad, so just spit it out."

Nicole swatted just in time so the pillow fell beside her on the couch. She toyed with a strand of hair and stared at Tenile contemplatively. She admired Tenile, although she'd never admit it. Even though she needed to re-think her hairstyle, her clothes, her makeup and her general appearance, Nicole had come to realize how strong and stable Tenile really was. Maybe that was why Landy had chosen Tenile over her. Landy had been from money and privilege, just like Nicole. Yet she'd chosen to befriend a nobody like Tenile Barnes whose parents worked at the docks.

During their freshman year, she'd resented Tenile for her closeness with Landy, but then the duo had let her in. They'd opened their arms to her, and she, because she felt it was their gain, had allowed herself to stoop to their level. Little did she know that over the course of those four years she'd learn more about herself and more about friendship and loyalty from those two than any book could ever teach her. After Landy's death, there'd been nobody left for her besides Tenile. And the girl had stuck. Even though Nicole had thought Tenile would be grateful to finally be rid of her—she'd never really been all that nice to her—she'd stuck around, offering her support, being Nicole's rock.

"There's this guy," she finally spoke.

Tenile grinned. "You are *not* here throwing my pillows around over some guy." Nicole never had a problem in that area. Men loved her, fell at her feet as she walked down the street and would drink from her shoe if they didn't fear she'd scratch their eyes out for damaging her Donna Karan pumps.

Nicole threw her a baleful look. "It's not funny, Tenile. This is very serious."

Tenile cleared her throat and straightened on the sofa. "Sorry. Okay, it's about a guy. A guy that you want and can't have. Why can't you have him?"

"Because he doesn't look at me that way."

"What way?"

Nicole never thought twice about her answer. "The way Nathan used to look at you."

Tenile jerked as if she'd been slapped. Why did she have to bring up his name? They were having such a good conversation—well, such an unusual one—but still *he* could have been left out of it. "I don't know what you're talking about." In the interest of self-preservation, Tenile kept her voice casual.

Nicole waved a hand. "Oh, get over yourself. You know exactly what I mean. You had that boy sprung ten years ago and probably still have him dangling from that thread around your pinkie." Nicole kicked off her sandals, propping her pedicured feet up on the table. "That's what I want. I want him to love me so much he can't see straight."

Tenile decided that the best way to get Nathan out of the conversation was to pretend that he'd never been in it. "Isn't that how you always have your men?"

"Usually, but I can't seem to bring this one around, and I really want to. I'm getting too old for these games and flings. Despite what everybody thinks, I would like to get married one day, settle down with one man and have a family."

Again Tenile had to laugh. "You do not want children. Your figure would never be the same again."

Nicole tried to rein in a snicker as her hand found her super-flat belly. "You're probably right." She sobered. "Still, that doesn't mean I don't want someone to love me. Nobody ever loved me."

Her voice was thin, shaky with emotion, and Tenile felt the impact of her words. Nicole was an only child, her parents either too rich, too busy or too selfish to give their one child the attention she so desperately needed. Mama had always said it was a shame that such a pretty creature had been spoiled from the inside out. "You can't make someone love you, Nicole. And if he doesn't, then that's his loss. Don't waste your time trying to make the relationship something it's not."

Nicole turned to stare at her in disbelief. "You should talk."

"What's that supposed to mean?" Tenile was a little insulted.

Nicole pointed towards the door. "You and teacher boy. You know damn well he's not lighting your fire. So why do you keep running around town with him?"

She had a point there, a point that Tenile had no intention of acknowledging. "You're delusional. Robert and I are perfectly happy." Now *she* was the one drumming her fingers over the pillow.

"Don't try to play me, girl. You know I know better. I've seen you happy. I've seen you madly in love. And that," she gestured towards the door again, "is definitely not happy."

"Whatever." Tenile rose again, this time going into the kitchen.

Nicole's bare feet padded across the carpet, then slapped daintily over the linoleum kitchen floor. She stopped and opened the refrigerator. "You eat like you're going through puberty," she said with disgust at the sight of sugared cereal and Kool-Aid in Tenile's refrigerator. "You never used to buy this stuff when we were in school."

Tenile opened a bag of potato chips and crunched on one. "You can get out of my refrigerator. Its contents are none of your business."

"Yeah, like the fact that your panties are in a bunch 'cause Nathan's back in town is none of my business either." Nicole pinned her with a lively smirk.

Tenile rolled her eyes.

"You are so predictable. The moment I heard he was back, I knew just the reaction you would have."

"And what reaction is that?" She bit into another chip, enjoying the salty alternative to this conversation.

"The 'I don't care, I don't love him anymore' one." She paused for effect. "You're still in love with him. You might as well admit it to me even if you're afraid to admit it to yourself."

Tenile balled up the bag and tossed it on the counter. "If we're done with your little problem, you can go." She stalked back into the living room.

Nicole sauntered behind her, a bottled water in hand. "Fine. My problem is much more serious than yours. You're too damned frigid to do anything about Nathan anyway. We need to figure out what I'm going to do to get my man."

An hour later, Tenile had showered and was attempting to style her hair. Nicole was stretched across her bed, poised like a lynx.

"So what I'm saying is, he sees me as a woman. A woman he likes to have sex with but that's all. That's the problem."

Tenile fussed with a hairpin and the uncooperative strands that refused to stay in place. "There's your answer right there," she said with a frustrated sigh.

"Good grief, what are you trying to do? Pull all your hair out?" Nicole peeled herself off the mattress and began undoing the progress Tenile had made. "If I stop sleeping with him, he'll just find someone else."

Tenile surprised herself by remaining still while Nicole brushed and clipped her hair. "If he finds someone else, then he didn't really want you in the first place."

Meeting her eyes in the mirror, Nicole looked at Tenile quizzically. "So if I cut him off and he backs away, that means he's not worth my time. Is that what you're saying?"

Not wanting to hurt Nicole's feelings but wanting to be honest at the same time, Tenile asked, "Who is this guy?"

Nicole picked up the curlers and twirled the straight wisps of hair she'd left free from the bun. "It's a secret."

"I hate secrets."

Nicole's hand paused in mid-air as she remembered. "That's right, you do. Well, he's somebody we've known forever. Somebody we both know very well."

Tenile's heart tripped, then almost stopped. Had Nathan gone from one of her friends to the other?

"What the hell's wrong with you? You look like you've just seen a ghost." Nicole gave her shoulders a rough shake.

Tenile pulled away from her. "Nothing's wrong." Taking a deep breath, she stepped further away. "Thanks," she murmured as she fingered her hair. Reaching for the dress she'd hung on the door, she pushed those thoughts out of her mind. She didn't care who Nathan was sleeping with. But she didn't want it to be with Nicole.

"That dress is hideous. It does nothing for your figure." Nicole clucked before moving to the closet to flip through Tenile's options.

"This dress is fine." But she didn't put it on just yet. She looked at it for a moment.

"Uck! You and I need to go shopping."

Tenile shrugged and removed her robe, prepared to put the dress on regardless. "I can't afford to shop with you."

Nicole pulled out a red low cut dress. "If this is the best you've got—and believe me it is—then you definitely need to go shopping with me."

Tenile didn't argue. Nicole had styled her hair in a very sophisticated style; the simple black coat-dress was not going to complement it. "It's just dinner. And you haven't said who your man is."

Nicole zipped her up. "You mean I haven't said that it's not Nathan."

Tenile tensed. Nicole knew her too well. "Don't be funny. Who is he?"

Nicole giggled, then went into the living room. By the time she reappeared, Tenile had on her shoes—which she'd changed from sturdy black leather pumps to strappy gold sandals—and was about to start her makeup.

"Uh-uh." Nicole motioned her away from the dresser. "You don't have anything up there worthy of this ensemble. Sit down and let me hook you up."

Tenile sat. "Hurry up. Robert will be here any minute."

"Please, school boy can wait. Especially since I've got more to tell you about how Eli likes to get down."

"Eli?" Tenile stared in shock at Nicole who was headed towards her with foundation in hand. "You are not serious."

Nicole smiled.

Tenile got comfortable in the chair. "Do tell. Robert will just have to wait."

The ride to Bangor was a shock to Tenile. She'd assumed they'd be dining in town. But she wasn't dissatisfied, and she and Robert took this time to get to know each other better. Since his earlier remark about being from Philly, she'd realized there were gaps in what she knew about him. If he was going to be someone she made a future with, she needed to remedy that situation as soon as possible.

He answered all her questions but seemed unwilling to go into any sort of detail. Finally, she decided she was being ridiculous. There was no way you could learn all there was to know about someone in an hour-long drive or even one night, for that matter. She'd known Nathan for five years and still hadn't known him as well as she thought.

After Nicole had finally left her alone, she'd thought a lot about those years they'd spent together, specifically how she'd never really noticed Eli and Nicole being more than friends. Yet Nicole had given her a detailed version of their first time together, which had taken place on Halloween of their sophomore year in the den of their house. On and off and between his girlfriends and her beaus, they'd drifted back to each other. Tenile wondered what type of person it took to sustain a relationship like that.

She wanted exclusivity, plain and simple. She didn't want, nor would she tolerate, someone dropping in between relationships. It was insane and she'd told Nicole that very thing. She deserved more, and if Eli wasn't willing to give it to her, then she needed to clamp her legs shut and move on to the next candidate. Nicole seemed to agree, but Tenile sensed a part of her was afraid. This was serious business for her; she'd never wanted anything permanent before. Apparently, she did now with Eli. Tenile wished her luck.

Luck. Ha, she needed some of that herself.

Tenile smiled as the car pulled into the parking lot. They were going to an Italian restaurant. She loved Italian food. Robert came around to the passenger side and helped her out of the car. "You look really good tonight," he told her for only the fifth time since he'd picked her up. He sounded incredulous, and Tenile tried not to be wounded. It wasn't like she was a troll any other time.

"Thanks, again." *Now buy me dinner so I can go home*, she found herself thinking as they walked into the restaurant. This was not the way she should be thinking about a man she wanted to get closer to.

The interior was dim, candlelight illuminating the spacious dining room. Tables were covered with red checked cloths, and high-backed dark wooden chairs eagerly awaited their patrons. It wasn't a packed house, but she heard the buzz of other diners while they waited to be seated. Robert touched the small of her back as they were led to their table. She jumped slightly, only because it was different. He didn't make a habit of being overly intimate in public.

He held the chair for her and waited until she was situated before looking at his watch. "I have to make a call. I'll be right back."

"A call?" She stared at him blankly. Who was he calling? He'd only lived in Tanner for a year, and as far as she knew, he didn't have any family nearby.

"It's nothing." He tucked a tendril of hair behind her ear. "I'll just be a few minutes."

"Fine." She didn't know what else to say, but he sure was acting weird.

Watching his retreating back, his tan slacks and white dress shirt moving effortlessly through the room towards the front entrance, she wasn't expecting anyone to approach, didn't imagine that anyone in Bangor would know her. When a hand touched her shoulder, ripples of panic streamed through her body. The eyes that met her gaze had an even more chilling effect.

Chapter 7

When she walked in, Nathan noticed only a siren-hot red dress, thin straps at the shoulders holding it in place and gold-tinged material falling sinfully over lush curves. He experienced a heat so fierce shooting through his loins that he'd been forced to stand. Imagine his surprise when his eyes made their way to the face of this delightful package only to find it was the woman who had invaded his heart.

Had she ever been this sexy before? Had he ever reacted to her this way before? He couldn't remember and didn't really care to. They were in the here and now. And right here, right now, he was rock hard, his erection leading him like raw steak on a stick—and he followed like a panting dog.

She was with a man. Robert Gibson, no doubt. The man had been foolish enough to leave that enticing beauty alone, and Nathan intended to take full advantage of that.

"I don't remember ever seeing you in that dress." His throat was raspy with desire that he'd planned to mask. It wouldn't do for her to think he was driven by lust only.

She tensed instantly. How had he found her here? Was he following her? "Wardrobes tend to change in ten years." Her tone was clipped even though her insides were swishing around in confusion—attraction or dread?

Nathan took the seat across from her, regrettably but wisely ending the contact of skin on skin. "Dining alone?"

"No, my date—my boyfriend—will be back momentarily. So whatever brought you here needs to take you back as soon as possible." She fidgeted with the napkin, unfolding it, placing it in her lap, finally balling it up in nervousness. Gracious, she hadn't been this unnerved by a man since…since—she'd never been this unnerved by a man. And damn Nathan Hamilton for being the first one!

look right beat." Oneil put a glass of orange juice and a
of Wheat in front of her daughter. Her baby girl. Tenile
been born three weeks premature, a tiny red bundle full
emembered the day clearly. Aaron, her oldest child, had
the week before, and his chubby little cheeks puffed up
wn at the baby as if she were an intruder. Calvin Barnes,
l, had adored their daughter, swearing she'd never have
ment in her life. Oneil sure was glad Calvin wasn't here
girl now.

ama." Tenile inhaled the wholesome smell of home—
heat for breakfast, the freshly squeezed orange juice, the
resting on the counter top near the stove, blaring the
imes she missed being home, missed waking up each
eone who cared about her and would talk to her.

rking those double shifts?" Oneil moved about the large
o keep herself busy. And she was trying not to look like
though that was her intent.

onths I'll have enough for the down payment on a house.
'll cut back on my hours." She knew her mother was
er, but owning her own home was a goal she wanted to
the year was out. As it stood now, she'd most likely be in
by the end of the summer—three months from now.
spoon of cereal, Tenile waited a beat, then put it into her
always put in just the right amount of sugar.

ieve whatever you put your mind to, baby." Oneil
hicken legs she planned to cook for dinner that evening.
really good now. She put up quite a fuss about staying
ut finally realized it was for the best. I'm sure Aaron's call
with that."

right on eating. "Maybe. It is better for her, though, and
got somebody to fuss over again."

s over people, I just take care of them." Oneil moved her
cken to the table and sat across from her daughter. "You
le taking care of yourself."

Nathan smiled, slowly, indulgently. She was shaking. He liked it, imagined those tremors increasing as his hands boldly raked over her body. "I simply needed confirmation."

Her brow furrowed and her hands stilled. "Confirmation of what?"

"That you're as beautiful now as you were then."

The compliment took her aback. The stinging edges of Robert's comment that she 'looked good' this evening dissipated as Nathan's smooth words washed over her like a dream. A dream that had turned into a nightmare, she quickly reminded herself. "I'm well beyond your flattery, Nathan. Now what do you really want?"

"You know, you looked pretty damn good the other day when I saw you too," he said conversationally. "And you weren't even dressed to impress then."

"I'm not dressed to impress you," she declared matter-of-factly.

"Pity."

She let out a deep sigh. "Nathan, this is ridiculous. We might as well put all our cards on the table right now."

Cards on the table. She had no idea what she was walking into. He sat back, lifted his hands then shrugged. "Ladies first."

Her lips formed a tight line. He was so damned cool, she wanted to strangle him. Why couldn't he be feeling the same tangle of emotions that she was? Why did he have to look as if he had all the answers? "What we had was nice while it lasted. But that's over and done with. We are two different people now with a lot of history between us. History I, for one, do not care to dredge up. Besides, I have someone in my life right now, so even if there were something left between us…." She clamped her mouth shut tight, then took a deep breath and tried again. "Whatever was between us before has long since fizzled. Why don't we just leave it at that?"

She was serious, he thought. Seriously delusional. The sexual tension between them was so thick right now a machete wouldn't cut through it. And as if that weren't enough, the overwhelming urge to rescue her from this hoax of a relationship with the poor, unsuspecting teacher clenched his heart like a tight fist. She was his, she belonged to him, and he had never been one for sharing. "Whew, that sure was a mouthful. I hadn't thought that deeply."

"You hadn't?"

"Nope. I just saw a really pretty lady and wanted to tell her so. The fact that I've known you intimately already didn't even enter my mind." He gave her a cheeky grin and felt sheer satisfaction as she squirmed with the memory. "Some things never fizzle, Tee."

She crossed her arms over her chest. "No, they just go away."

It was a cheap shot, but it hit its mark and he sobered instantly. "I cannot apologize enough for that mistake, so I won't do so again. Just know that I'm back now, and I intend to make things right this time."

"And how do you propose to do that?" His eyes had softened, searching hers for something she wasn't sure she had. He wore all black, his short-sleeved shirt displaying huge biceps that her fingers tingled to touch. He'd taken really good care of himself. For that alone she wanted to curse him.

"I'm going to find out who killed Landy and clear my name." He let the words hover over the table and settle between them. "I didn't kill her, Tenile. It's very important that you believe that."

She believed it. She always had. "I know you didn't, Nathan."

Relief, pleasure, love, lust—all those emotions soared through him simultaneously. Acting on instinct and pure need, he reached across the table, rubbing her arm until she reluctantly put her hand in his. "And I'm going to get you back."

"No. We can't—" Because he looked too sexy, too comfortable with his declaration, she got to her feet. "I should go and find Robert."

He rose, watched her eyes go wide and watchful as he shifted just an inch closer. "He can't stop what's between us."

"Don't."

"I can't help it." He was so close to her now that the tips of her breasts brushed over his chest. His hands found her waist, and he held her to him. It took a lot of carefully controlled emotions to keep him from kissing her right there in the middle of that restaurant with her date quickly approaching them. "And neither can you."

Before she could speak, before she could make any attempt to move away—even though their closeness felt all too right—Robert appeared.

"Is something wrong, Tenile?" [...] to-face.

She looked at Nathan, admiss[...] "Ah, no, Robert. Nothing's wrong. [...] didn't move away.

"I'm Robert Gibson and you ar[...]

Regardless of how much he wa[...] had to acknowledge him. If not as a [...] never accept that— then as her date[...] he'd seen confirmation in her eye[...] tonight, that would have to be enoug[...] as he pulled them away from her. E[...] eye. "I'm Dr. Nathan Hamilton."

He saw the second Robert co[...] moment his defenses went up. Relu[...]

"Tenile and I were just about to [...]

The man didn't want him aro[...] didn't want any man within an inch [...] been gone. Robert could have this e[...] vowed. "Surely. I was just finishing [...] "I'll see you at work, Tenile."

She cast him a baleful look. "Yes[...]

"Have a good evening," he said[...] before leaving them alone.

Robert helped Tenile back into [...] not so long ago vacated. "I see his [...] yours."

Tenile groaned inwardly as thoug[...] the man she was supposed to be da[...] going to be a long evening.

"Chile, you[...] bowl of Cream[...] Rose Barnes ha[...] of tears. Oneil [...] just turned thre[...] as he looked dc[...] her late husbar[...] an unhappy m[...] to see their littl[...]

"Thanks, [...] the Cream of [...] small televisior[...] local news. At[...] morning to sor[...]

"You still w[...] kitchen trying [...] she was prying[...]

"In a few r[...] At the point, [...] worried about [...] achieve before[...] her own hous[...] Blowing on th[...] mouth. Mama[...]

"You'll ac[...] seasoned the c[...]

"Tracy's doing[...] here with me [...] had a lot to dc[...]

Tenile kep[...] for you. You'v[...]

"I don't fu[...] pan of raw ch[...] could use a li[...]

"I'm fine, Mama."

"You ain't fine, and don't sit there and tell me that bald-faced lie." Big hands flipped the chicken from side to side as she continued seasoning it.

Tenile took a sip of her orange juice. "Mama, please don't start." She'd managed to go an entire week without hearing about Nathan and her mother's thoughts on his return. Now, on her first day off this week when she'd ventured out of her house early in the morning to visit with her mother, she feared she'd not dodged the bullet but walked right into the line of fire.

"I knew when I heard that boy was back it would be bad feelings for you. I remember how the both of you were back in school." Oneil let her words settle. "I also remember what happened that made him leave town in such a hurry. Now, I want you to be careful around him."

"Mama, Nathan is not dangerous. He wasn't then and he certainly isn't now." At least, not in that way, she thought dismally.

"Seems to me people don't run away unless they're trying to hide something."

Tenile opened her mouth to speak again, but Oneil silenced her with one look. "I ain't convicting the boy. All I'm saying is something made him run. And we still don't know who killed that girl. That's all I'm saying."

"Alright, Mama. I hear what you're saying."

Oneil rolled her eyes. "You never had a problem with your hearing. It's your listening that could use some tuning up."

Tenile got up from the table, put her bowl in the sink and leaned over the bottom cupboards.

"What are you over there doing? Trying to ignore me in that quiet way of yours?" Oneil accused her.

Tenile had begun to hum "Someone to Watch Over Me," a song that had played in her head throughout the night. It was an old song, and she wondered why it was on her mind this morning. She didn't give it too much thought, just kept on moving. "I'm getting the pot to start the barbeque sauce. You'll need it for the chicken when you get finished."

"Hmph. Yeah, you fix the sauce. I'm gonna keep right on talking."

Tenile proceeded to the top cupboards, pulling out the brown sugar and tomato sauce. Mama was right. She'd keep right on talking, whether Tenile listened or not.

⋙⋘

"She was the closest one to her. If anybody knows, she'll know." His tone was brisk as he paced the length of the room.

"But if she hasn't talked in all these years, what makes you think she'll say something now?"

"Because he's back. He's poking around trying to find something. Trying to find me. And if she joins up with him, that's exactly what they'll do. Now I'm paying you good money to see that this doesn't happen. I don't want Hamilton uncovering what I've worked so hard to hide. What's done is done, and I want to keep it that way."

The second man shrugged. He'd gotten into this by sheer greed. For him, a product of the projects with a drug-addicted mother and a philandering alcoholic father, money was the answer to everything. He was getting paid pretty well from the man pacing the room, the man who was deathly afraid that his sins of the past were about to resurface and smother him. He didn't care either way, as long as he got paid. He hadn't broken any laws...yet. But if this man was saying what he thought he was saying, that would be changing soon enough.

"That house, that girl and Hamilton. They all hold the answers. I want them taken care of, and I want it done immediately. I can't stand this hick town, and the longer I have to stay here, the more I hate it." He clapped the other man on the shoulder. "I'm trusting you to take care of this."

"I'll handle it, boss. You don't have to worry. But you know my payment will have to be increased."

Greedy son of a bitch, he thought. "Yeah, yeah. Whatever." He waved his hand. He didn't have time to think about what he'd pay the man, probably because he had no intention of paying him anything. Fool that he was, he thought he was making big moves, securing himself financially for life. There was no need to burst his bubble just yet. No need to tell him that after all was said and done he'd have no need for money. "Whatever you want, you'll receive."

The second guy smiled. "Then I'll take care of Hamilton and the woman pronto."

"Don't forget the house. There's something in that house."

"I won't forget."

Standing at the end of the soft drink aisle, Nathan watched Tenile as she carefully selected a two-liter bottle and put it into her cart. He'd been following her around the market for the last fifteen minutes. Not two seconds after he'd entered the store with the intention of stocking his own refrigerator, he'd seen her. She was clad in jeans—dark denim that molded and shaped that amazing body of hers—and a red button-down shirt tied just beneath her breasts. What was it with her and red? Somehow that color seemed ten degrees hotter when she was the one wearing it.

She moved to the frozen foods, selecting vegetables and those low fat dinners that looked appealing on the cover but sucked big time in the taste department. His cart was still empty, but he didn't care. It was exciting to watch her walk, see, think, concentrate. He studied her move-ments—the bend of her knee as she stooped to get something on a lower shelf, the curve of her arm as she read the nutritional facts on the back of a box, the tilt of her head as she decided what to put into the cart next. She was mesmerizing him, and he wasn't putting up any fight at all.

Just that quickly, while he was transfixed by the inch of skin her shirt revealed, she turned and saw him. He felt her heated gaze and looked up to meet it. He smiled, her sexy-as-hell scowl preventing him from doing anything else.

He didn't have time to move away, although he wouldn't have even considered it, before she was headed straight for him.

"You *are* following me, you stalker!" she exclaimed when their carts were touching end to end.

"I'm not stalking you," he replied calmly, though he was walking a thin line. "I'm grocery shopping. A man's gotta eat."

Her eyes narrowed on him. "Your cart's empty."

He looked down and felt laughter boil inside. "You've got a point there."

"Having trouble finding what you're looking for?" she asked icily. His eyes were amused, his lips faintly curved. And then she saw what she'd been rebelling against for the last week. Pure, unadulterated lust.

"I know exactly what I'm looking for. And conveniently enough, it's managed to walk right up to me without much effort on my part." His eyes raked over her.

"You're disgusting. And you're bothering me. I'm trying to shop." In an irritated gesture, she pushed her purse further up on her shoulder and attempted to maneuver her cart.

He swiveled so that he was now facing in the same direction as she was, standing alongside her. "That's good because I'm trying to shop too." He walked beside her, effortlessly keeping up with her quick stride.

"Nathan, this isn't funny."

"I'm not laughing," he said but couldn't help smiling.

She gave him an accusatory look. "You're not?"

His hand went to his mouth as he tried unsuccessfully to cover the grin. "Nope. I'm just really happy to be so close to you." It was the truth and she didn't like it. He could see the tension in her shoulders and longed to kiss her right there in the hollow where her pulse thumped wildly. "Anyway, finding you here is a two-fold blessing."

She turned quickly down another aisle. "How do you figure that?" She was annoyed that he was walking with her but even more annoyed at her body's reaction to his close proximity.

"I can't seem to figure out what to have for dinner tonight. Maybe you could help me?"

"I don't know what you like."

"I'm not hard to please. But then you knew that already, didn't you?"

She did know. Whatever she or one of the other girls had cooked in that house, Nathan had always been the first at the table to scarf it down. But she remembered that his favorite was pot roast and potatoes, mac and cheese, collard greens, iced tea and apple pie for dessert. Like a blast from the past, those dishes, those smells, coursed through her, causing her to stop quickly.

"Are you trying to tell me canned soup would be a good idea?" he asked, his eyes scanning the shelves she'd stopped directly in front of.

She followed his gaze, sucked her teeth and rolled her eyes. He was an infuriating man. It was probably best that they just get this shopping excursion over with so she could be on her way...alone.

He read her expression and moved around her and her cart. Lifting a can in each hand, he said, "I never could quite decide between vegetable and alphabet vegetable. What do you think?"

The breath she huffed out ended on a laugh, and she finally gave in. "You should be pretty adept at spelling by now, so I'd say be mature and get the plain vegetable."

He turned to face her, pleased as punch at the pleasant smile she wore. "Only if you say you'll share it with me."

She took the can of vegetable soup out of his hand, unceremoniously dropping it into his cart. "I'm having dinner with my mother and Tracy this evening."

She'd started moving again so he followed. "So have lunch with me."

She looked at her watch. "It's past lunch time."

He chuckled. She wasn't going to make this easy. But that was okay because he loved a challenge. "Then come by tomorrow after church."

She stopped again, just as they were about to turn into another aisle. "You remembered I go to church on Sundays?"

She looked so incredulous and extremely vulnerable that his heart skipped a beat. "I remember everything about you." They were in the middle of the supermarket, but he didn't care. He took a step closer to her, cupped her cheek with his palm. "I remember how you smell." He inhaled deeply, closing his eyes to the intoxicating scent. "I remember how you felt beneath me." Opening his eyes, he watched hers darken as the memory crept over her too. "And I think I remember how you taste, but I'd love a refresher." He leaned closer and was about to take her mouth when a voice interrupted from behind.

"Well, well, well. It's like déjà vu seeing you two together again." Geraldine Finley was upon them like a lightning bolt, effectively shattering the moment.

Chapter 8

Tenile jumped, moving away from Nathan as quickly as her feet could manage without landing her on the floor. Nathan turned slowly, ticked that he'd been so close to tasting her again only to be hindered by a woman whose voice was a blast from the past.

"I was just tellin' your mama I knew it wouldn't be long before you two picked up where you left off." Geraldine's eyes pinned Tenile, ignoring Nathan for the moment.

"Hello, Mrs. Finley. It's a pleasure to see you again. I swear, I don't think you've changed one bit since I last saw you." Nathan moved closer to the woman he'd always thought was built like a football player—which was exactly what he meant by saying she hadn't changed. He dropped a kiss on her weathered cheek and draped his arms around her. It was a good thing he was tall with long limbs, else they both would have been embarrassed when his arms didn't fit around her width.

"I'm glad you've finally realized this is where you belong, son. And I see I'm not the only one." Her eyes cut toward Tenile again.

Tenile was tempted to turn tail and run out of the store but thought better of it. That would give Mrs. Finley too much to talk about. She'd stand strong today then be sure to stay the hell away from Nathan. The last thing she wanted or needed was for talk about her and Nathan reuniting to circulate through town. She needed to focus on things with Robert. She'd been way too close to falling under Nathan's spell…again.

"Mrs. Finley, it's always good to see you. I see you've got a full cart. Why don't you go ahead of me in line? Wouldn't want to hold up your dinner preparation," Tenile said sweetly, eyeing the overflowing contents in the woman's cart. No wonder she stayed so big; she had enough food in there to feed an army even though all her kids were grown and out of the house.

"Oh, I've got plenty of time to chat."

Didn't they know it.

Nathan smiled and cast Tenile an apologetic glance. "Well, we don't, Mrs. Finley. We have plans, and if we stand here talking any longer, we'll be pretty late. So we'll bid you goodbye until the next time we see you around." He moved his cart and started walking away.

Tenile started to follow Nathan, but Mrs. Finley moved her cart in front of hers and smiled. "Juggling two men, are we? Now you know that's not a good reputation for a woman to have in a town this small. What would your mama say?"

Tenile felt a shiver down her spine and longed to tell the woman where she could go with her assumptions. Instead, she gave her mother's friend a polite smile and spoke in a carefully controlled tone. "I don't think I have to worry about my reputation, Mrs. Finley. I've been in this town since I was a little girl. Everybody knows me and everybody respects me. The decision about what men I associate with is my business and mine alone. My mother respects that, and I would hope that the town citizens would as well." Moving her cart in a wide circle to escape the woman's barricade, she walked away.

Nathan went through the checkout counter—quickly since he only had the can of soup and the loaf of bread he'd picked up when he walked away from Tenile and Mrs. Finley. He now stood outside the store waiting for Tenile to come out. From the look on her face when she exited the store, lips in a tight line, brow furrowed, he could tell that Mrs. Finley's comments had made her uncomfortable.

"How could you just let her make that assumption and not correct her? How could you let her believe that we were seeing each other again?"

"It's not—"

"We are *not* seeing each other!"

Nathan arched a brow. "C'mon, Tee. Since when do you worry about what that old biddy says?"

"Since I have a boyfriend and a reputation to protect. I *do not* sleep around, nor do I date two men at the same time. But she'll no doubt have the entire town thinking that I do." There was a slight breeze, and strands of hair blew across her face into the corners of her mouth as she spoke.

Nathan reached out, smoothed those strands away, letting his fingers graze the soft flesh of her cheek. "I know you don't sleep around. As for the boyfriend part," he shrugged. "I don't know how long you plan to keep up that charade, but in my opinion, you should just put old Robert out of his misery now." He wanted to smile but thought better of it. This was a serious moment, at least for her.

"Now you get this straight. I have a boyfriend, and I have no intention of putting him out of his misery, as you say. You and I are not seeing each other now or anytime in the future. You got that?" With a quick step forward, she extended her finger and poked his shoulder repeatedly for emphasis.

Nathan grimaced. What he was getting was a sore shoulder, thanks to her. Casually and with deliberate restraint, he took her wrist, bringing it—to her dismay—to his lips, kissing the rapid movement of her pulse before letting go. "I'm seeing you pretty clearly right now, and what I see I'm liking more and more."

She wanted to scream. She wanted to scratch his eyes out and yell to all of Tanner that she wasn't seeing him, that she didn't want to see him, that they were over. Instead, she wrenched out of his grasp and picked up her bags. She turned to stalk away, but he grabbed her arm.

"Calm down, Tenile."

"I won't calm down. I don't want to be the subject of town gossip again." She did cease trying to pull away. His grip was too tight, and she probably looked more foolish for attempting an escape. "I don't like being talked about and stared at. It wasn't easy for me before—" Her voice broke.

"I know. I'm sorry." His grip loosened and his hand moved up and down her arm in a familiar motion.

"I knew the moment you came back the talk would start again. I don't want to go through that again."

He saw the hurt in her eyes, the pleading for him to make this go away. But before it was all over, talk was going to get a lot worse. He

71

couldn't stop that from happening, and he wouldn't promise her something he couldn't come through on. "My being back stirs up a lot of things for a lot of people. And while I have no intention of hurting anyone, I'm not leaving and my search for Landy's killer won't be dismissed."

"But do you have to involve me? Can't you just forget I was part of it?"

He rested one hand at the small of her back while he cupped her neck with the other. "I can't forget any part of you. You are embedded in me, and no amount of time or distance can ever change that."

She knew she wasn't on solid ground anymore as she shifted closer to him. "I don't know if I have the strength to go through all this again. You have no idea how long it took me to move past Landy's death, past you."

He had some idea; he was still trying. "You were alone then, and I know it was very hard for you, but I'm here now. I'm not going to leave you again, and I'm not going to let anybody harm you with words or any other way." He brought her closer and her eyes widened.

Her free hand slapped against his chest as alarm bells went off in her head. "What are you doing?"

"Relax, baby. I need to taste you again. It's been way too long."

She didn't want his kiss, didn't want this scene that they were making in the grocery store parking lot. She didn't want any of this. And yet she found herself moving closer, lifting her chin to receive him, anticipating. "You hurt me, Nathan."

He closed his eyes to her words, lowered his head. "This won't hurt. I promise." Then his lips touched hers.

She melted into him, her senses acutely aware of every place his fingers touched, and his tongue stroked sleekly against hers. He was right; it didn't hurt—it pleased, soothed, assuaged.

He pulled back. "The memory is no comparison." His hands continued to rub and stroke her neck and back.

"Nathan, I have a boyfriend." She stepped back in defense.

"I'll give you twenty-four hours to remedy that situation."

She didn't like his tone. "And if I don't?"

He grabbed his sole bag and prepared to go to his car. "I'll do it for you."

Tenile rolled her eyes. He'd grown quite bossy in ten years. "I'm a grown woman."

"I don't deny that. In fact, you're a very sexy grown woman who will be joining me for lunch and probably dinner tomorrow."

He was walking away, just leaving her there as if the conversation were finished. "Nathan?" she called to him.

He turned. "Tomorrow, Tee. And if you don't tell Robert, rest assured, I will. As a matter of fact, I'd prefer he hear it from me. But I'll let you decide."

And just like that he proceeded to his car. She hadn't confirmed she was going to his house, she fumed as she made her way to her own car. She hadn't said she would break up with her boyfriend. Why should she? He'd assumed an awful lot from just one kiss. She tossed the bags in her backseat and got in the front. One kiss that hadn't been all that—all that long, her mind translated. She slipped the key into the ignition. He was out of his mind if he thought he could waltz back into town and order her about, uproot the life she'd built for herself, kiss her outside for everyone to see.

When she reached home, she walked into her kitchen and put the bags down. Pulling out a chair, she let her shaky legs bend until she was seated. Dropping her head into her hands, she sighed. She was out of her mind if she thought they were truly, finally over.

❧

"Her trust fund amounted to more than two million dollars and is still collecting interest," John Lange, private investigator, spoke into the phone.

Nathan sat in the executive black leather chair he'd purchased for his home office, one hand holding the phone to his ear, the other stroking contemplatively over his bearded chin. "Who holds the account now?"

"It looks like the beneficiary hasn't been changed—Byram Connor."

"Byram Connor died in our junior year." Nathan's confusion was evident in his tone.

"Then it appears this financial data hasn't been updated since then. Landy Connor died a year after her father. The family attorneys should have long since had these beneficiaries changed, most likely to Miranda Connor since Landy's biological mother was already dead."

His office light was the only light on throughout the house, and Nathan felt lulled by the darkness. He'd come home after his scene with Tenile and enjoyed a good run. His muscles had been taut with desire for her and frustration at his inability to act on that desire. After his run, he'd prepared his lonely can of soup and attempted to enjoy a solitary dinner in the kitchen that had once been filled with people and laughter.

After doing some medical research, he'd decided it was time to get down to the real business of being back in Tanner. He wanted a future with Tenile but knew they'd forever have Landy's death and his implication in that situation looming over them. She didn't want to be dragged into this again, didn't want people talking about her. He was going to do everything in his power to minimize that and settle the matter once and for all.

"Where is Miranda Connor now?" He remembered Landy's stepmother vividly from the funeral where she had shown up dressed in royal blue, hands, neck and ears jeweled, face as cold as ice.

"Mrs. Connor relocated to the South of France immediately after her husband's death. Her son, Donovan Connor, has a home there as well."

Nathan sat up in his chair. "Donovan Connor. I remember him. He visited Landy quite frequently here in Maine." A visual of the man appeared in his mind.

John must have been going through his file because Nathan heard papers shuffling. "Yeah, he travels a lot."

"What kind of work does he do now? Before Mr. Connor's death, he had been a certified flunky going through his five figure allowance as if it were cheap beer." Nathan rose from his chair, walked into the living room and switched on the CD player. It was too quiet in this house; he didn't like it this quiet. The slow piano solo coasted through the room, and he leaned against the wall, letting the sound move over him.

"It doesn't really say what kind of work he does."

"Figures. He's probably still a flunky. I'm interested in knowing where he traveled in the months leading up to Landy's death. I think the last time we saw him was at her twenty-first birthday party, which was about six months before her death."

"I can do some research and get back to you."

"Do that. Have you had any luck finding the origin of that letter?"

"No, the sender's address was a vacant building, and the envelope was dropped off at a street-side box, so there were no witnesses. I'll dust the FedEx envelope again for fingerprints and give it to my guy at the station, but we're probably not going to find anything."

"You're probably right." Nathan mentally prepared a list of possible persons who could have sent him the letter.

"But if he sent one letter, my bet is he'll send another. This one will have to come to you there and may narrow down our list of suspects. How many people in New York knew you were going back to Maine?"

"I didn't tell any of my colleagues where I was moving. I left my dad a note. There was no one else, and I left a couple of weeks after I received the letter."

"If you get another letter there, then it's safe to say somebody's keeping close tabs on you. All we'll need to do is figure out why."

Nathan smirked into the phone. "We? That's what I pay you for."

John laughed. "Speaking of pay?"

"Yeah, your check's in the mail." They talked for a few more minutes about unrelated issues before disconnecting. Nathan went back to his office to place the phone back on its base. The music followed him, a jazzy melody that made him feel like dancing with a woman—Tenile— with wine chilling, lights down low and bed waiting. His mind was steadily exploring those options when out of the corner of his eye he saw a movement at the window.

Instinctively, his head turned, eyes narrowed at the pane and the darkness beyond. He didn't see anything. Moving closer to the window, he thought he caught a flash of white, a shirt maybe. His long legs took him into the kitchen, to the drawer by the refrigerator where a flashlight waited. Grabbing it, he made his way out the back door and onto the porch. Motion lights came on, and he slipped through the night air to the side of the house with his office window. A part of the bush had been cut away, a section that would accommodate a body getting closer to the window. He angled the light to the ground and wasn't surprised to see the grass had been trampled on. Somebody had been there, watching him.

He turned, flashing the light towards the water, then towards the woods, the perfect shelter, the perfect hiding place. Nathan walked to the edge of trees and realized that going in would be futile. His Peeping Tom was well gone by now, but he'd sparked something in Nathan's mind— something he hadn't given much thought to…until now.

Chapter 9

H e's in the dark," Landy's voice echoed throughout the room.

Tenile moaned, refusing to open her eyes but hearing the words all the same. "Go away!" her mind screamed to no avail.

"He's out there, Tee. In the dark. He's waiting. You must be careful."

Tenile opened her eyes then and saw Landy perched at the bottom of her bed, her expression serious, her eyes almost fearful. "Who's there? Who's in the dark?"

"He wants you now because he thinks you know. You and Nathan." Landy's hands were folded in her lap.

"Me? I don't know anything. Does Nathan know?"

"You have to help him. You and Nathan are the key. He knows that and that's why he's come back."

Tenile's heart beat frantically. Who the hell was in the dark? And why was he waiting for her? And why in God's name was she sitting up in her bed talking to a damn ghost?

"I don't know what's going on. I don't know what you're talking about." She took a deep breath then exhaled. "What am I supposed to do?"

"You and Nathan are the key." Landy's voice seemed to echo, her body becoming transparent and vague until she was no more.

Tenile fell back down on her pillows. "Damn you, Nathan Hamilton! I knew your return would be a big pain in the ass!"

Within the Shadows

A light breeze and the smell of newness wafted through the air as Nathan snapped open the white linen cloth and spread it over the dining room table. He'd been cleaning fiercely throughout the morning. His mother would be proud. He wanted everything to be perfect for his first real date with Tenile in ten years. He hummed with the lyrics of Nancy Wilson's sultry voice while he worked.

Since he hadn't purchased nearly enough food yesterday at the market, he'd had to make another trip early this morning. He could cook, he'd been feeding himself just fine for all these years, yet when he thought of preparing a meal for Tenile, he'd felt a little uneasy. So he'd enlisted some help. Mrs. Myers lived down the road a bit, but she remembered him and remembered that he used to mow her lawn and run errands for her while he was in school. She had been more than happy to prepare the meal for him.

Now all he needed was to set the mood. Not that his intention today was to seduce Tenile. While he wouldn't mind breaking in his new sleigh bed with her, today meant something more. If she came—when she came—it would mean that what was between them before was still alive and that she was willing to give them another try. He'd realized sometime in the wee hours of the night that he needed her desperately. This search for Landy's killer was as much justice as it was vindication for him. He hadn't liked leaving town with Tenile thinking him guilty, and he'd hated that accusatory look in her eyes the day he returned even more. So to some extent, it seemed that without her by his side, without her as the prize, this crusade would all be for nothing.

He heard a knock at the door and jumped—he actually jumped. Moving through the large rooms that led to the foyer, he chastised himself for being so silly. He and Tenile had once lived together; they'd been as close as a married couple, without the rings. There was no need for this nervous jittering in the pit of his stomach.

When he pulled the door open, his eyes barely registered the female standing there, instead focusing on the red, white and blue FedEx truck pulling away from the curb. Another package, another letter.

"Are you even going to acknowledge me, or is there something else that interests you today?"

His gaze shifted and he took in Tenile and her attitude. He smiled. She was so cute when she was agitated. One hand was on her hip while she looked him up and down in question. She was still wearing her church clothes—a plain black dress that seemed to fit her like a second skin. He licked his lips, wondering how such an ordinary piece of material could be so damn enticing. When she shifted, folding her arms over her chest, pushing her already plump breasts up until he thought they would spill right over the bodice of the dress, he sucked in a deep breath to keep from falling at her feet.

"Calm down, Tee. I have every intention of acknowledging you, today and well into the night if I'm lucky."

He'd been examining her, looking at her as if he were ready to take her to bed that very moment. Her heart soared, and though her legs shook with anticipation, her anger rose with each passing second. She wasn't there to sleep with him; she'd been trying to convince herself of that fact on the ride over. She was there because Landy said they were the key, that only they could figure out who killed her. She owed it to her friend to find her killer, even if it meant succumbing to Nathan, again.

"You are not now, nor were you ever that lucky." She thrust the package in his direction. "Here's your package." Then she pushed past him and made her way into the house.

Everything was the same, and yet there was something different. She remembered the layout of the house as if she'd just been here last night. She knew that if she took another step to the right, towards the stairs, the floor would creak. She also knew that the kitchen was straight ahead. Its yellow walls were still clear in her mind.

Nathan fumbled to catch the package before it hit the floor since she hadn't made sure he had it before she'd moved on. Quickly, he looked for a return address but wasn't surprised to find none. Closing the door, he threw the package on the entry table and moved to stand behind her. He'd look at it later. Right now was for Tenile and their new beginning. "How was church?"

Tenile turned, not surprised that he stood so close, but unnerved just the same. Remarkably, she didn't take a step back. She was in his house, alone. Running from him was pointless; she'd admitted that. "Church was fine, full of sinners and saints. I don't smell any food." She didn't smell anything but him. All male and an enticing cologne that she couldn't quite name. He wore navy slacks, a white polo with navy trim, his shoes—most likely Kenneth Cole—expensive and casual all at the same time. His arms seemed to bulge with muscle as her eyes fell to the spot where his sleeves ended. God, she wanted him.

"Which one are you?" He reached out, touched a hand to her cheek, lightly gliding over the smooth surface. His finger slid along the narrow line of her neck, to the protruding bone of her shoulder, along the swell of her breast. Her hand quickly came to cover his.

"My salvation is not in question. Yours however…" She let the words linger.

Nathan grinned, happy that they'd slipped back into their easy banter. "Jesus didn't say saints couldn't be horny."

"Whatever. I didn't come here to see how horny you were. We've got some things we need to get straight." She moved into the living room, dropping her purse on the end table before taking a seat on the chocolate brown sofa. This was new. Its soft leather cushioned her as she sat.

Nathan joined her, taking a seat—to her dismay—right beside her. "I agree."

"You agree that I don't care if you're horny?" She lifted a brow in question and crossed her legs.

Nathan couldn't resist her teasing grin. He leaned in quickly, planting a chaste kiss on her waiting lips, then pulled back to survey her reaction. "You care that I'm horny; you just don't want to discuss it right now. That's fine with me. We've got time." He grinned at her astonishment. "But there are other things we need to talk about first."

She was not going to fall for his charm or her own need to feel his hands on her again. "Nathan, about Landy. There are some things we need to get straight."

He sobered instantly. "I didn't sleep with her, Tenile. Nicole was drunk the night she told you that. She was grieving, like we all were, and she lashed out. I don't blame her for it, but I was angry that her words hurt you, especially since they weren't true."

An unknown weight lifted from her shoulders, and she sighed with relief. "I did believe her and that was my fault. I should have asked you. I should have given you a chance to tell your side, in that and in the other." Nervously, she began to wring her hands. "About the murder."

He wanted to tell her he didn't do that either, but he waited for her to continue.

"I know you didn't kill her. You loved her just like we all did. It's just that everything happened so fast, and we were all in shock and you didn't say anything. You didn't deny or confirm. And then you were gone." She said the last quietly, almost as if she didn't want to relive those feelings again.

He moved closer, wrapped one arm around her shoulders and pulled until her head lay on his shoulder. "I was wrong for leaving. I was selfish. I had my career to think of, and my father made a way for me to escape. I thought of you because we were supposed to go to New York together, but I thought you believed them. I thought you didn't want anything to do with me. So I left when I should have stayed."

She started to shift, realized there wasn't any place to go and relaxed. It felt so right to be in his arms. It felt safe. So she didn't move; she didn't speak; she didn't let herself think of where this might lead.

"I've never stopped thinking of you—never stopped loving you." He spoke the words he'd wanted to say that morning in the hospital. She tensed in his arms, and he held her tighter. He'd planned to give her room, to let her gradually get used to the idea of them being together again, but now that she was here in his arms, he couldn't bring himself to back away.

Instead of exploring her own feelings for him, she blurted out, "I tried to call Robert, but he wasn't home. I left him a message."

Nathan's chest rumbled with laughter. "I told you I would take care of Robert."

She slapped at his chest. "I don't need you to take care of Robert. I can handle my own affairs."

"Is that what it was with him, an affair?"

"I wanted to make it more. I wanted it so badly because that would prove I was over you."

His hands rubbed up and down her arms as he kissed the top of her head. "Are you over me, Tenile?" He held his breath in anticipation.

The ringing phone stayed her tongue. Nathan swore as he rose to answer it, fully intending to blast whoever was on the other end. His time with Tenile was precious, so this had better be good. "Hello?" he barked into the receiver.

"Did you get your package?" a muffled voice asked.

Nathan was immediately alert. "Who is this?" He turned his back to Tenile, not sure he was ready for her to know all that was going on.

"You have to find him. He's still out there, ready to kill again. You have to stop him."

Before he could ask another question, the caller disconnected. He replaced the receiver and turned, almost bumping into Tenile.

"Who was that?" He'd gone still as stone, the tone of his voice chilling the room.

"Nobody." He moved around her, going into the foyer and grabbing the FedEx package. He pulled the tab and extracted the letter.

Tenile came to stand beside him, reading the words along with him. *He killed her and he'll kill anyone who figures out why. Be careful.*

❧

"Where have you been? I've been calling you and leaving messages for days." Eli barged past her, ignoring her shocked expression. Damn it, he had been calling her repeatedly, more than he'd ever called any other woman in his life. He'd finally had enough of her answering machine and decided to pay her a visit.

Nicole wore gray slacks and a fuchsia blouse. Her feet were bare because she'd removed her shoes moments before Eli knocked at the door. The clip in her hair was bothering her, so after closing the door, she pulled it free and walked over to plop down on the couch. "Hello, Eli. It's nice to see you too."

Eli pulled off his suit jacket and stared down at her. She was a damn infuriating woman. But when he saw her full breasts heave, his groin tightened. She was a damned sexy woman. "If it's so nice to see me, why has it been days since we're together? One minute you're at my house every night, and the next you disappear."

Nicole would have laughed but for that huge vein pulsing in his neck. He was pissed and she...she was liberated. "Darling, I'm so sorry. I've been extremely busy."

Busy with what? Nicole modeled, mostly for catalogues and mostly seasonal. She didn't have a regular nine to five as he did. And to him modeling wasn't so serious that it could keep her busy. She wasn't a supermodel, though her fine features made her just as beautiful. She stretched and he moaned. A model—Hugh Hefner would pay millions to photograph her nude. At that thought, a jealous streak soared through him and he cursed.

"You could have returned my calls." His voice boomed throughout her apartment.

"Why Eli, did you miss me?" *Oh please say you missed me. Please.*

Eli paced the floor. "Well, yes...I...I guess I sort of did miss you. We've never gone days without talking to each other." With a start he realized how true that statement was. In the fifteen years he'd known Nicole, they'd remained in close contact with each other. Even when she went away on photo shoots, he called her and she called him. It had been almost as if they were husband and wife—and that thought scared him to death.

Nicole crossed her long legs, let her fingers comb through her thick hair. "How do you feel about that, Eli? How do you feel about missing me?"

A thick blade of lust stabbed through him, and he began pulling at his tie, moving closer to her. "I feel like I always feel when I'm around you."

When her hands paused and her lips parted slightly, he stopped right in front of her and unbuttoned his first button.

Nicole swallowed the desire she too felt. Eli was a fine specimen. Tall, broad, dark and sinister. It was that bad-boy sparkle in his eyes that had always appealed to her, called to her.

But they weren't kids anymore. She wanted more from him than a quick romp in bed. "Think beyond the sex for a minute, Elias. How does it feel to really miss me?"

"Elias? You never call me Elias unless we're in the groove." He paused, his fingers shaking slightly over the next button. "What's going on with you?"

She puffed out a breath and stood, pushing past him. "I need a drink."

The corner of her living room contained a huge curving bar complete with the best and most expensive wine she could find. She turned over a glass and poured one her favorites, Cabernet Sauvignon. Swirling her glass, she watched the dark ruby wine move along the sides. Fastening her eyes on him, she took a long drink before setting the glass down with a clang. "Where is this going, Eli? Where are we going?"

"Alright," Eli swore. He snatched his tie off and threw it on the chair with his jacket before moving to sit on the barstool. "What drama are we about to go through now?"

"Drama?" Nicole cocked her head. "Since when have I ever given you any drama? You're usually in and out of my bed so fast there's no time for me to come up with any drama."

He couldn't argue that fact. He'd never liked cuddling with Nicole. It felt too permanent, too much like a relationship, a relationship they couldn't have. "Okay, then what's with the questions about missing you?" He reached out, grabbing her wrist, massaging gently. "You know I miss you whenever we're apart."

Nicole pulled her arm away. "Whenever we're not in bed you mean?" She took a few steps until she stood on the other side of him. "Look, this is not good for me anymore."

Eli turned, confusion etched all over his face. "What's not good for you? Woman, I swear you're confusing the hell out of me."

"That's exactly it! You shouldn't be confused. You should know exactly what I'm saying because you should be feeling the same thing. This sex game has got to end." She folded her arms across her chest and tried not to pout. She was a grown woman, and he needed to see her as that. He needed to take her seriously.

"What?" He grabbed her at the waist and pulled her until their fronts were touching. His hands found her butt, and he massaged the pliable skin. "Baby, if you want it now, here I am. We don't have to play no games." He caught her mouth for a greedy kiss.

Nicole took the kiss because, damn, he could kiss her into an orgasm, and if she wasn't going to feel him inside her, she could at least get some pleasure. When his hand found her breast and his fingers expertly toyed with her nipple, she moaned. Then she heard Tenile's words roaring through her mind. She flattened her hands on his chest and pushed away. "No. Not this time," she said adamantly. "I don't want just sex anymore, Eli. I want something more. You and I have been sneaking in and out of each other's beds for years now, and it's time for it to stop. I want a real relationship. Real dates, real communication—the whole nine yards."

Eli stared at her, bewildered and hard enough to come right this very moment if she didn't open up and give him some. He saw her mouth moving but couldn't believe he was hearing her words correctly. Relationship? Since when did she want a relationship? And with him? Nicole had always been fickle about her men, choosing only the flashiest, wealthiest dudes to escort her. He'd never been like that, and until he'd become a doctor, he hadn't been able to afford the places she liked to go for dinner. They had good sex. Damned good sex. And that was all. At least he thought that was all. "Nicole, what are you talking about? Are you feeling alright?"

Nicole rolled her eyes. "I feel fine, Eli."

He shifted and the bulge in his pants positioned itself securely at her center. He throbbed with need, his heart pounding with the anticipated release. He hadn't been inside her for days, and like a damned crackhead, he was *feenin'* for her. "Baby, please. Can we talk about this later?" He ground her onto his erection, feeling the pleasurable sensations rocket through him. "I need you."

Lord help her, she needed him too. Her panties were so wet she was sure a stream of desire would trickle down her legs at any moment. But this was how it always went with them. He'd touch her; she'd melt. He'd stroke her, she'd moan. He'd come and she'd soar right beside him. As wonderful as that was, it wasn't enough. Not anymore. "I'm serious, Eli. I want more than this. The question is, do you?" She looked at him seriously then. His eyes had darkened with lust but now cleared as realization sank in. His hands that had just gripped her in passion loosened until she was standing on her own, no longer being held up against him. She stepped back to steady herself.

"That's not how things are between us and you know it. We have an arrangement. An arrangement that has suited us just fine for years. Why do you want to change that now?"

"We're not kids anymore. Everybody around us is either getting married or at the very least shacking up. All we're doing is having sex, and it's not enough anymore."

"You don't like sleeping with me?" He asked the question but couldn't believe that was true. She'd all but trembled in his arms just now.

She gave a wry smile. "I love sleeping with you. More than with any other man I've ever slept with. And that's why I want more. I want something more permanent. Something more exclusive."

"We will always be together, Nicole. You know that. No woman, no man, has ever been able to take that from us, at least not for long."

She shook her head from side to side. He was determined not to understand, and her resolve was weakening. He had to leave. She walked to the chair, grabbing his jacket and his tie on her way to the door. "I don't want to always be your piece on the side. I don't want to ride this wave until the next man or woman comes along, Eli." She opened the door. "I want more from you than that, and if you can't give it to me, then we have nothing."

Eli moved across the room, amazed at what she was saying. "Nothing? How can you say we have nothing?"

She stood by the door, emotion welling up in her throat. "With all the pain that I've felt for loving you all these years, that's how."

Oh God, had she said *loved*? That was impossible. Nicole did not love him. He was sure of it. He wasn't her type. He couldn't give her what she wanted, what she needed. She couldn't possibly love him? Could she?

He snatched his stuff from her hands. "There's no going back, Nicole. If this is how you want it, then it's done. I won't be back."

It took all her strength to hold onto the tears that burned her eyes. "If this is how you want it, then I don't want you to come back."

He stalked off. She slammed the door.

He sat in his car fuming, anger and unquenched desire rampaging inside. His hand went between his legs, trying to soothe the painful bulge while his heart battled with an unfamiliar feeling.

Nicole ran to her bathroom, turning on the hot water and reaching for her bottle of bath salts. She stood, stripped then stepped into the heated bubbles, allowing the steam to scratch the itch she'd been forced to deny. She'd done the right thing; she knew it to be true. But damn, she felt horrible—tense, horny and horrible.

Chapter 10

Tenile walked into the hospital lounge on Tuesday evening. Any minute now her mind would start to focus on work instead of her personal life.

After having dinner with Nathan on Sunday and discussing her eerie feelings and his leads in Landy's murder, she'd been even more confused. And if that weren't enough, the scorching kiss they'd shared at his door before she left was permanently emblazoned in her mind.

"Tee, this feels so right. So good," he whispered in her ear as his hands explored her backside. She hung on to him, trying to remember why she needed to leave.

"Let's take this slow, Nathan. There's a lot going on now."

He pulled back, still holding her in his arms. "I don't want you to worry about any of that. I'm going to handle it."

"How can I not worry? Whatever is going on involves me too. I want to find her killer just as much as you do."

"You're one stubborn ass chick. Have you always been like that?" he joked.

"Don't try to change the subject." She smiled, enjoying how good it felt to be with him.

He pulled her closer, desperately wanting the feel of her soft curves against him. "The subject is you joining me upstairs in my new bed." He nuzzled her neck.

"You've got a new bed?"

"Oh yeah, and the right side's designated just for you."

"I have to stay on the right side?" Her hands roamed over the muscles of his back.

"Oh no, the first round we're bound to be all over the place. But when I decide to let you rest, the right side's all yours."

She giggled and snuggled against him a moment longer. Then she pulled away. "Good night, Nathan."

He held on to her hands until his arms couldn't stretch any more because she was too far away. "C'mon, Tee."

"Good night." She waved and walked to her car, half praying he'd call her back. Instead, with a dangerous smirk on his face, he'd watched her climb into her car.

He hadn't called on Monday, and she'd tried to keep busy so as not to emphasize that fact. She'd tried to call Robert again, just so she could get that over with, but hadn't reached him.

Now she was at work for the first time since her and Nathan's new connection. How would they work together with that sexual tension buzzing between them? The odds of avoiding him were slim.

After labeling and placing her lunch pail in one of the few remaining spots in the refrigerator, she glanced at her watch. She had a few minutes to spare before she was expected on the floor. Crossing the room, she took a seat on the couch, the same couch where Nathan had found her sleeping the day he'd returned to Tanner.

Her thoughts drifted to Landy and the message her ghost was trying to pass to her. It appeared someone was also trying to give Nathan a lead to the killer. She felt a momentary bolt of fear. The note had said the person would kill anyone who figured everything out. What if that were true? Hot shivers moved down her back, so intense her palms began to sweat.

Was Landy's killer still lurking around Tanner? Nathan seemed to think so. Landy's ghost hadn't seen fit to visit her since Saturday night. Obviously, she didn't have any more leads for her. Tenile wondered if there were some way she could summon her to appear. That made her chuckle, effectively taking away the fear. She'd go right home, light some candles and have herself a good old-fashioned séance. Her mother and the gossip committee would get a kick out of that.

The door to the lounge swung open, jarring Tenile from her thoughts. With undeniable joy, she watched Nathan walk in, closing the door behind him. Immediately, his tall frame seemed to fill the room, crowding her. He saw her and instantly moved in her direction, as if they were naturally connected. Though he'd just been on her mind, seeing him brought a rush of new emotions, and her pulse quickened.

A smile broke over his face as he stood in front of her, sliding one hand into his pant pocket. "Hello." His voice was smooth and husky, as if they were alone in his bedroom instead of in the employee lounge of the hospital.

"Hello," she replied, feeling her heart pound at his closeness.

"How are you today?" His question was casual and innocent, but his eyes were dark and intense.

"I'm fine." Tenile spoke from her spot on the couch. Seeing him, she felt weak and didn't quite trust her legs to hold her should she stand up.

"You're not," he said quietly, seeing the lines of worry in her face.

Tenile was reluctant to hold his gaze. He seemed to possess the ability to see right through her. She looked down, rubbing her hands over the maroon scrubs she'd worn today. "I'm fine."

She was lying and he knew it. Removing his hand from his pocket, he adjusted his pants and squatted directly in front of her. "You're not." Placing one hand gently on her knee, he urged her to look at him. "You're worried. Don't be. Everything is going to be fine. I won't let anything happen to you."

Reluctantly, she stared at him, trying like hell not to focus on those smoldering eyes that warmed her to her toes. "It's not just about me, Nathan. There's a killer on the loose."

"I know that and I'm going to find him."

"You're not invincible, you know. He could come after you." She hadn't wanted to admit how real that fear was to her. "Maybe we should go to the police."

After she'd left his house the other night, he'd thought about that for her protection. "We don't have enough to go to the police. They won't take you seriously, and they might get around to charging me."

She didn't have a rebuttal. Instead, she found herself falling deeply into those bottomless pools of warmth. He looked at her with such adoration, such caring, her heart swelled with need; she fought the urge to throw her arms around his neck and take all that he offered.

He loved her so much. The fact that he was this close to her, touching her again after all these years, would be enough if he died tomorrow. Yet he knew he'd fight the devil himself for their future together. "I missed you." He didn't want to talk about killers, didn't want to think about death. All he wanted was Tee.

She felt his warm breath over her face as he moved closer, his lips brushing lightly against hers.

His pager went off, beeping loudly, successfully ending the connection before it really began. Nathan swore and snatched it from his belt. "I have to go." He stood, still staring down at her.

Tenile cleared her throat and stood with him. The beeping pager had snapped her back to reality. It was time she started acting like a woman, not a dazzled teenager. "I should get to work too." She tried to push past him to the door.

He grabbed her arm, turning her to face him. "We need to be alone."

He was really getting to her. She sighed. "Right now we have to work." She bit her bottom lip to keep from moving into his arms, into the warm embrace she knew she'd find there.

She was right, he knew, but he didn't have to like it. "We'll work now and then we'll concentrate on us. Deal?"

Just his simple gaze warmed her. Alone. Nathan wanted time to recapture what they'd had, that feeling that had lived inside them all the years they were apart. She wasn't even going to front. She wanted that too. "Deal."

"You've got it bad, Nate," Eli said with barely restrained disgust as he and Nathan sat in the hospital cafeteria.

Nathan grinned. "Whatever I've got is nothing compared to the bug up your butt." Nathan put two packs of sugar into his coffee. "You going to tell me what's gone wrong in the wonderful world of Eli?"

They'd both been on duty all day, and in that time, they'd had numerous emergencies and just managed a moment for a break. Eli's brow was furrowed, his mouth fixed in a snarl. Something was definitely going on.

"My world is just fine, thank you very much. Unlike you, I don't wear my heart on my sleeve."

"No, you wear it in your pants. That's why none of your relationships ever last long. Sooner or later it gets soft." Nathan sipped his coffee.

Eli grunted, picked up his own cup then set it down again. "Hearts and sex don't mingle."

"Sex doesn't love and respect you."

"Nate, I don't need this. Not right now and not from you."

Nathan sat back in his chair, eyed his friend suspiciously. "She wants a commitment and you're too chicken shit to give her one."

Leave it to Nathan to figure it out and attempt to analyze him. Old habits really did die hard, he admitted. "Christ! Were you hiding in her bedroom? Or did she just come running to you like old times?" Eli slammed his big hands on the table and leaned in closer.

"Whoa!" Nathan raised his hands, a look of surprise on his face. "Who are we talking about, and why would she come to me?"

"Nicole, dammit! She's got it in her head that we should be something more than sex partners. Isn't that a laugh for you? I can't begin to please her!"

Nicole and Eli were still sleeping together. This was a shock, but Nathan didn't let on. "It seems to me you've both been pleasing each other for quite some time. Now it's time to try something different."

"I don't want something different. I want sex," he declared. "With Nicole."

"You're too old for just sex."

"Bull! You're chomping at the bit waiting to screw Tenile again."

Nathan stiffened. Some topics were off limits with him. "Tenile and I have never just screwed. And unlike you, I'd give her whatever she asked for."

"Then that makes you a gullible fool." Eli frowned. "Nicole's fun. Sex with her is phenomenal. But that's it. There's no happy ending or wedded bliss in our future."

Nathan stood, frowned down at his friend. "I'll pick you up some extra hand lotion."

Eli emptied his cup before following Nathan to the elevators. "Hand lotion? What for?"

"With that attitude, you sure as hell won't be getting pleasure the traditional way. Might as well stock up. You're a crabby bastard when you're backed up!"

Nathan laughed as the elevator doors closed them in. Eli, however, didn't get the joke.

⨯⨯

Just before ten that evening, Nathan began to feel the exhaustion kick in. He'd been at the hospital since ten this morning, working nearly twelve hours. Flipping through the chart he'd just picked up guaranteed relief was nowhere in sight.

In Room 4 was a high-risk pregnancy. The mother had developed gestational hypertension over three weeks ago, and efforts by the clinic doctors had proven futile. Three days ago, the patient had presented to labor and delivery with swollen ankles and legs and a weight gain of thirteen pounds since her last clinic visit, two weeks prior. Yesterday, her blood pressure had seemed to stabilize, but a check just an hour ago showed her pressure was up again. With the diagnosis of preeclampsia pretty clear, he'd ordered a sonogram.

Reading over the technician's report, his worst fears were realized. Compared to her sonogram of four weeks ago, this one showed that although the mother was rapidly gaining weight, the baby was not. The placenta was no longer providing nourishment.

With a sigh, Nathan prepared to tell the middle-aged woman that induction was necessary. Her baby was in danger and needed to be delivered as soon as possible. Bad news never made him happy. With constant neonatal care, at twenty-eight weeks the chance of the baby surviving outside of the uterus was fairly good. Still, a premature baby was never really out of the woods.

His feared that the mother's increased blood pressure might cause her to have seizures or, worse, a stroke. The baby's immediate danger was possible brain damage from the lack of nourishment over the last few weeks. Overall, the diagnosis was not good, and he walked toward the room with a weight on his chest.

"Hello, Mr. and Mrs. Gonzalez," Nathan greeted the couple as he walked into the room, chart in hand. Mr. Gonzalez stood to shake his hand, and Nathan obliged with a friendly smile.

"So Doctor, what's the news today?" Mr. Gonzalez stood beside his wife, staring at Nathan expectantly.

They expected him to have all the answers, to know the right thing to say. He expected that of himself, but in cases like these, the truth was that all he could do was get the baby delivered. The rest was out of his hands.

"Unfortunately, Mrs. Gonzalez, your blood pressure has escalated again, and the sonogram shows that, even with your recent weight gain, the baby has not sustained any significant growth in the last month, which leads us to believe that the placenta is no longer providing enough nourishment for the baby." Looking from husband to wife, Nathan struggled to stay calm, focused, detached. The last was always the hardest in his line of work because the birth of a healthy baby was an overwhelming joy to him.

"The baby needs to be delivered. We're still at a safe enough point that we do not need to perform an emergency cesarean, but I am suggesting immediate induction. I believe it's the best option, definitely the safest one."

"So will the baby be alright?" Mr. Gonzalez asked, concern written all over his face.

"As a result of modern medicine, the survival rate for babies born at twenty-eight weeks is surprisingly good. There may be complications with the baby's breathing since the respiratory system is the last to develop. The baby might need the assistance of a respirator to breathe. But we've given you steroid shots to help speed up the lung development."

"But it can survive?" Mrs. Gonzalez whispered.

"Yes, it can," Nathan told her. "But we must start the induction now. If your pressure gets any higher, vaginal birth will be out of the question, and I'd like to spare you the surgical procedure of a cesarean."

"Will her pressure return to normal once the baby is delivered?" Mr. Gonzalez, who had taken his wife's hand in his, stroked her fingers gently and looked at Nathan anxiously.

"Usually, the pressure returns to normal once the baby is born. If it doesn't, then there are stronger medications we can give the mother to assist in the transition back to a normal pressure. As it stands, we cannot give her those medications now for fear of further harming the baby."

"Then let us proceed," Mrs. Gonzalez announced. Her husband looked down at her, questions clearly visible in his eyes. With a nod of her head, she acknowledged his fears while affirming her own. Giving him a wan smile, she squeezed his hand and shifted her attention to Nathan. "What's the first step?"

"I'll have one of the nurses come in to insert a suppository called Prostin to soften your cervix. She'll also start to administer a small dosage of Pitocin intravenously to stimulate contractions. Once we've developed normal contractions, you'll begin to dilate, and your labor should proceed normally. I know that you wanted a natural birth without any pain medication, but with preeclampsia patients, I generally recommend a low level epidural because increased pain tends to raise blood pressure. Once you've reached four centimeters, we can send for the anesthesiologist."

"That doesn't sound too bad," Mr. Gonzalez said.

Mrs. Gonzalez cut her eyes at her husband. "I guess not since you're not the one who has to go through it."

Taking his wife's hand, the burly Mr. Gonzalez smiled. "I'll be with you every step of the way. I'll feel every pain you feel," he told her.

"Well, hop on up here and let them insert a suppository inside you," she laughed.

Nathan chuckled along with the couple, glad that they could remain lighthearted at a time like this.

Within the hour Mrs. Gonzalez had dilated two and a half centimeters. Nathan had the nurse slightly increase the Pitocin and assured the couple that things would soon start moving quickly.

As if his prediction had been etched in stone, Mrs. Gonzalez immediately dilated to five centimeters, and he paged the anesthesiologist.

"Almost there," Nathan told her as he examined her again. "Your baby will probably be born before eleven o'clock," he told her, looking at the clock on the wall.

"Care to make a wager on that, Doc?" Mr. Gonzalez attempted to lighten the serious mood that had settled in the room.

"I'm not a betting man, Mr. Gonzalez, but I'm pretty sure it's going to be soon." Nathan smiled and walked out of the room, feeling a little more comfortable with the situation.

He still hated the idea of facing another premature birth, but he had no other choice. Her hypertension had been caught as soon as possible, and every measure had been taken to bring her blood pressure back down to normal. It was out of his control now, and that was what scared him most. He could do everything the textbooks and his gut instinct told him to do, but in the end, whatever was meant to be was going to be. He just prayed that he was meant to help things turn out right.

His mind on Mrs. Gonzalez and her impending delivery, Nathan walked down the hall, scarcely paying attention to anything around him. Turning the corner swiftly, he collided with a soft female form, which snapped him out of his thoughts.

Blinking in confusion, he inhaled her scent before actually realizing it was Tenile. As a result of their collision, she wavered and he reached out to steady her.

"Sorry," he murmured, his hands protectively on her waist.

"No, I'm sorry," she spoke at the same time. "I wasn't looking where I was going." Tenile tried to back away when she had her footing, but he held her firmly. Her hands, which had grabbed the lapels of his jacket, still rested on his chest.

"Actually, I'm glad we ran into each other." He smiled slyly.

"Why?" Tenile eyed him suspiciously, even though she'd wanted to be near him again.

"I know you're going to be off duty soon, and I wanted to get this before you left." Before she could protest, he gave her a loud smacking kiss.

She couldn't hide her pleasure and wasn't sure she wanted to, but kissing here was not appropriate. "Okay, now that that's done, you can move out of my way."

There were sounds in the hallway, sounds of people who were actually doing their jobs, unlike them. His shoulders rose and fell heavily as reality set in. They were at work. No way could he touch and kiss her the way he wanted. They both had jobs to do and reputations to uphold. Still, she felt so good, looked so tempting. "I can't wait to get you alone." His gaze held hers, making silent promises and hoping she agreed.

She couldn't resist. She tried, oh how she tried. But those liquid pools of brown melted all her resistance, and she sighed again. "My next day off is Saturday. I could meet you somewhere."

He shook his head vehemently. "That's too far away. How about I bring you lunch tomorrow?"

She considered his offer. They'd be on her turf, and she'd be able to set and control the mood. She readily agreed. "That sounds good."

Already he was craving the feel of her lips against his again. The passion he saw in her eyes, felt emanating from her body, beckoned him. The sound of someone being paged over the intercom was like a splash of cold water. Nathan let his hands drop from her waist. Tenile took a much-needed step back. He breathed heavily, trying to regain some semblance of control.

"Dr. Hamilton?" Nathan heard a voice behind him and was grateful that he'd just moved away from Tenile so that they now stood a respectable distance apart. Turning in the direction of the voice, he closed his white coat to conceal his arousal.

"Yes, Rosie?" he answered the redhead who stood about six feet from him.

"Mrs. Gonzalez is complete."

"Mrs. Gonzalez is on my roster," Tenile told Rosie. "I was on break and just going back to check her again." She stepped from behind Nathan and walked toward her fellow nurse.

"Okay, her water broke about ten minutes ago and the baby's crowning." Rosie continued the rundown. "Her epidural was administered and has been keeping her comfortable. Her husband's in the room with her, using Lamaze techniques to get himself through each contraction."

"This should be good," Tenile giggled. Expectant fathers were often a great source of entertainment for the staff. "Okay, I'll get a cart and go on in." Nathan had been about to kiss her again, she knew. Thankfully, Rosie had appeared. Nathan's kisses were lethal and were bound to lead to even more pleasurable things, things they couldn't do in the hospital hallway.

His voice interrupted her retreat. "She's only twenty-eight weeks. Call NICU and tell them to be prepared. I want two neonatal nurses down here for the delivery. I'll get scrubbed and be right in. Have her start pushing but not too hard," he instructed, as if she didn't already know.

The passion they'd shared only moments ago was temporarily forgotten. It was time to get down to business, and they both switched roles quickly and efficiently.

"I know. Premature babies tend to fly out quickly and, with too much pushing, too fast. I'll take it slow until you get there," Tenile assured him before walking down the hall with Rosie.

Nathan headed toward the surgical rooms to scrub. As he scrubbed his arms up to his elbows, he looked at himself in the mirror above the large sink. His eyes were clear, his features unaffected, but on the inside, where it was harder to see, things were different.

He was so close to reuniting with his one true love—so close to having everything he'd ever wanted. But something stood in the way. Something lurked in the shadows, waiting for him—waiting for them— to stumble upon the secret that had haunted Tanner for years.

Grabbing the antiseptic soap again, he scraped the rough bar over his hands and arms viciously to get rid of bacteria. As he did, his mind whirled with determination to find Landy's killer as soon as possible. Things wouldn't be right until he did. He and Tenile wouldn't be right until he did.

By the time Nathan made his way to the birthing room, Tenile had uncovered the cart, inspected all the instruments, dropped the lower half of the birthing bed, propped Mrs. Gonzalez up and strapped her legs into the stirrups. Mr. Gonzalez stood to her right side, garbed in green surgical scrubs and holding his wife's hand.

"Okay, with the next contraction, I want you to grab hold of your thighs, put your chin on your chest and push," Tenile instructed the patient.

Mrs. Gonzalez nodded her head and prepared for the next contraction. The epidural was working well, and except for pressure in her bottom, she didn't feel any pain.

Rosie took a position to Mrs. Gonzalez's left and counted through the pushing effort while Tenile crossed the room to tie the back of Nathan's surgical gown. He lifted the mask to his face, and Tenile tied the strings behind his head, her hands brushing against the exposed skin at his neck. Warmth eased down her spine and her stomach twisted. Pulling two large gloves from the box, she held them open for him to slip his hands into. When they were on, her eyes held his. Silently, they acknowledged their unfinished business before attending to the matter at hand.

"Three, four, five," Rosie was counting. Mr. Gonzalez whispered the numbers in Spanish. Since his wife spoke fluent English, as did he, this was a sure sign he was nervous, Tenile thought.

Nathan moved to stand between Mrs. Gonzalez's bent legs. Right behind him, Tenile stood next to the table, ready to hand him whatever he should need. Glancing over at the monitor, Tenile nodded to Rosie and announced, "Okay, Mrs. Gonzalez, with this next contraction, I want you to push with everything you've got. The head's right here. One good push and it'll be completely out."

"The baby has lots of hair, Mrs. Gonzalez, lots of curly black hair," Nathan announced. "Come on, give me a good push," he urged her.

Mrs. Gonzalez pushed until tiny beads of sweat dotted her forehead. Her husband supported her with one hand behind her back and the other one clutched between her tightening fingers.

With her pushing and the tightening of the uterus, the baby's head popped out slick and wet. "Don't push! Don't push!" he instructed Mrs. Gonzalez, who fell back on the pillows breathing heavily.

"Okay, one more little push to deliver the shoulders, Mrs. Gonzalez," Tenile said when Nathan had finished.

Mrs. Gonzalez had barely squeezed her husband's hand before her face became distorted with the next push. The rest of the baby's body slid out quickly and, if not for Nathan's agility, the baby would have landed on the floor.

"It's a boy!" Tenile yelled. The sight of a new baby always excited her. Moving to the side, she motioned for Mr. Gonzalez to stand next to her.

Nathan reached for the suction bulb to clear the baby's mouth and nose. "I'm going to clamp the cord, and you cut right here, Dad," Nathan told the man.

With wobbly hands, Mr. Gonzalez held the scissors, aimed them and cut the cord, severing his son's dependence on his wife.

Moving quickly, Nathan passed the baby to Tenile, who had a blanket already open for it. She wrapped the baby and passed it on to one of the neonatal nurses who had been standing by.

They rushed out of the room, headed for intensive care. Tears streamed down Mrs. Gonzalez's face.

"Give me a check on her pressure," Nathan ordered.

"145 over 92 and falling," Rosie told him.

"Good, good. You didn't tear at all, Mrs. Gonzalez; I suspect because the baby was still so small. I'm just going to deliver the afterbirth now, and we'll get you cleaned up," Nathan told her.

"When can I see my baby? Is he okay? Where did they take him?" she asked.

Tenile put a hand on the patient's knee. "He's going to the NICU to be checked out. As soon as I get you cleaned up, I'll check on him for you."

The woman wasn't satisfied, but she lay back on the pillow and tried to relax. When the afterbirth was delivered and Nathan was assured that her bleeding had stopped, he removed his gloves and circled to the side of the bed.

"Mrs. Gonzalez, you did a good job," he told her, taking her hand in his. "This was for the best. Now both you and your son have a better chance at living."

Mrs. Gonzalez couldn't speak, her tears building and spilling onto her golden cheeks.

"Thanks, Doc." Mr. Gonzalez extended his hand over his wife's chest. "Thanks for all your efforts. We both appreciate everything you've done for us."

Nathan took the man's hand and shook it heartily. "You're welcome. Mrs. Gonzalez, I'll be back in a bit to check on your pressure again." She only nodded in response.

Nathan moved toward the door, ripping the mask and cap off as he reached for the knob.

"Let's get you cleaned up and comfortable, Mrs. Gonzalez." Tenile's voice had him turning before leaving. His eyes searched for and found hers; she smiled at him. His heart tightened in his chest, and he felt the corners of his mouth turning up in response. Breaking the eye contact, she moved briskly, wiping and cleaning her patient.

Within the Shadows

As if he didn't already know, he acknowledged that he loved this woman and couldn't wait until they started their own family.

Chapter 11

Nathan's adrenaline buzzed in the enclosed atmosphere of the car as he drove down Main Street. A call to the NICU had informed him that the Gonzalez baby had weighed in at three and a half pounds. As expected, he wasn't able to breathe on his own, so they had put him on the respirator. They were still running tests to discover whether there was neurological damage.

He'd tended to one emergency, and now he was on his way to another. The message had been clear—for him to come immediately and to come alone.

He pushed his car to limits most likely unfamiliar to the citizens of Tanner, but he didn't care. The threat was real; the sick churning in his gut proved it. He pulled up by the park and barely had his seatbelt unbuckled before his door was open, his feet pounding on the sidewalk. He felt in his front pocket to make sure he had his cell phone and that it was on and easily accessible. His legs carried him swiftly past the town monument and over the stretch of grass that led to the gazebo.

He slowed as he approached the white structure. It was almost midnight, and except for the occasional fireflies, the area was dark. The ripe smell of freshly cut grass tickled his nose. The message had said to meet the sender at the gazebo. He stepped onto the old structure, grimacing when he saw no one. Cursing, he jammed his hands deep into his pockets and looked around.

The town picnic would be held here in a few weeks. If he remembered correctly, this gazebo would be decorated with ribbons and balloons, and the mayor and his wife would sit up here, along with the sheriff and his deputy. All across the lawn, tables draped in white cloths and covered with food would stand waiting for attention. Children would run rampant while the older folk gathered in groups to gossip and gripe.

What would they say about him this time?

A look at his watch and a yawn that couldn't be suppressed had Nathan walking away from the memory-filled structure. He'd missed him. Or had his mysterious informer even bothered to show up?

At this point he didn't care. He got in his car and headed west, home. He was beat and this wild goose chase had made him grumpy. All he wanted now was a hot shower and his bed.

Tomorrow he'd spend time with Tenile. That thought soothed him, comforting him as he drove through the deserted streets. They'd worked well together. She'd been so in sync with what he needed. It had been that way during Tracy's surgery as well.

Reluctantly, he admitted that any skilled nurse would have done the same thing. But the thought of the two of them working side-by-side, performing medical wonders, was a better thought, a more pleasant thought.

In no time he found himself pulling into his driveway. He didn't bother to grab his briefcase from the backseat since he'd have time to look over his grant papers tomorrow. His shift at the hospital didn't begin until eight tomorrow night, coinciding exactly with Tenile's hours.

It must have been the exhaustion that had him moving so slowly, that had him fumbling to get his key into the door, and that made him oblivious to his surroundings. The blow that blindsided him seemed to come out of nowhere. He fell against the door just as strong hands grabbed his collar, spinning him around. This time he saw the fist coming and had the good sense to lean to the side. His hands fisted and he landed a good shot on his assailant's chin. The guy stumbled backward, and Nathan leapt on him, grabbing a fistful of his shirt and lifting him slightly off the ground to see his face.

"Jesus! Remy, is that you?"

Kareem twisted and struggled until Nathan let him up.

"Get your damn hands off me," Kareem yelled and finally broke free.

Nathan rolled to a sitting position, staring at the slender man he'd once called his friend. "What the hell is your problem? This sure isn't a welcome home party."

Kareem snarled, turned his head away and spit the taste of blood out of his mouth. "I'd have to be some kind of idiot to welcome a murderer back."

Nathan bit back his retort, struggled to his feet and walked toward his front door once again. "C'mon, have a drink. It'll make your mouth feel better." He didn't wait for Kareem to accept or decline, just kept on walking until he was in the living room, pouring himself a shot of vodka, straight.

"I'm not drinking with a killer," Kareem said when he sauntered into the room.

Nathan took a swallow and braced himself for the heat that spread throughout his torso. "Why not? You're in my house. You slept in the bed next to mine for four years."

"You had us all fooled, especially Landy." Kareem fell back onto the couch, his hand smoothing over his jaw. "And you hit like a bitch."

Nathan couldn't help grinning. "I cracked your jaw, didn't I?"

"Lucky shot."

"At least I don't run up on a man in the dark of night."

"No, you strangle innocent women after you've had your way with them."

Neither Nathan's stance nor his features changed. Once again he didn't admit or deny it.

Nathan's fingers clenched the glass tightly, an act Kareem couldn't possibly see. His jaw tightened and he reined in his own anger. Kareem hadn't changed much. His mustache had finally grown in, but his ears were still too big for his peasy head. Yet there was an edginess to him, a bitterness that had been left to fester. Nathan chose his words carefully as this admission meant a lot to him and probably to the man sitting across the room. "I didn't kill Landy. She was one of my best friends. If you reach back and remember what we were all like together, you'll realize I'm right. I could never have hurt her in any way."

"But you could sleep with her!"

Those words hit him with as much venom as had the murder accusation. Nathan could have told him to take a hike, that whom he slept with was his business. But because he'd known Kareem a long time, known how deeply in love with Landy his friend had been, he decided to give him the truth.

Dragging his hands over his face, Nathan moved to sit in the chair across from him. "Look man, I know how you felt about her. For that reason alone I would have never pushed up on her. We were just friends. That's all."

Kareem couldn't look at him. He heard the words but couldn't digest them. "It shouldn't have happened. She should still be alive."

Nathan lifted his glass, stood and extended it to Kareem. "I feel the same way."

Reluctantly, Kareem took the glass, rapidly drank it down then choked.

Nathan laughed, moved closer and clapped his old friend on the back. "You still drink like a punk."

"Shut up, man." Kareem coughed again.

❧

Pulling out of the parking lot of Riverside Pizza, Nathan inhaled the succulent aroma coming from the two boxes beside him. A 2-liter of Pepsi, a pleasant white wine and a triple layer chocolate cake from Annie's Bakery would do just fine. Tenile loved dessert more than anything else. He remembered that about her. When he'd glanced into the window of Annie's Bakery, the chocolate confection appropriately named Temptation had whispered her name.

That's what she would forever be to him—his one temptation. He'd had a taste of her before. Now he longed for more. Everything about her tempted him: her smile, her voice, her intelligence. She inspired him to be all that he could be, made him want to be so much more.

A few minutes later he pulled up in front of her building. Taking the keys out of the ignition, he sat there a moment, pondering the step he was about to take. Had Landy never been killed, he and Tenile would have undoubtedly been married by now. As he stepped out of the car and the glove of humidity threatened to strangle him, he felt something, something that drove thoughts of Tenile out of his mind. Looking around, he saw nothing out of place. Cars drove up and down the street. Trees stood in the same spot they'd been in for years. But he couldn't deny a feeling of dread. The killer was near, the day of reckoning close and inevitable.

∽

Tenile showered and changed into jeans and a clingy shirt that tied up in front. She'd brushed her hair, pulling it up into a ponytail but leaving a few loose tendrils at the nape of her neck. Moving to the phone, she tried to call Robert again. He still wasn't at home. Tapping a fingernail on the receiver, she wondered at that. He hadn't returned any of the four messages she'd left over the last couple of days. Robert always called her, at least once a day. She roamed through her living room, wondering if he had somehow got wind of the fact that she'd been seen with Nathan. That was entirely possible in a town the size of Tanner. Her mother had already called her with a barrage of questions regarding her and Nathan's shopping expedition. Robert could have easily heard the same nonsense. But why wouldn't he call her or come over to confront her?

Absently, her fingers parted the mini-blinds at her front window, and she spotted Nathan's car. Thoughts of Robert quickly vanished as her heart fluttered at the sight of the man she'd once loved, and maybe still loved, walking towards her door carrying bags and pizza boxes. She smiled. How could just the simple sight of him make her smile, make her insides turn to mush?

The buzzer sounded and she moved to the front door. Anxious for him to be close, she had the door already open when he stepped off the elevator. As he approached she took note of the black jeans, leather loafers and black fitted T-shirt—an Adonis in black. Her mouth all but watered.

"Pizza." He held his arms up, offering the boxes. His eyes danced at the sight of her, and suddenly, the nonchalant mood he'd worked so hard to construct on his way up here slipped. "Are you hungry?" His voice lowered, his eyes darkened.

Tenile swallowed hard, begging her tongue to remain quiet. If she were forced to answer that question, she'd be inclined to admit that nothing in those boxes could feed the hunger she felt right now.

"I got pepperoni and extra cheese, your favorite." His words seemed foreign as his mind clouded with her scent. She looked so fresh with her makeup-free face, the crisp white shirt—which, by the way was sexy as hell. It circled her breasts and came to a tight knot just above her navel, leaving an inch of mocha-colored skin visible. He wanted to drop everything and drag his hands and tongue over that enticing display.

Her lids seemed way too heavy, and her legs felt unsteady. "You know me too well." She moved aside, flattening her back against the door jam, more to keep her body upright than to allow him room to go inside, but he didn't have to know that. "Come in."

Nathan entered her home, the place where she came to relax, to be herself. His eyes quickly took in the surroundings. Art deco was her style. He almost smiled as he looked around at all the eclectic pieces that so reflected the woman—the huge colorful pillows that lined the cobalt blue couch, the fuzzy peach-colored rug on the floor. She had an abundance of candles in different shapes and colors strewn throughout the tiny space. Her living and dining room were one and the same, a cheerful spot.

"The kitchen's that way," she said from behind him, slightly unnerved at his perusal of her apartment. She walked toward the kitchen herself so he could follow.

"I'm sorry I took so long. I stopped for dessert." Following her into the kitchen, he couldn't help watching the sway of her hips in her tight jeans. Either it was the small space or the humidity had followed him into the building, he didn't know, but it was getting increasingly difficult to breathe.

"Dessert?" Tenile beamed when they were standing near the kitchen table. "What'd you get?" Ignoring her instincts, she moved closer to him to get a peek at what was in the smaller box he held.

"It's a surprise." He held the box just out of her reach.

She looked at him suspiciously before making a grab for the box again. Failing, she frowned.

"What's the matter? You don't like surprises?" With a lopsided grin he eyed her pouting lips.

"Nope, I'm way too impatient." She smiled reluctantly.

"I'll make you a deal," he began, the idea forming quickly in his mind. "I'll give you a peek, if you give me…a kiss." Nathan grappled for control; he was definitely going to explode if he didn't get his hands on her soon. He was craving the feel of her lips against his. He hadn't known how badly until now.

A kiss? Hadn't she been dreaming of that? The thought crossed her mind that this might lead to something else, but her traitorous body took over, and she found herself moving closer. "That's blackmail," she crooned.

Nathan took a step closer until the tips of her breasts touched his chest. Shrugging his shoulders he whispered, "Take it or leave it."

"I'll take it," she said without hesitation.

Nathan needed no further urging. He lightly cupped her chin, holding her gaze. Her lids fluttered as yearning rose within her. His tongue lightly traced the line of her lips, probing until she parted them. Delving inside, he stroked and soothed. Their tongues dueled with a slow heat that threatened to burn them both.

She jerked in his embrace, unprepared for the warmth spreading quickly throughout her body. She leaned even closer, feeling his strength. He groaned. Wrapping her arms around him, she knew she was giving too much, feeling too much. But it had been so long since she'd felt this way, almost like a lifetime, and she was determined to make it count.

Eyes closed, she willed the sensations rippling through her to last forever. She'd dreamed of touching his hair again, and her fingers splayed over the close cut softness at the back of his neck. Her arms slid from around his neck to grasp the strong muscles of his arms. She relished the hardness, the strength that made him all man. Need sprang alive and the pounding of her heart left her weak, vulnerable. At this moment she would have given him whatever he asked for, but slowly, reluctantly, he pulled away.

Nathan trembled. Her taste lingered on his lips. She had been soft and warm and clinging in his arms, just what he wanted, what he'd waited so long for. She smelled so good, a clean, fresh scent like just washed clothes, an aroma he knew would haunt him for the rest of his days. His blood roared in his head as memories of them making love fused in his mind.

While he still possessed the strength to move, he backed away from her, returning his attention to the box that had led to the kiss. He dislodged the tape and flipped the lid open.

Tenile was still a little dreamy after the kiss, but her eyes immediately found her prize, and she squealed like a child. "Mmmmmmm, that looks scrumptious."

Nathan almost moaned himself. The cake wasn't nearly as scrumptious as the treat he'd just indulged in. "Temptation," he whispered.

When she looked at him in question, he smiled. "It's called Temptation."

"Oh?" She looked away from him quickly, not sure he was talking about the cake.

"Where are your glasses?" he asked when he saw her back away.

Slowly, Tenile closed the lid of the cake box then dared to look in his direction. He had a strong jaw, chiseled and masculine. His nose was a little crooked, which only added to the allure of his features, and his eyes…those dreamy, dark liquid pools seemed to swallow her whole.

"Um, glasses?" he reiterated when she only stared at him in response to his question.

"Oh, that's right, glasses," she stuttered. In all her lifetime, she never remembered stuttering, especially not in front of a boy or, in this case, a man.

"Yeah, that would be good, and plates." He smiled to himself at the knowledge that she'd been just as affected by that kiss as he had, if not more. She raised her arm to retrieve plates from the cupboard, and he turned away. Her shirt was too tight and cut too low. He could see the creamy swell of her breasts and imagined his tongue trailing the path between them. The shirt tied together right down the center, somebody's idea of fashion—his idea of torture.

"The glasses are over there, in the cupboard just above your head," she directed, still trying to get a grip on her own tumultuous emotions.

While they gathered the dishes, mindful to stay a good distance away from each other, the same thought went through both their minds—this was going to be a long afternoon!

With the sun high and hot, the air conditioner, thankfully, cooling off the interior of her little apartment, they settled in for a nice comfortable afternoon.

"So how'd you end up in obstetrics? I thought you were aiming for surgical nurse." Nathan said after swallowing a bite of pizza.

She shrugged, propped her elbows on the table. "I don't know. I just sort of fell into it. I started out on the surgical rotation but midway switched over to obstetrics, and I've been there ever since. It was the right choice for me."

"I understand. I always knew I wanted to be a part of the most important event in a woman's life," he replied.

"You were always pretty certain about everything in your life." That was just one of the things she loved…liked about him.

He watched her lift another slice from the box. Tenile had never been shy about eating. "It really throws you for a loop when those careful plans are derailed."

"Yeah, I've learned that everything can't always go according to plan. But change sometimes is good and needed."

"Change?" he chuckled.

"What's so funny?"

"I was just thinking of how some things change drastically and others, despite the world, stay exactly the same."

She was curious, and her head tilted to the side. "Like what, exactly? You seem to be thinking of something specific."

"Eli and Nicole. Did you know they were still sleeping together?"

Had it been anyone else asking her besides Nathan, she would have choked, then denied it. But since they all knew each other as well as siblings, that was pointless. "Yeah, she told me about it. She wants the brass ring though."

Nathan nodded, took a drink and set his glass down. "Eli's scared to death of rings of any kind."

"That's sad."

"Why do you say that?"

"Because he doesn't know what he's missing by being afraid. They could be so good together." She'd come to that realization after thinking about Nicole and how sincere she'd looked when she'd talked about Eli. She really loved him, and he was too dumb to see it.

"Are you afraid?"

His question threw her for a minute since she was sure they weren't still talking about Eli and Nicole. But what was he talking about? Was he asking if she was afraid of finding Landy's murderer or if she was afraid of the changes that were going on with them? "Am I afraid of what?"

"Of me. Of what my coming back into your life means."

She lifted a brow. "And what does it mean?"

He smiled. She was so smart, so sure of herself and so sure she was treading lightly where they were concerned. And oh-so-wrong. "It means that now you have to stop hiding behind your work and your nice comfortable apartment. You have to get back out there and live the way you were meant to."

"I am living my life just as I want it."

"You're living safely because you don't want things to come crashing down around you again. You shifted from surgical nursing because that's what you had discussed with Landy. You stay cooped up in this apartment so you don't have to hear the gossip or become a part of it anymore."

"How dare you come here and talk as if you know all about me?" She stood and stalked into the living room. Her hands trembled, and she couldn't tell if it was because he'd been dangerously close to the truth or if it was simply his nearness. Either way, she didn't like the feeling of helplessness that lurked beyond her anger.

He'd pushed her too far; he realized that the moment he spoke. Yet he was glad to finally have approached the subject. She was hiding, had been hiding since the day he left, and he wanted her to know that it was safe for her to come out now, to start living the way she was intended to live. He moved slowly, deliberately, giving her a few moments to get herself together before he jabbed at her again. He knew she'd be angry, and would quite possibly lash out at him, but it was for her own good, for both their good.

"When Landy died and I left, you felt abandoned by the two people that were closest to you. Landy couldn't help what happened to her. I could have. I should have. But that's no reason for you to continue carrying that pain and disappointment around with you for the rest of your life." She faced the window, staring out, not moving, not speaking. He stood directly behind her but didn't touch her. "You know what attracted me to you initially?" She didn't answer. He knew she wouldn't—she was stubborn as hell.

"You had spunk and determination. You wanted that freshman English class and you stood in that line that stretched around the corner and back. You wouldn't move and when that tall dude tried to get in front of you, you slit his throat with words and sent him cowering to the back of the line. I knew then that you were special, that you were a person worth knowing."

She finished the memory. "So you joined me in line and kept me company until I registered and gave you my phone number." Nathan had seemed to appear out of the blue, his calm tone soothing her frayed edges and finally making her laugh at some silly remark he'd made. She'd known then that he was special too.

He saw the tension ease in her shoulders and moved closer. He didn't give her any more room; he figured he'd already given her plenty. "If ever two people were meant to be together, it's us. I believe that just as I believe you're selling yourself short."

"Nathan." She started to shift then realized there was no place for her to go. Her backside began to heat first as he pressed closer to her. She felt she was suffocating, fighting for every breath that came, but she didn't panic, wasn't afraid. She was okay as long as he didn't touch her—but she craved his touch, willed with her mind that he would simply put his hands on her. As these thoughts fought in her mind, his hands were on her shoulders, running down her arms. Everything inside her began to pulse, to vibrate with desire. "I can't deny this…this connection we have. But so much time has passed. We've changed…"

She was trembling. His palms, the simple touch of his hands to her skin, was so wonderfully arousing. Then he leaned close to her ear, his breath warm and intoxicating against the sensitive skin. "You looked so tidy and crisp when I arrived today. Calm and cool on the outside, and on the inside…I wondered what was going on inside your mind, inside your body." He kissed the side of her neck, his hands rubbing her arms more insistently. "I wondered if you were feeling just half of the desire that I was. If you wanted me as much as I so desperately want you."

Involuntarily, her body leaned against his, her head falling to the side to rest on his shoulder. He kissed her neck again then suckled not so gently. "I was nervous." *Still am*, she admitted to herself.

"Don't be. At one time we knew each other better than we knew ourselves. It can be that way again. Let your defenses down, Tee. I want you back."

She whimpered with indecision. "If I let my defenses down, I'll be exposed." Her hands fisted at her sides. "I won't be able to stop you from hurting me again."

His hands finally moved to circle her waist, his thumbs brushing against the exposed skin at her midsection. "I won't hurt you again. I can't live without you. Ten years was a long time to learn that lesson, but

I did, baby. I learned that you are everything to me, and I was a fool to let you go. I won't let you go again, Tenile. I won't."

Weak knees and all, she turned to face him, had to see him as this moment intensified. "Nathan."

He saw the moment her mind was made up, the second her eyes shifted from question to acquiescence. "I am so completely in love with you, Tenile," he moaned.

His admission left her breathless. "I'm trying to decide if the time is right." *Trying to decide if surrender makes me weak.*

His fingers found the knot of her shirt, undid it and pushed the material aside. "Keep thinking about it," he said as his lips began to trail hot kisses down the front of her neck to the hollow between her breasts and further down until his tongue plunged into her navel. "Let me know what you decide."

In answer, she grasped his head between both hands and pushed his face closer to her skin, moaning his name as his tongue continued to lavish her.

"I haven't done this in a while."

He unsnapped her pants. "It'll come back to you."

She responded with a sigh and he scooped her up. "Which way?" he asked when her languid eyes stared at him.

She pointed, leaned in and captured his lips, sucking his tongue into her mouth. Groaning, he walked and kissed simultaneously.

Her bedroom was different. The cheerful personality in the other rooms hadn't quite made it back this far. Her bed, dresser, nightstand and blinds were all black, cold and void of any feeling. So unlike her. Dropping her on the bed released a small giggle from her.

"What happened? Your decorator quit?" he asked as he pulled his shirt over his head.

She barely looked around, already knowing what he meant. "I don't know. There's something to be said for all black." She was having a difficult time dragging her eyes away from his half-naked body.

With a grin quickly spreading over his face, he undid his belt, then the snap to his pants and pushed the material over his thighs. "You always did have an exceptional eye for style."

He was gloriously naked in front of her, and nothing else seemed to matter, not the color of furniture, the color of the sun—nothing mattered but Nathan. Extending her arms, she beckoned him. "I've always had an eye for you."

One knee touched down on the black comforter as he brought the other around to straddle her. "Then I'm the luckiest man alive."

Nimble fingers removed her shirt, unclasped her bra and smoothed over the delectable mounds. He tried not to shake with joy. Lowering the zipper on her pants, his knuckles grazed against her. She purred, low and catlike.

When she was free of her clothes, he stared down at her, his eyes roaming freely. "I dreamed of you." Flattening a palm over her belly, he sighed. "Sometimes we'd be in school." The skin here was so smooth, so soft.

She squirmed, her center beginning to ache.

Taking in extra air, he let his hands roam the mocha valley, exploring, marveling. "Most times you'd be just like this." His hand moved further south until soft dark curls gave way to heated moisture. "Open and waiting for me."

When one finger dipped inside, she began to quiver. "Oh God, yes. I've been waiting for you." Admission came quickly. For ten years she'd been waiting for him to come back to Tanner. To come back to her.

With each stroke of his finger over the swollen folds and moist heat, his stomach tightened and clenched, his groin pulsating until he was sure he'd burst.

She looked at him, looked closely into the face she'd thought she'd known so well. His features were tense, as if he concentrated solely on her. His desire was evident, yet he touched her with infinite slowness. Her breath hitched as he grazed her clit—softly, almost like it wasn't really there. She would have thought that ten years away would have made him a ravenous beast; instead, his movements were measured, as if she were glass and would shatter.

Heat swirling in the pit of her stomach slowly began to grow, forming a large pool of sensations spilling over to every part of her body. With one hand she cupped his face, and with the other, stroked his penis. His lips parted slightly, his eyes growing darker.

Emotion welled up inside him, and he wanted to find the words to explain just what he was feeling to her. Instead, he lowered his head, kissed her lips, emptying his confession into her.

Feeling as if she were sinking into the soft mattress, Tenile moaned. Her bones were pliable, her insides like Jell-o, her world complete.

Ending the kiss, he framed her face with his hands and smiled down at her. She lifted her arms, wrapped them around his neck, shifted and clasped her legs around his waist. She smiled even as she made sure his arousal brushed over her dampened sex.

As if on command he slipped inside her, pleasure washing over him in one furious wave. Her back arched and her hips began to rock.

Nathan held her tightly, afraid that if he let go she would vanish. He moved slowly inside her, giving them both time to consummate the memories with the here and now. Had she always been this wet? This inviting? This passionate?

Her nails raked over his bare back as spasms of delight coursed through her. He knew exactly how to move, which places to stroke—any and everything that brought her pleasure, he knew.

He reared up, unwinding her legs from his waist, propping each ankle onto his shoulder. As he slipped deeper inside her, the ten years seemed to vanish. She was still his as if this were their first time. They were connected, their bodies touching. They were one.

Tenile gripped the sheets, her head flailing from side to side. Beyond sex, that's what this was. Sensations swirled through her, new and ripe, covering every inch of her body. He claimed her, and she was allowing herself to be claimed. He filled her and she allowed herself to be filled.

He pulled out, plunged in, pulled out, plunged in.

Darkness began to surround her, a cloudy haze hovering at her feet, a cushion for when she fell.

His thrusts were slow, purposeful and on point. Her moans echoed throughout the room, a symphony of her love for him. "Nathan." A sigh. A groan. It was all about him.

He would remember this always, and when she closed her eyes, he demanded she open them. This would be a memory for both of them. He would make sure of that.

He grabbed her ankles, spreading her legs slightly apart as his pace increased. "Say my name."

The pressure built inside her until she was ready to beg for release. "Nathan."

Sleek wetness sucked him in, grabbed him fiercely and wouldn't let go. "Say it again."

"Nathan." The name tore from her like a raged cry.

Her legs had begun to shake and he knew she was close to the edge. He put her legs down, pushed her knees to her chest and kissed her, his tongue sinking into her mouth the way his penis had invaded her womanhood. She whimpered, opening wider to accept him. He sucked her bottom lip, bit down and rammed into her forcefully, more forcefully than he ever had before. "Come for me," he ordered her. "Come for me."

Bright lights burst before her eyes when she obeyed his command. She went limp and his hips slowed to a gentle rocking. His kisses softened, raining freely over her face.

He was murmuring in her ear, something, everything. It didn't matter what he said as long as he remained here while saying it. She hugged him tightly, repeating his name, convincing herself that this was not a dream.

He sensed her need, felt the urgency in her grip. "I'm right here, baby. I'm not going anywhere."

His words relaxed her and she realized he was still hard and throbbing inside her. She picked up a slow motion of her hips, rotating against the swollen rod so that it hit her walls at every angle.

His own desire continued to build as she flexed her muscles, constricting against him with excruciating pleasure. He was going to explode. The tip of his penis was so hard, so ripe for release. Her hands found his butt, holding him still, holding him inside her as she worked her magic. His breathing grew erratic, his heart performing a dance all its own. She was so wet, so hot; they fit perfectly. His arms wobbled as the spasms racked through him. Release was coming; his body was preparing for it.

A ferocious groan built in his chest as he looked down at her. She watched him intently as if she knew exactly what she was doing to him. Again, he wanted to speak, to tell her what effect she was having on him, but couldn't seem to come up with the words.

He was standing at the edge, ten years behind him and Tenile in front of him. Tenile, open and waiting for him, hot and ready for him, a smile on her face, her undulating hips and soft words beckoning him to join her. Every muscle inside him tightened, and his hands fisted in the pillows around her head. That groan that had been building escaped as he cried out with the force of anticipation. She held him tightly, edging him, pushing him. And then he fell, long and hard. He fell. It took a few moments before he realized he'd hit the bottom because the impact had been so soft, so comforting, so Tenile.

Chapter 12

W"e have to get to work."

Her words were true, yet she kept her legs wrapped around him, pulling him closer. He groaned, his arms encircling her. They'd been in bed all afternoon. The sun, which had been high when he arrived, was now low on the horizon.

Nathan inhaled the sweet smell of her hair, which was now tickling his nose. They were twined together so that it was impossible to see where she started and he ended. He'd waited what seemed like an eternity for this. He'd come back for this, to lie here with her in his arms.

Tenile had never been so content in her life. Nathan was holding her. A few minutes ago Nathan had been inside her, carrying her to higher heights than she'd ever reached. Their lovemaking had been unique, the feelings, the motions, nothing like they'd experienced before. Yet the hint of familiarity lingered long and strong. She'd been his before; she'd given herself to him long ago. And now she was doing it again.

The logical part of her questioned her sanity, questioned why she would put her heart on the line again. Just as his hand cupped her right breast and squeezed gently, the very illogical but sexually contented part of her sighed, happy that the only person who could make her feel this way was back in her life. But was he back for good?

Nathan felt her body tense, felt her shifting away from him even as he held her in his arms. "What is it? What are you thinking?"

She was quiet, unsure of what her words should be, unsure of whether she should speak them at all.

"Tee, talk to me." He shifted so he could see her face. Looking into eyes full of sadness caused a tightening around his heart. "What can I do to make it better?"

"I didn't want anything the way we planned. I left that house and swore nothing we planned would ever happen." She bit her bottom lip trying to regain some composure.

She needed to say this, he knew, but he wanted to stop her. To tell her it wasn't necessary, that everything was different now. Instead, he brushed her hair behind each ear and waited patiently for her to finish.

"I changed my studies, going back to school at night to take classes in obstetrics and gynecology. I worked at the hospital as an assistant until I had enough credits to go on the floor in labor and delivery. I got my own apartment because I couldn't stand the thought of living with my mother, with all her questions, all her friends' questions about what happened. I didn't date for years." Her hands rested on her chest. She felt the rapid heartbeat as she watched his deep brown eyes watch her. *Could he understand? Would he believe how hard being without him was? And would that be enough to keep him here this time?*

"In the back of my mind, I thought it was all a bad dream. That Landy would turn up alright and you…you would walk through that door with that easy smile and calm me the way you used to." She willed herself not to cry and took a deep breath instead. "When I finally realized that wasn't going to happen, I started to focus on myself, on what I wanted from life. Surprisingly, all those plans we'd made together vanished. I didn't want any of that anymore. I was perfectly content being single, working and coming home. That became my life, my only goal to buy a house of my own. When I met Robert and he seemed so intent on dating me, I figured, why not? I hadn't been out with a guy in about a year at that time. Hadn't been with another man in a year." Satisfaction made a quick appearance as she admitted to him that she'd gotten over him long enough to sleep with someone else. There was a glimmer of hurt, a second of anger, then it was gone, and his eyes were calmly fixed on her again.

"Tenile—"

Two fingers to his lips stopped his words. This was her time, her words, her release. "I wanted so desperately for Robert to wash all memory of you away. He was stable and level-headed, and he wanted us to be together." She shrugged because this part she still didn't really understand. "I just couldn't make it work. His touch, his words, never really moved me. And when you showed up, I knew why." Her thumb traced the outline of his lips, smoothed over his mustache, his goatee. "For whatever reason, I'm stuck on you, Nathan Hamilton." Cupping his chin she grinned. "And I'd like to know what you plan to do about that."

He could have called it relief, but somehow that didn't seem to be enough. Her beginning words, full of all the turmoil his departure had put her through, had made him sure she was planning to send him packing, although he had no intention of leaving her. But had she felt that way, recapturing her heart once more would have been a little harder. Then she'd touched him, and in that moment, he knew she still loved him as deeply as he loved her, even though she'd yet to say it.

"First, I intend to make love to you again." He covered her body, pushing her legs apart with his own. "And this time while we're making love, I'm going to tell you how much you mean to me." He slid into her in one slow, tortuous motion. "I'm going to tell you how much I love you." *Stroke.* "How I've never stopped loving you." *Circle. Stroke.* "How I'm never going to let you go again."

She opened wider, wrapping her arms securely around him, waiting for the precise moment to match his motions. *Stroke.* "Mmmmmm, Nathan."

His arms folded around her, pulling her close as he buried his head in her hair, then turned to her ear. *Stroke.* "I love you, Tenile." *Stroke, circle, moan, stroke.* "I love you. I love you."

❧

The doorbell rang and Eli silently prayed it was Nicole. It had been days since he'd seen her, days since he'd talked to her, and he was afraid he was beginning to miss much more than just their sex. He grabbed his jacket. He wouldn't have a lot of time to talk to her; he had to be at the hospital in half an hour.

"Hello, Elias."

Eli stood perfectly still. The tall, thin man who stood in front of him was certainly a blast from his past, one he wasn't too keen on dealing with again. "Donovan. To what do I owe this pleasure? I didn't even know you were back in Tanner."

Donavan smiled, a cold calculating move he'd been used to doing all his life. "Invite me in, Eli. What I have to say can't be discussed out here."

That was exactly what Eli had been afraid of. Still, he did have manners. He stood to the side and closed the door when Donovan stepped through. Tossing his jacket on the chair, he turned and waited for the shoe to drop.

"I see you're living quite comfortably." Donovan looked around Eli's spacious condo, admiring the expensive art and sculptures. He walked about slowly, fingering the pieces of the *All That Jazz* collection that Eli owned. "Still into jazz music, huh? These are some pretty expensive pieces. Are you on your way to collecting the entire set?"

"I like art. But that's not why you're here." Eli stood, his legs slightly parted, his hands in his pockets. Something had to bring Donovan Connor out from under the rock where he'd hid after his sister's death. And Eli was afraid he knew what that something was.

"You can afford all this on a doctor's salary?" Donovan lifted his arms, sweeping the rooms.

Eli grinned. Donovan hadn't changed much. He was still almost rail thin, his boyish features masking the evil creature Eli knew him to be. "I'm head of the department. There's a pretty reasonable salary that goes with that title."

Donavan laughed, moved to the bar and proceeded to fix himself a drink. "You *were* head of the department. Your old friend has that position now, doesn't he?"

Oh yeah, he knew exactly why Donovan was back, and it didn't look good for any of them. "Yes, Nathan has recently taken over that position. I have some other things that I'd like to do."

"Like open your own practice, be the sole private obstetrician in Tanner. But you can't quite do that with the meager sum you have in the bank. Have you thought about investors?" Donovan took a swallow of the clear liquor and bit back a grin.

Eli grimaced. "It's a little early in the evening to be drinking so hard, don't you think?" He decided this was going to take a moment, so he went to the couch, took a seat and watched Donovan finish off the vodka. "What is it you really want, Donovan? I know the last place you'd want to be is Tanner. So you must have a reason. What is it?"

Donovan laughed. "Yeah, I see you remember me well. I do hate this hick-ass town of yours. Never could understand why Landy wanted to stay here. Anyway," he sauntered over, took a seat on the barstool, "I figured you and me got some things to discuss. Since we're both looking for the same thing, it makes more sense that we simply help each other."

Eli was careful. He held himself perfectly still, not wanting to give anything away. "And what exactly is it that you think we're both looking for?"

Donovan's grin never wavered. "I'd say about half a million in cash and twice as much in jewelry."

"I don't know what you're talking about."

"You're such a piss poor liar, Grant. Landy's stuff. I know she took it to that shack y'all shared and called a house. I know she told all of you in that clique of yours where it was. Funny thing is, none of you have made any big purchases since her death. You all seem to be making honest livings for yourselves. So that leads me to wonder exactly which one of you knows the whereabouts of money that should have been mine." Now Donavan changed. The smile was gone, and a sinister gleam entered his eyes as he looked at Eli.

"How do you know what we've all been doing?" Eli suddenly felt nervous.

"Oh, I've been keeping close tabs on you and the crew. But now it's time to stop messing around. I want my money and those jewels, and I'm not leaving Tanner until I get it."

"I don't know what you're talking about."

"Oh, you don't, huh?" Donovan stood, walked over to the window, then turned back to Eli. "Then maybe that little slut you're still bangin' knows something. She's really grown into her looks; her body is tight as shit. I have to admit when I saw her last night, she made my dick hard."

Eli was out of his chair, grabbing Donovan by his collar and shoving him against the wall. "She doesn't know anything. And if you go near her, I'll make you pay."

Donovan laughed, his vodka-scented breath going directly into Eli's face. "Man, I don't want your leftovers. She looks good but she's still a hick, just like the rest of y'all. Still, if that's the only way I can get you to cooperate, then maybe I'll pay her a visit next."

Eli let him go, stalked across the floor and swore. "You will leave her the hell alone. She doesn't know anything."

"And you do?"

Eli took a deep breath and prepared to make a deal with the devil.

❦

Tenile's shift was over, for which she was profoundly thankful. Side-by-side, she and Nathan had delivered three babies that evening and additionally performed one cesarean. He'd requested she attend, to observe, since she didn't have the surgical credits. She felt the little push and respected it for what it was. Nathan always made sure he pushed her to her limits—in everything.

She'd gathered her stuff and was boarding the elevator when Myla, the head nurse, stepped inside with her.

"Leaving for the night?" Myla questioned, although she already knew the answer.

"Yeah, I'm on a little earlier tomorrow. Karen needs to leave at four, so I told her I'd cover for her."

Myla grumbled a bit before folding her arms over her chest. They were almost to the bottom floor when Myla abruptly said, "Don't think I don't know what's going on with you and that doctor. I'm not blind nor am I stupid."

Tenile had wondered how long it would take for her and Nathan to be exposed. This was a little sooner than she'd anticipated, but she was determined to deal with it.

"I would never assume you were, Myla. But what Dr. Hamilton and I do on our own time is our business."

Myla sucked her teeth. "You bring it on my floor, it's my business."

"We haven't brought anything to your floor."

"Haven't you? For the last three hours, I watched those lovers' looks and shared touches in the hallway. And all I'm saying is, it don't look good. Plus, I ain't too sure I trust him."

For the second time in as many weeks, Tenile found herself thoroughly annoyed with the small town gossip and opinionated prejudice in Tanner. Myla was her supervisor, so she'd respect her, but she would not be bullied or chastised for looking at someone.

"Again, what Nathan and I do in our private time is our business. As for happenings on your floor, the doctor and I are too busy to do anything other than deliver babies. If you have an extra three hours to watch us, then I believe your services should be re-evaluated."

Ding! The elevator stopped and Tenile made a move to step out.

"It's a cryin' shame what happened to that gal. And you called yourself her friend. Hmph. Looks like you wouldn't want to be sleepin' with her killer."

All bets were off now! Tenile turned, sticking her foot against the door so it wouldn't close. "You'd do well to mind your own business, Myla. Slander is a serious offense and is punishable under the law. So keep your opinions and accusations to yourself."

She couldn't get away fast enough. Adrenaline flowed through her in hot rushes as she made her way to her car. She was relieved when she saw Nathan sitting in his car beside hers.

"Hey, beautiful. What took you so long?" The moment he looked at her heknew that something was wrong and stepped out of his vehicle. "What happened?"

Normally, she didn't squeal with the intent of getting a co-worker in trouble, but Myla had been vicious, and she couldn't let her words rest. "It seems our secret is out and someone's not pleased."

He'd begun to rub her shoulders, but now he frowned at her. "I take it somebody said something to you."

"Yes. It appears that your head nurse is not pleased with us being intimate since she believes you killed Landy." She moved, unlocked her back door and threw her stuff into the backseat.

Even though his jaw clenched, Nathan was sure not to show any other emotion. He'd deal with Myla later. "Forget about it, baby. We'll go back to your place, and I'll give you a nice massage."

"Nathan, a massage won't make the town forget, nor will it prove your innocence."

He opened her door and urged her to get in. "Nobody can prove my innocence but me, and I will in time. Until then, it's best to ignore the gossip."

Tenile sat behind the steering wheel. "I don't know if I can ignore it."

"You can." He leaned into the car and placed a light kiss on her pouting mouth. "And you will. Now drive home. I'll be right behind you."

A couple of blocks away from the hospital, she started to believe his kiss had some type of healing power. She felt lightheaded and excited. And each time she glanced in her rearview mirror and spotted his car, her heart hammered with anticipation.

They approached her building hand in hand, exchanging smiles and knowing glances. In the elevator, he took her in his arms and kissed her until her knees went weak. She leaned on him all the way to her apartment door.

Nathan stiffened and she raised her head from his shoulder to see why.

"Wait here." He pushed her aside and moved closer to the door.

It wasn't closed all the way.

Slowly, he pushed the door open and was prepared to walk in when he felt her right behind him. "I told you to stay out here."

"This is my apartment, my home that I know I locked up when I left. I'll be damned if I'll stand out here while you go in to see what happened."

Her eyes were bright, her chin jutting forward, and he knew there was no point arguing with her. "Stay right next to me."

She waved a hand at him.

"Tenile, I'm serious. I want you to stay near me while we're in there."

She saw a bit of panic in his eyes and realized this really could be serious. "Okay, I'll stay near you."

She gasped once they were inside and the light was turned on. He took her hand, rubbing his thumb over her skin before taking another step.

All her colorful pillows were in shreds and strewn across the room, looking as if someone had taken a razor to them before tossing them about. Her pictures were pulled from the walls, her dinette set over-turned.

"I'm going in the bedroom," he told her and intended to tell her to stay there.

"I'll be right behind you."

He sighed and walked towards the bedroom, holding fear at bay.

Neither one of them was prepared for the scene. All her clothes were thrown about the room, her drawers broken and tossed in the floor, her blinds torn from the window and crushed. And the bed...the mattress was ripped to pieces just like her pillows in the other room.

Nathan took a step forward, careful to move stuff only with his feet.

Tenile was trying to hold on to her composure, trying not to act too female and scream. Nathan had moved away from her, leaving her to stand in the midst of the wreckage by herself.

"The sheets aren't here."

Tenile heard his words but didn't understand. "What?"

"The sheets. Did you take the sheets off before you left?"

She looked toward the bed again. "No." She shook her head. "No, I didn't."

"They're gone. Why would somebody take your sheets?"

Tenile wasn't really paying attention to Nathan. She'd picked up a piece of her mini blind.

"He's watching," she whispered and turned towards the window. "He wants me to know he's watching. He tore down the blinds so I'd know that he can see me."

Nathan went to the window and didn't see anything out of the ordinary, but he did remember the person who'd been at his window a few nights ago. "Grab what you can; we're leaving."

"Leaving? Where am I going? This is my home."

"This is your home, but he's been here. Do you really think I'm going to let you stay knowing that?"

"I'm pretty capable of making my own decisions. He's been here and now he's gone. Why shouldn't I simply clean up and stay here?"

Across the room his gaze shifted and focused on the mirror on top of the dresser. Slowly he moved to Tenile, put his hands on her shoulders and turned her around. "That's why you shouldn't stay."

She gasped, her eyes going wide with terror. Grateful that he was behind her, she let herself fall against him, for she was sure she couldn't stand another moment on her own.

JUNE 18

It was written with lipstick, blood red lipstick that she was positive she didn't own.

"The date of Landy's death. He's reminding us," Nathan said solemnly. "I'll get your things."

She couldn't speak, only nodded in agreement.

Chapter 13

Oneil Barnes was fit to be tied. Geraldine's words were still ringing in her ears. Her only daughter up and moving out of her apartment to shack up with some man. Not some man, that man! She hadn't raised her child that way. She and her husband had overlooked the fact that she'd lived with three men in college because there were two other girls there too, but this was different. The man she lived with now was a murderer…or at least he hadn't been proved differently.

She didn't like it. No, she didn't like it one bit. She moved around her kitchen like a woman on a mission, chopping vegetables, seasoning meat, making iced tea, mixing the cake batter. They were coming to dinner. That's what her daughter had said when she called this morning. "Mama, I know you've heard some stuff, and we're coming to dinner tonight to explain."

Then, just like that she'd hung up the phone, like it was over and done with. Oneil's nostrils flared so wide she was sure either smoke would come out of them or she'd suck something up before long. Tenile had plumb lost her mind. That's what it was. She'd always gone off and done things her way and in her time, and just look where that had gotten her. Into the arms of a murderer. A man who murdered her best friend at that.

So flustered and bothered by Tenile and her decision, Oneil picked up the wrong shaker and shook too much pepper into the vegetables. "Oh shoot!" She shrugged her heavy shoulders and looked down at the mess. "Well, serves 'em right for gettin' me all upset." She stirred the vegetables, resisting the urge to sneeze. She'd make sure Nathan Hamilton got a healthy helping of vegetables tonight. She chuckled to herself.

"What did your mother say?" Nathan asked as he entered the kitchen. Tenile had gone in there to make the call to her mother. It had been three days since she'd moved in with him. Three days since someone had broken into her apartment.

"I didn't give her much chance to say anything. I told her we'd be there for dinner." She absently flipped through a magazine, trying not to think about tonight or the events that had led up to it.

"You're positive she already knew you were staying here?"

She cut him a glaring look. "I don't know why you insist on acting like you've never lived here before. As soon as you packed my stuff and sped over here, Mrs. Finley was probably on the phone to two or three people, telling all she thought she knew." She rolled her eyes. "Besides, my mother calls me every morning like clockwork."

Nathan filled his bowl of Raisin Bran with milk and sat at the table across from her. "Why does she call you in the morning? She knows you work the night shift." He took a spoonful and almost sighed. It was the same bittersweet taste he remembered sharing with her in this kitchen so long ago.

"Because she's my mother and that's the way her mind works. I know it's strange, but I don't think there's a cure for it."

He chuckled. "You don't seem too bothered by it."

"I'm used to it now." She kept looking at the magazine, ignoring his crunching and munching. She hadn't been able to bring herself to eat Raisin Bran since leaving this house ten years before. Her first night after she moved in with Nathan, she'd been sure she wouldn't survive. She'd endured an onslaught of memories that she'd feared would never stop. But once in the bed beside Nathan, once he'd put his arms around her, whispering that she was safe with him, she'd fallen asleep. And since then the memories had been okay, not gone, but safely appearing at intervals, allowing her time to recover.

Now, the Raisin Bran was something altogether different. She smelled the sugar-coated raisins and listened to the crunch. He kept eating as if there was nothing wrong with what he was doing until she slammed her magazine down.

"What?" He looked puzzled and his spoon dripped milk inches from his mouth.

"The least you could do is make me a bowl too. That is so rude of you to sit in my face and eat and not offer me some." She stood, yanking open a cabinet that housed his only four bowls. "And when are you going to buy more dishes? You have exactly four of everything. I sure hope you don't plan on entertaining anytime soon."

Nathan smiled. He'd suspected she hadn't had the cereal since he'd left. Offering her some would have made her think about it too seriously. Waiting until the decision was hers had allowed her time to digest the memory and move on. He kept right on crunching while she slammed cupboards and made her own bowl.

❧

"Well, Albert, you finally made sheriff. Congratulations." Nathan held his front door open, studying the short, round man. When he'd left Tanner, Albert Ross had been just a deputy trailing behind Sheriff Hilcott in his starched uniform and thick glasses. Now he stood as tall as his frame allowed, hat atop his head, badge shinning on the pocket of his shirt. They were both around the same age, give or take a year or so. Nathan had sensed then that, like many of the townfolk, Albert thought him guilty of killing Landy. The tight look on Albert's face now confirmed he still believed it.

Albert nodded stiffly. "Nathan Hamilton. I heard you'd returned." Albert faced the much larger man, trying like hell to hold on to his nervousness. He'd never been this close to a killer before. But he was the sheriff now; Nathan Hamilton should be the one nervous, not him. His nervousness turned to anger and disgust as he remembered the luxury car parked out in the driveway and looked at the starched casual black pants and cranberry polo shirt, the gold watch at Nathan's wrist and the expensive looking shoes on his feet. Money and privilege, that's what had gotten him out of the murder rap—that's what made Albert sick to his stomach.

"I came down to the precinct the other night with Tenile, but you were already gone." Nathan suspected this was the reason for Albert's late afternoon, weekend visit to his home today. Tanner was a small town, not used to things such as murders and break-ins. It was only right that the local authorities took such things seriously.

Albert removed his hat, scratched his already balding head and looked around the hallway. Nathan hadn't invited him to go any further. "Ah, have you seen Ms. Barnes? I went by her place this mornin' and nobody was there."

Nathan slipped his hands into his pockets, raised a brow. "Have you found the man who broke into her house?"

Albert's eyes narrowed on him. "What makes you so sure it was a man?" He'd read the report, knew it was Hamilton who had accompanied Ms. Barnes back to her place and found the mess. Still, he didn't put anything past Nathan, past a murderer.

Nathan didn't flinch even though the hint of suspicion in Albert's tone bothered him. He was still a suspect, and as a result of his running away instead of proving his innocence, would probably always be considered one. "Would a woman steal the sheets from another woman's bed?"

"Jilted lovers do strange things."

Nathan grinned at the other man's stupidity. "Yeah, like leave the date of another woman's murder scrawled on the mirror in lipstick." Albert didn't know anything. He simply wanted to talk to Tenile, to find out if she believed Nathan was somehow involved in the break-in and, undoubtedly, Landy's murder.

Just as he'd assumed, his return had re-opened Landy's case, and he was still the number one suspect. But not for long; he'd see to that personally.

"I'd rather discuss the particulars with Ms. Barnes."

"Here I am. Let's discuss it." Tenile appeared in the doorway leading to the kitchen. Both men turned to her now, staring as if neither of them had expected her. "We can talk in the living room." She moved slowly, carefully, as two sets of eyes paid close attention to her every movement.

"Can I get you something to drink, Sheriff?" she asked when she was standing in the middle of the living room floor.

"Ah, no. No, thank you. If you don't mind, I just have a few questions."

Nodding, she caught Nathan's speculative glare over Albert's shoulder and dismissed it. She took a seat on the couch, knowing Nathan would join her. When he did, she noticed the uncomfortable shift in Albert's eyes and wondered if Nathan had seen it too. Would they ever prove his innocence? And what would happen to their future if they didn't?

"So what do you need to ask me? I already gave an account of what was missing and damaged. I don't know what else I can tell you."

Albert fidgeted with his notepad, his cool eyes moving from Tenile to Nathan, then back to Tenile again. "I'd rather we talk alone."

Nathan put a protective arm around Tenile. "I'm not leaving and that's not negotiable."

"You have nothing to do with this," Albert began to protest.

Tenile interrupted the two men in the midst of their pissing match. "Nathan was with me when I found my house in disarray. He has also been gracious enough to let me stay here until my apartment is up to par."

Albert looked at her with clear disagreement.

She straightened her back, meeting his cold glare and holding it. "I want him to stay."

There was a deafening silence.

"Your questions?" Nathan prodded.

With barely restrained contempt, Albert lifted his pen and spoke directly to Tenile. "Have you been seeing anyone? An old boyfriend?"

She hated that Albert had accused, tried and convicted Nathan already, without any doubt of his guilt. But she'd answer his questions if that would make him go away sooner. "I was dating Robert Gibson."

"And Mr. Gibson doesn't mind that you're staying with Mr. Hamilton now?"

Nathan tensed beside her, and she put a hand on his knee. She would handle the sheriff her own way. "Mr. Gibson doesn't mind because he doesn't know. I've been unable to get in touch with him for the last week or so."

"Really?" Albert's brow went up. This was very interesting. He made a note on his pad to check on the whereabouts of Robert Gibson. "Isn't that…convenient?" Again, his eyes shifted to Nathan. "You've wasted no time getting back into the swing of things, Hamilton."

Only good home training and the desire not to make things worse for Tenile kept Nathan from wrapping his hands around Albert's thick neck. Instead, he tightened his grip on Tenile and smiled. "Don't fault me. I'm not the one who left such an attractive woman alone."

Albert stood, obviously irritated by Nathan's comment. "That is so true. I remember you having a fondness for attractive women."

Nathan stood as well, tired of being the accommodating host and equally tired of Albert's veiled accusations. "I believe you have some things you'd rather say to me, Sheriff."

Albert folded his notepad, placed it in his shirt pocket. "Not unless you have something you want to tell me."

Tenile stood then, placing her hand on Nathan's arm. He was tense, his entire body rigid beneath Albert's steely glare. "I hope you plan to focus your energy on who vandalized my apartment, Sheriff."

Albert let his gaze fall from Nathan. He surveyed the room, taking in the sparse but expensive furnishings. "I'll be focusing my energy on lots of things, especially things of the past."

There was no doubt the sheriff's words were meant for Nathan. "The past should be re-visited. I've been thinking that myself." Even though his hands fisted and released at his sides, Nathan kept his face blank. Albert was watching him closely for any sign of guilt, any moment of weakness. He wouldn't give him the pleasure.

The room filled with such a thick cloud of hostility Tenile thought she'd suffocate. "If there are no more questions, I'll see you out, Sheriff."

This didn't need to go any further. Albert was clearly baiting Nathan, and Nathan, despite his efforts, was about to lose control.

The last thing she wanted was a confrontation between the town sheriff and Nathan in Nathan's house where she was staying. They'd be the talk of the town…again.

"I can reach you here if I have more questions?" Albert inquired.

Tenile moved from Nathan, grabbed the sheriff's arm and led him out of the living room.

Nathan didn't move. He couldn't. Rage simmered inside him, boiling and churning like a dark storm. He didn't kill Landy, but he might as well have since everyone seemed so convinced.

He walked to the bar, gripped a glass in his hand then pushed it aside. Tenile hadn't told the sheriff they were together, that they were a couple again. She hadn't made any comments about the past, any defense towards the allegations that hung in the air. She'd told him she believed in his innocence. But in a town full of doubt and rumors, could he trust the honesty of that statement?

He trusted her. That would have to be enough.

"Ms. Barnes. Tenile, I have to be straight with you." Albert turned at the door, looked at her earnestly. "Are you sure you should be staying here? With him?"

Tenile couldn't tell if that idea repulsed or worried him. Either way she wasn't going to concern herself with it. She'd made her decision, and she had to stick by it—no matter how much the hatred in Albert's tone caused her to worry. "Sheriff, I assure you I am safer here than anywhere else in town." And she believed that, or at least she had before the sheriff's visit.

Albert stared at her, unsure if he believed her but determined not to have a repeat of what happened at this house ten years ago. "I'll be keeping a close eye on things."

"You mean on Dr. Hamilton?" she corrected him. Then she gave him a smile that was sure to tick him off even more. "I'm sure you will, just as I'm sure you'll be disappointed in your findings." With her hand on the doorknob, she nodded her head and with a voice laced with honey said, "Have a good day, Sheriff."

✎

The Barnes house hadn't changed much since the last time Nathan had been there. The hedges surrounding the long front porch were thicker. The rose-covered trellises climbed a little higher, passing the second story windows now. The same, yet different.

The dirt driveway seemed strange without the old beat up yellow truck Mr. Barnes used to drive. Tenile had told him of her father's massive heart attack three years ago, and he'd been sorry to hear it. Memories of himself and Mr. Barnes sharing cold drinks and baseball games filled his mind as his booted feet took the steps to the front porch.

The moment they entered the foyer, they heard the television and smelled the aroma of a home-cooked meal. Mementos, knick-knacks and pictures still crowded the hallway. The living room was to the right; that's where the TV was on. To the left were the stairs. He'd ventured up them only once or twice. Straight back was the parlor, where Mr. Barnes used to smoke his cigars because Mrs. Barnes wouldn't allow them anywhere else in the house. And past that room was the kitchen, from which the succulent smells wafted.

Suddenly very nervous, Tenile turned to Nathan. He looked so handsome in his dark pants and crisp shirt. His goatee was growing thicker, giving him an air of maturity that she admired. "I should probably talk to Mama first. You go on in the living room. Tracy's probably propped up on the sofa. That sounds like those action movies she loves watching."

She was fidgeting, her anxiety clearly written on her face. She'd been really quiet since the sheriff's surprise visit. That, coupled with her mother's reaction to them being back together, was more than enough reason for her to be a bit jittery.

He moved closer, took both her hands and brought them to his lips for a quick kiss. "We'll talk to your mother together. Then we'll check on Tracy."

Despite the warmth he stirred in her, she wasn't so sure his reception in the Barnes household would be warm. "Nathan, you don't have to," she protested.

Tucking her arm into the crook of his own, he was already headed towards the kitchen, towards those wonderful smells, before replying, "Yes, I do. She needs to hear it from me. That's the only way it'll truly matter. Besides, I'll have to remind her how charming she always thought I was."

Despite her reservations, Tenile grinned. "She never thought you were charming. She thought you were a starving boy who talked too much."

They entered the kitchen laughing and arm in arm, only to stop abruptly at the sight of Oneil, knife in hand.

"Good evening," Oneil said with a frown.

"Hi, Mama," Tenile responded with less trepidation. Nathan's presence, his persistence and the simple act of kissing her hand had all succeeded in melting away some of the stress she'd allowed to build up in the last few hours.

Nathan watched mother and daughter embrace as Oneil's eyes stared him down over Tenile's shoulder. She was going to be tough, but winning her over would be worth it. "Mrs. Barnes, it's nice to see you again." Nathan moved a step closer as they broke the embrace. Oneil's gaze narrowed on him, sizing him up. He'd put on a little weight since she'd seen him last, probably from all that fast food up in New York. He probably hadn't eaten home cooked vegetables and meat in all the years he'd been away. Still, he'd filled out nicely. Had grown a mustache and a little beard too—made him look distinguished. Or possibly mysterious. Her thoughts brought about an immediate frown. He looked mysterious alright. "It was nice seeing you before things got bad. But now, I don't know." She spoke her mind, as always.

Tenile took his hand in hers but remained quiet. Nathan had noted Oneil's assessment, felt the battle going on inside her. She remembered the boy he'd been, the murder, his disappearance and now, just now, the connection he had with her daughter. She had a right to be angry, a right to be defensive. And he had a right to knock all that down and give her his honest commitment to the truth. "Things did get bad, ma'am. But I can assure you I had nothing to do with that."

"Runnin' is for the guilty." Oneil moved to the table where the pineapple and brown sugar ham sat.

Tenile sent him a baleful look, and he shooed her away. Moving to the counter, he picked up a platter. "I believe you're right," he told Oneil as he placed it next to the ham. "That's why I came back."

Oneil mumbled something, dropped the first few slices of ham onto the platter. "Opening old wounds is what you're doing."

Nathan couldn't resist; he plucked a piece of meat and stuck it in his mouth. "No, I think I'm about to enjoy me a fabulous meal," he said, savoring the sweet flavor.

Oneil never looked at him, never stopped slicing. "About to get your fingers slapped, I'd say."

Behind them, Tenile's shoulders relaxed. He tossed her a smile, and she stuck her tongue out at him. She was going to the living room to see Tracy. Nathan's charm with her mother was about to get nauseating.

Dinner progressed with pleasant conversation and light banter with a few chuckles sprinkled on top. Nathan and the three ladies sat at the heavy oak table in the dining room for what seemed like hours. Nobody mentioned Landy or the murder or the break-in at Tenile's, even though it was likely on all their minds.

Oneil watched him like a hawk, he noted. Tenile got her looks from her mother. She had the same almond-shaped eyes the color of a shiny penny. Oneil's eyes, however, were wrinkled at the edges with lines that spread outward towards high cheekbones. She'd endured a lot over the last years, and a part of him longed to ease some of that worry, to make her future years just a bit happier.

He turned slightly to his right and watched Tenile sip lemonade. He found and held her eyes. His heart sped, tripped and all but skidded out of his chest at what he saw in them. When she lowered her glass and licked her lips, heat pooled in his groin.

❦

He'd been watching her. She caught his gaze and felt the warmth emanating from him clear across the table. Had it ever been like this before? No, she didn't think so. Whatever was between her and Nathan now was new and, while a tad familiar, totally different from the youthful love they'd shared so long ago.

In his eyes, beyond the lust she identified easily, she suddenly saw something else, a wariness, a suspicious edge she couldn't quite fathom. And questions began to surface. That visit from the sheriff had her thinking crazy. Doubts she knew she shouldn't have suddenly seemed more fact than fiction. Was Nathan still hiding something about the murder?

Then he winked at her and the Nathan she knew was back. Her hand went to her temple, and she swayed in her chair, almost swooning in relief.

"Tee, what's the matter with you?" Oneil hustled from her spot at the head of the table to stand by Tenile's side.

Nathan reached for her hand, clasping it in his. Her hand was cold. One moment she'd been staring at him with what he was sure were the same thoughts in his own head, and the next she'd gone pale, her eyes glassing over mysteriously.

"She'd better not be pregnant." Oneil frowned at him.

"Can I get you something, baby?" He ignored Oneil, his focus solely on the daughter, the woman.

Oneil rubbed her meaty hands up and down Tenile's arms as if the problem were a simple chill. "Shackin' up in that old house again. The both of you should know better. You're a baby doctor; you know how it works."

Tenile sighed at her mother's words and quickly tried to pull herself together. This conversation could go really bad, really fast, if she didn't put an end to it. It was too hot in here; she couldn't breathe, couldn't see straight. "Mama, I'm not pregnant."

"You look like you need some air." Nathan stood, pulling Tenile up to stand beside him.

Oneil held on to one of Tenile's arms protectively. She didn't like how Nathan had stood beside her baby, taking hold of her like he owned her. "She needs to come back home and stop causing so much talk. I swear, if Geraldine calls me one more time with news about my daughter and her friends, I'm gonna scream."

"Mrs. Finley needs to keep her mouth shut," Tracy quipped. "She minds everybody's business but her own. Ask her about her oldest son, Johnny, the one that moved up to Canada. That'll shut her up."

Nathan sent a look of gratitude to Tracy, who hadn't gotten up from the table but had stopped eating to see what was wrong with Tenile.

Oneil looked from Tracy to Nathan, disdain clear in her eyes. "Geraldine's my friend, and she's just looking out for me and mine."

"Mama, please. I don't care what Geraldine or anyone else is saying. My life is my business." Tenile stood on shaky legs but felt her wits slowly returning. "I'm going into the kitchen to get us some leftovers," she said to her mother. "Then I'll be ready to go." She turned to Nathan before walking away.

He was relieved. For a minute there, he'd thought she might consider her mother's words and refuse to go back to the house with him. In that case, he would have had to throw her over his shoulder and exercise his brute strength against her. Looking at Oneil and her unconcealed anger, he was grateful that he hadn't had to go that route.

"Just what do you think you're doing, carrying on with my baby, bringing all this bad talk around again?"

Oneil was in his face now, those eyes he'd admired a moment ago were sending sparks of anger directly at him. For a moment he thought the ground he'd gained with her was lost. Then he remembered the woman he was dealing with. This woman had raised the love of his life, and he knew just how to handle her. "I'm looking out for me and mine."

Tracy snickered.

Oneil huffed.

He bent down, planted a quick kiss on her cheek and gave her shoulders a reassuring squeeze. "I'm not going to hurt her, and I'm not going to see her hurt. Trust me." He knew he was asking a lot, knew that it was a long shot she'd give her trust that quickly, that completely where her only daughter was concerned. But she needed to hear the words; she needed to know his intentions.

Oneil turned away, grumbling and clearing the dirty dishes from the table, then moved toward the kitchen. Tracy sent Nathan a thumbs-up and cheerfully consumed her apple pie. He went into the kitchen to join Tenile. He took the containers she'd packed, put them in a bag and headed for the car, leaving her and Oneil in the kitchen alone, giving them the privacy they needed...and escaping another possible run-in with the mighty Oneil.

Chapter 14

W e need to talk right away." Eli spoke into his cell phone as he drove toward Bar Harbor.

Nicole rolled her eyes. It had been two weeks since she'd talked to Eli. Two weeks since he'd refused to commit to her, and here he was calling her, expecting her to drop everything and come running to him. "When I thought we needed to talk you had other ideas. Now you expect me to follow your lead because you say so. Just who do you think you are?" She drummed her nails over the black lacquer table in her dining room.

"Nicole, this is serious. We need to talk about—"

"What I had to discuss was serious too," she interrupted him, growing angrier by the second. "If you don't think committing to each other is serious, then I don't know why you're calling."

Eli took a deep breath. She could be an exasperating woman at times. Someone had threatened him and his livelihood, and she was the only one he could turn to. But would she listen? No, she wanted to go on and on about a commitment that just wasn't going to happen. "Nicole! Please be quiet for just one minute."

Her mouth opened then snapped shut. He sounded intense and she wondered if he were calling about their relationship at all. "Eli, what's going on? Where are you?"

"I'm on the road, on my way up to Bar Harbor." He took a deep breath. "We need to talk about the trunk."

She hadn't thought about that trunk in almost a month now, so it took her a few seconds to figure out what he was talking about. "The trunk? Why? Have you found it?"

"No, I haven't found it. But it appears that we're not the only ones looking for it."

"What? I didn't think anybody else knew about it. Who could possibly be looking for it?"

"Donovan Connor paid me a little visit. He's back in Tanner."

Nicole sank into a cushioned black chair, her free hand going to her forehead. "Why would he come back now? It's been ten years."

"He knows Nathan is back, and he suspects we're close to finding the trunk. He wants it. Badly."

"Tell me something I don't know," she huffed.

Eli shook his head. "No, Nicole you don't understand what I'm saying. He's threatened to destroy my entire career if we don't get it for him."

"Eli, that's ridiculous. He can't touch your career. Your reputation in town is impeccable, and there's nothing he can do about that."

"My reputation may be impeccable, but the skeletons in my closet have a few blemishes."

"He doesn't know about that. Or did you tell him?" Nicole panicked. Most of Eli's skeletons involved her as well.

"I didn't tell him anything. But he suspects something. He's a powerful man, Nicole. Money can buy you all sorts of information. I can't afford to take that chance."

She thought about the repercussions for a minute and agreed with him. "So what's in Bar Harbor?"

"I'm following up on a lead to the trunk. But we need to meet when I get back. We've got to come up with a plan. And we've got to find that trunk before Donovan does."

"How long are you going to be there?" She wanted to see him now. She wanted his assurance that things were going to be alright. "Maybe I can join you."

"No. You've got to stay put, keep an eye on things there. Have you seen Tenile?"

"I've talked to her, but I haven't actually seen her. You know she moved in with Nathan."

Eli sighed. "Yeah, I know, back at the old house. That puts a huge damper on things. It was okay when it was just Nathan, but now that Tenile's there too, it makes things a little tricky."

"I can handle Tenile. It's Nathan I'm worried about. Tenile says he's very intent on finding Landy's killer."

"I figured as much when he came back. I can't believe this is happening. After all these years, I just can't believe it. I thought bringing Nathan back to town would help us find the trunk sooner. Instead, it's opened up a whole new can of worms."

Nicole stood and began to pace. Her heart pounded and her fingers shook on the phone. This wasn't good. She and Eli had worked long and hard on this and couldn't afford for anything to go wrong. But with Donovan and Nathan in town digging up old memories, something bad was bound to happen. "I'm scared, Eli."

Her voice had gone to a whisper. He caught the hint of despair and cursed to himself. He hadn't meant to get her involved. All those years ago when they'd started sleeping together, it had been just fun and games. But then he'd started to confide in her, and she'd offered her help. They had been on the same page, wanting the same things. Now he thought it was funny that she wanted something different from their relationship after all this time, while he was content with the arrangement they had. Or was he?

He felt a nagging sensation that he needed to turn his car around and head straight for her house. To head straight for her. He wanted to hold her, to smooth the kinks in her shoulders that he was sure were there now with this new information. She didn't do well under pressure; he'd seen that the night of Landy's murder. She'd been a mess, clinging to him for dear life. He'd helped her then, helped them both with soothing words and gentle stroking. Now, this time, he was afraid that his words and touch were no match for what they were about to face.

"Don't be. Fear causes mistakes, and we can't afford any mistakes right now. I'll be back in a couple of days, and we'll work this out."

She felt so vulnerable, so alone. "Okay, a couple of days. And you'll come here as soon as you get back?" To her own ears she sounded weak, but she didn't care. She needed Eli; it was that simple.

"I won't make any stops until I get to you." He wouldn't, and he found himself thinking that he didn't want it any other way. He wasn't really sure what that meant but decided not to analyze it for now.

"Call me when you get settled."

"I will."

∞

Nicole took a long hot bath, donned her robe and stretched out across her bed, thinking about the news from Eli. She was dozing when the doorbell rang.

Cursing, she raised her lithe body up from the bed and pushed her feet into her slippers. She didn't even bother to stop by the mirror to check her appearance. She didn't care how she looked and prayed the person at the door didn't take too much of her time. She needed to get back to her worry session, and she wanted to do that alone.

"Hi." Tenile gave Nicole a smile before brushing past her and dropping her purse on her couch. "I need a drink."

There goes my alone time, Nicole thought as she shut the door and turned to face the bar. "It's a bit early for a drink, don't you think?"

"It's seven-thirty, and if I don't have a drink, I'm going to break something. Would you rather I visit your china cabinet?" Tenile arched an eyebrow.

"Do and you'll die a very slow death." Nicole joined her at the bar. "Pour me one too."

Tenile did just that, filling both their glasses to the rim with a dark burgundy. They sipped in silence, Tenile leaning both elbows on the bar as she stood and Nicole sitting on one barstool with her feet propped up on the other.

"So what crawled up your butt?" Nicole asked first.

Tenile grimaced. "Let's see, where do I start? Nathan walks back into my life, touching me and making me feel things I'd long since buried. Rumors about us being together have spread throughout the town like wildfire. Somebody broke into my house, my so-called boyfriend, or should I say ex-boyfriend—only he doesn't know it yet—is missing in action." She took another drink. "Oh, and I keep having really vivid dreams about Landy." She prayed they were just dreams, even though the last time she'd been fully awake.

Nicole stared at her a moment. Was she falling apart? She looked closer. Tenile was always under control. She had a calm and sincere personality. This babbling, almost hysterical woman with the now half empty wine glass in her hand was someone totally different. She did need a drink. She watched as Tenile emptied the glass. And she'd probably need another one pretty soon. "Um, how 'bout we tackle those things one at a time? What's up with you and Nathan?"

Tenile rolled her eyes and poured another drink. "Nathan and I have unfinished business," she stated simply.

Nicole nodded. "And you're finishing it now?"

"We're doing something." She took a sip and contemplated what was really going on with her and Nathan. She enjoyed being with him, coming home from work, usually a half hour behind each other, climbing into that bed together and snuggling through the night. It felt good, she admitted, really good. At work they were professional, working side-by-side as Nathan continued to encourage her surgical studies. She hadn't made a decision regarding that yet but felt that yearning inside pushing her towards her original goal.

"It just seems different than before."

"It is different. Both of you are older, worldlier." Nicole tossed a glance at Tenile. "At least he's worldlier. You, I fear, have had yourself all bottled up since Landy died."

"Shut up." Because she was right, Tenile refused to look at her. "I haven't been bottled up. I just didn't want to go through the pain I went through before."

Nicole swung her legs over the side of the stool and stood. "Oh get over it, Tenile. We all lost a friend that night, but we didn't stop living."

"I didn't stop living either. Maybe her death hit me harder than it hit the rest of you guys."

"Why? Because I told you Nathan slept with her the week before she died?" Tenile had never said a word when she'd told her that. Over the years, Nicole had wondered what effect it had really had on her.

Tenile put her second empty glass down on the bar. If she weren't careful, she'd end up drunk as well as confused. "Why did you tell me that? Did you have any proof or was it just an assumption?"

Nicole hunched her shoulders, moved to the couch. "Neither. I was bored. You and Nathan seemed so happy. Landy seemed happy; although looking back, I don't really know why. She'd just broken up with that older guy a few weeks before, but she was really happy about something. One night when I was leaving Eli's room, I heard noises downstairs." Nicole tucked her legs up under her and ran her fingers through her hair. "I came down the steps determined to bust you and Nathan for necking on the couch since that was against the rules. Everybody knew you two were doing it but couldn't catch you in the act."

Tenile frowned. "Everybody knew?"

"Oh please. You two were inseparable, like two peas in a pod. Most mornings you'd wake up smelling just like him."

Tenile smiled at the memory.

"Anyway, imagine my surprise when I get downstairs and it's Landy on the couch with Nathan, her legs thrown over his, his hand on her knee."

"That's all you saw?"

"That was plenty. You were on your high horse about how committed he was to you and how you two were always going to be together, and I was sick of it. I wanted you to see that you could be played for a fool just like the rest of us."

Tenile read between Nicole's words to what she suspected was the real driving force behind her lie. "Just like Eli was playing you? He never would claim you as his girlfriend but didn't have any problem calling you to his room at night. How did that make you feel?" Because it had angered her when Nathan told her, she wondered now how Nicole had dealt with it.

Like crap, she wanted to say. Like she was worthless and undesirable, just as her parents had always told her. "I didn't like it. Just recently, I realized how much it bothered me. That's why I told him things had to change."

"And what did he say?"

Nicole emptied her glass, shrugged her shoulders. "He's not ready. I don't guess he'll ever be ready."

"And how do you feel about that?"

"I feel like crap, Tenile. Is that what you want me to say?" she yelled.

Tenile moved over to sit on the couch beside her. "No, that's not what I want you to say. But if it helps, you can yell it out as much as you like. It's crappy the way he's done you all these years. But at least you had the guts to stand up for what you want. Unlike me," she said in a whisper.

"You've always known what you wanted." Nicole looked at Tenile. She looked different. Her skin was even a little brighter. Being loved right would definitely do that to a woman.

"But I never had the guts to go and get it. When he left I just let him go. I should have gone after him. But I didn't. I couldn't." And now that he was back, she was still questioning him.

Nicole sat up and turned to the side so that she was completely facing Tenile. "Do you think he killed Landy?"

She thought about it, laced her fingers together, then took them apart. Did she? "How could I be in love with a man who might have killed my best friend? That's what I kept asking myself that night. "

"And now?"

"And now I've told him I believe him. When people accuse him, I stand up for him. I defend him. But in the back of my mind, some nights when I'm lying in that bed beside him, I think about all the unanswered questions."

Nicole put a hand on her shoulder. "Be careful, Tenile. I don't know if he slept with her or not. That was just a cruel joke on the two of you.

But what I do know is that Nathan was the last one of us to see Landy alive. She was wearing his jacket when they found her body. I can't tell you what to believe, but I can warn you to be very careful."

Tenile let her words sink in. Everything Nicole said was true. She was so conflicted. She loved Nathan—her heart was a true testament to that. She trusted him, or else she wouldn't have moved in with him. But there were still so many questions, so many unanswered questions. Part of the reason she was so supportive of his crusade to find the real killer was she desperately wanted to get rid of those questions in her own mind.

Driving home from Nicole's house after two more drinks and three hours of conversation, she still hadn't managed to quiet the flurry of doubt. She drove through familiar streets unaware of her surroundings. Unaware of the car that followed her closely.

※

It was Tenile. She was going to Nathan's house, where she lived now. He'd watched her go into her friend's apartment. Nicole, the hottie he'd always wanted in his bed. Too bad she was so stuck on that doctor dude who screwed around on her every chance he got. As he'd waited for her to come down, he'd thought about going up and enjoying them both. That would have been some kind of bonus, he thought with a lustful smile. The only thing that had stopped him was that he had a long night ahead.

But now she was alone. He could take care of her tonight and then deal with Hamilton. It wasn't the right time, but he was getting tired of waiting. Tired of hiding until the date rolled around again. He'd end this now, once and for all.

Her car swerved as she took the right turn too fast onto the deserted road that led to Hamilton's house. She must have had a pretty good time up there with Nicole. He licked his lips as he thought about how good a time they would have had together. He switched on his high beams, moved closer to her bumper. She swerved again, going off on the shoulder of the road before regaining control. He followed her, his heart thumping loudly in his chest.

Warm air whipped around him. His windows were down because it had gotten really hot in the car while he'd waited for her. He pressed down on the gas, moving close enough to read her tags. They were up for renewal next month, but she wouldn't have to bother with that.

There was one more turn; then she'd be less than a mile from Hamilton's house. Wouldn't it be special if she died in his arms? A smile came to his face as he drove even faster. She must have realized he was on her tail because she sped up also. His foot pressed harder on the accelerator, closing the little distance she'd put between them.

⊱∾⊰

She was driving too fast. Tenile knew this because trees were whizzing by her at an alarming rate. But the sense that she wasn't alone and the car steadily riding her tail had her rattled. She wanted to hurry to the house.

He's coming.

She heard Landy's voice as clearly as if her friend were sitting in the seat right beside her. Tenile chanced a look to the passenger side but saw nothing.

Hurry up. He'll hurt you too.

Although there was no one there, Tenile obeyed the voice and increased her speed. The lights coming through her back window were blinding, and she blinked several times to refocus.

You've got to get away. He'll kill you too. Hurry, Tenile! Hurry!

Tenile saw her turnoff, knew she was almost home. She maneuvered the wheel, never slowing, knowing she'd be there in a few minutes. Knowing Nathan would be there in a few minutes.

The lights seemed to grow, invading the back of the car, flooding its interior. She gripped the steering wheel, trying to focus on the road ahead of her. Fear and anxiety swelled inside as she struggled to stay calm. When his bumper connected with hers, she was terrified but not surprised. The car jolted and her head snapped back so hard she heard the discs in her neck crack.

Tenile, he's going to kill you!

The car rammed into hers again and she braced herself, felt her own vehicle spinning, heard the tires screaming in protest against the sideways movement.

Suddenly her car seemed to take on a mind of its own and lifted from the pavement only to smash into something solid. She heard metal screeching and glass shattering just before the airbag opened, slamming into her with such force that great bursts like fireworks danced in front of her eyes. There was a heaviness in her chest she couldn't relieve, and pain seemed to spread throughout her body like wine spilling across the floor.

I'm so sorry, Tenile. I'm so sorry.

Tenile heard the voice again, Landy's voice. She struggled to open her eyes, to see her friend just one more time, but she couldn't. She wanted to move, to run to Nathan because she knew the house was right there.

Then she went numb. No pain, no fear. Nothing but blackness, which seemed so much more alluring than the light. It was quiet, very quiet as she drifted. A hand seemed to brush her shoulder. In the distant darkness there was a glimmer of light, a smile, familiar and comforting, beckoning.

Landy. Her best friend. They were together again, at last.

Chapter 15

Nathan was in his office trying to work, trying not to think of Tenile and where she might be. She'd left the house right after dinner, mumbling something about needing some air, some space. He didn't want her to be alone. Whoever had broken into her house had been angry. The violent slashes in her pillows had proven that. Still, he couldn't hold her hostage. So he'd let her go.

Propping his elbows on the desk, he steepled his hands and rested his chin against them. His thoughts shifted to how fast things seemed to be moving between them. He'd only been back in Tanner for six weeks, and in that time, a lot had changed. He sensed that there were many things going on in her mind that she hadn't told him about. Just this morning she'd been in his office fingering the notes that had come from his informant. He hadn't heard from him since failing to meet with him in the park.

Like him, she probably wondered how close the killer really was and if he planned to attack again. John hadn't provided much more information, and just this morning, Nathan had called to alert him to Robert's disappearance. While Tenile didn't say much about her ex-boyfriend's quick departure, it had nagged at him for some time now. It was time to find out all he could about Robert Gibson.

His eyes were tired from reading all the research material he needed to be familiar with for Monday's meeting with the hospital's board of directors. The house was dim and quiet, reminding him of the fact that he was there alone. Absently, he wondered if his Peeping Tom would pay another visit and turned towards the window where he'd previously seen him.

The sound of screeching tires instantly alerted him. He swiveled in his char, turning his attention now toward the front of the house. Since his office door was open, he could see eerie shadows dancing across the living room walls as headlights came through the front windows. On instinct, he jumped out of his chair and ran to the front door, wrenching it open in time to see a big car deliberately ram a smaller, dark car, spinning it out of control.

Above all the other noise, he heard a scream that sent his heart into overdrive. He flew off the porch and down the driveway just as the dark car spun into the trees and came to a rest with the front end wrapped sickeningly around a tree trunk.

With an arm shielding his eyes against the headlights, he'd just started for it when suddenly a long luxury car roared past him so fast and so close he rocked in its wake. He barely glimpsed the license tag before the car was gone. When he got close enough to recognize the smaller car, his pounding heart leapt into his throat.

"No. No. Oh God, no."

Somehow he made his way to the driver's side and saw her.

"Tenile!" he yelled but knew she didn't hear him. He reached for the door handle, but it was crunched into the metal of the doorframe. He pounded on the driver's window, which was cracked but held. "Tenile!" Frantically he searched for something to break the window. Spotting a big rock, he grabbed it and struck the window with all his might.

With a horrendous cracking noise, the glass shattered into a thousand pieces. He reached inside to touch her. "C'mon, baby, answer me. Tenile, answer me." He shook her slightly, not wanting to move her too much since he was unsure of her injuries.

Blood was oozing from her forehead, and she looked like a rag doll with her body twisted between the air bag and the seatbelt. Calling on all his medical training, he swallowed the tears that threatened to fall and reached to his side for his cell phone. It wasn't there. He'd taken it off when he got home. He'd have to leave her alone to call for help. The awful realization was like a body blow.

He leaned into the car. "Baby, I've got to leave for a minute. Just a minute." He lifted her hand and held it tightly for a moment. "I'm going to get some help. I'll be right back." He spoke to her as if she were going to answer him. God, he wanted her to answer him. He wanted her to look up and shout some smart remark about how long he was taking. Something, anything. He prayed for any sign that she was alright.

But as he ran across the road, he knew she wasn't alright. It didn't take a doctor to see how serious her injuries were. The force from the airbag alone could have broken ribs, punctured a lung. A host of life-threatening things could be going on. The fact that she was unconscious was a bad sign.

He took the steps two at a time, found the phone in the darkness of the living room and punched in the emergency number. He was back at her side in seconds, holding her hand, talking to her, reassuring her, trying to reassure himself.

It seemed hours before he heard the sirens. Then he was pushed to the side as the fire department worked to get her out of the car. He trembled as he watched them pull her from the car. Her head lolled to the side, and blood ran down the side of her face, forming ugly rivulets on her neck and chest.

The police wanted to ask questions, Albert leading the pack, but he brushed them off, moved them all to the side with a flourish of his arm, making it known he wasn't about to talk right now. He heard whispers about alcohol and speeding, but he didn't give a damn, didn't care what any of them thought. His only concern right now was Tenile, whether she'd ever look at him again, whether he'd ever hear that voice he loved so much. He watched the paramedics work, barely conscious of the stats they yelled and recorded. The second they lifted her into the ambulance, he jumped into the back with her, grabbing her hand again, talking to her as they sped off.

His mind whirled with memories of when they first met, first made love. He cursed himself for being so foolish to leave her for ten years, cried out with the stupidity of everything. He'd come back for her. She'd been the driving force behind his decision to prove his innocence. She was a part of him, a part that he wasn't willing to live without any longer.

He couldn't lose her; he just couldn't. It would all be for nothing if he did.

❧

"She had a couple glasses of wine while we talked and that's it. Her mind was as clear as yours and mine when she left. I'm sure she wouldn't have run herself into a tree on purpose." Nicole was outraged. The sheriff had questioned her a billion times since she'd been at the hospital today, and last night, he'd made her come to the precinct to tell him what she and Tenile had been doing before she left her house.

Nathan had been frantic when he called her. She'd jumped out of bed, almost in a drunken stupor, threw on some clothes and met him at the hospital. Tenile's mother and Tracy were there, tears falling freely. She took a seat and joined in.

"I'm just trying to get an accurate picture of what happened." Albert wrote in his little book as he talked.

Nathan had just come from Tenile's room, and overheard Albert and Nicole's heated exchange. He had managed to avoid talking to Albert by staying at Tenile's side the entire time and forbidding any law enforcement to enter her room. Now he needed to tell him what he knew. In the early morning hours he'd called John, given him the partial license number he remembered from the other vehicle, and instructed him to get him a name and address before the end of the day.

Albert was so set on pinning him for something, anything, that Nathan knew he wouldn't look into the situation thoroughly. He wouldn't pay attention to what Nathan was going to tell him. John would find the info, and they'd find the person who'd run Tenile off the road. Then he'd decide what he was going to do with him. The right thing would be to turn him over to law enforcement, but Nathan felt a burning need to wrap that person around a tree the same way Tenile's car had been. Banking those emotions, he made his way into the waiting room. Leaning down, he kissed Oneil's weathered cheek. "She's stable now. A broken rib, a concussion, four stitches to the gash on her head and she woke up for a few minutes." Oneil stared at him blankly. She didn't want to hear medical jargon or prognosis. "She's going to be alright."

Tears streamed down her face as she pulled Nathan into a big hug, clapping his back with her large hands. "Thank you, Jesus. Thank you, Jesus." She released him and stood. "Can I see her?"

Normally, it wouldn't have been his call, but Dr. Traviotti had extended professional courtesy to him and allowed him to deal with family and prospective visitors. "You and Tracy can go in for a few minutes."

Nathan helped Tracy and her now bulging belly out of the chair. "And then I want you to take Tracy back home and deposit her in the bed. Get yourself some breakfast and a hot bath and some sleep; then you can come back." Oneil looked as worn out as an old dishrag. "You can't do anything for her if you're not well-rested yourself."

To everyone's surprise, Oneil nodded her agreement and took Tracy's arm to lead her towards Tenile's room. When they were out of earshot, Nathan stood next to Nicole, taking her hand in his and kissing her forehead. "She's going to be okay. We'll go back in after her mother has some time with her."

Nicole nodded, tears of relief filling her eyes.

"You seem to be handling things very well, Hamilton." Albert eyed him. He hadn't missed the way Nathan had taken control of the scene both last night and now. He resented it. This was his investigation, his town. He hated the idea that this man, this murderer, could waltz back in and move around barking orders like he was the mayor or someone else with authority. He intended to knock him down a notch. "Now how about you tell me exactly what happened? I already know that Ms. Barnes was drinking. Did you and her have a fight? A lover's quarrel?"

A wicked gleam shadowed Albert's face, and Nathan struggled not to punch him. "Tenile and I are just fine, no need for a fight of any kind. She went out after dinner, went to see Nicole, as you already know. They shared a girl's evening and she came home."

Albert didn't take his eyes off Nathan, but he wasn't writing in his notepad.

"I was in my office when I heard tires screeching. When I got to the door, I saw a car ram her car, and she crashed into the tree. The car sped off as I ran to see if she was alright." Nathan paused, gathering more control. "It wasn't drunk driving. She wasn't distraught. She was run off the road, maliciously rammed by another driver. I would call that attempted murder, Sheriff."

Nicole gasped. Albert stared, his face blank, his hand still not writing down Nathan's words.

Nathan put an arm around Nicole as she cried. "I saw only part of the license plate. The last three digits were 238, and it was a Maine tag. Write it down, Albert. You'll need to go call the station and have them run a tag check. The front end of the car should be pretty banged up, shouldn't be too hard to find if he's still in town. It was a luxury car, white or silver, one person inside."

He moved away before Albert could gather his wits and come at him with anything else. He didn't have any more patience to deal with Albert and his suspicions. He and Nicole went to stand outside of Tenile's door.

Nicole turned to him. "My God, Nathan! Why would somebody run her off the road?"

"We must be getting close to something," Nathan said absently. He'd gone over the facts with John and had turned up some pretty disturbing stuff, but he hadn't had a chance to piece anything together yet.

"You mean to finding out who really killed Landy?" She folded her arms and took a step away from him.

Nathan watched the cautious move. He and Nicole had been friendly enough. He thought she had much more potential than she dared to explore, but that was her call to make, not his. The thing with her and Eli had been going on for years, and he wondered when it would either go forward or end for good. Although he'd never been attracted to her—to her great displeasure—he could certainly see why Eli was. Nicole was a beautiful woman with a sharp mind but a vengeful heart. For those reasons, he would tread lightly. "Yes. It's important to Tenile and me to find out who really killed Landy. I've hired a private investigator who's been working on the case for a while now. I think we're getting close."

"There's something that's always bothered me about Landy's murder," she said matter-of-factly.

"What's that?" He knew. He'd always known. But he wanted her to tell him. To stand face-to-face and tell him that she thought he was the killer.

"Why was she wearing your jacket? You and Tenile were an item back then, not you and Landy."

Nathan gave a half smile. Nicole definitely needed to be watched, he thought as he calmly calculated his answer. "So the story that Landy and I slept together a week before the murder, is that all of a sudden untrue?"

Nicole rolled her eyes. "Good grief, how many times do I have to admit to this. Look, I made it up to get back at Tenile. I told her that last night. But that doesn't change the fact that Landy was wearing your jacket when they found her body."

So Tenile had gone to Nicole to talk about the murder and him being with Landy. That would explain her drinking. "I don't know how she got my jacket. We all did live together remember. It wouldn't have been hard for her to walk into the closet and pick up my jacket. And no, I don't know why she would do that, but that's only circumstantial evidence. That doesn't make me guilty."

"No, it doesn't. But it rubs a lot of people the wrong way, including Tenile."

Nathan leaned against the wall, let his head fall back as he closed his eyes. She was telling him things he already knew, a battle he was already fighting. "Look, Nicole, all I can say is that I didn't do it." He looked at her again. "And I'm going to prove it."

Her head hurt like hell. To blink almost brought her to tears. The pain in her chest was almost gone, but she grimaced when she felt the thick white bandage on her forehead. She'd have a scar, probably a very ugly one at that. She was going home today, actually to Nathan's house because he insisted. Her mother had clucked a bit but resigned herself to it. That in itself was unusual, but so was getting run into a tree by a complete stranger.

Even as she thought it, she knew it was a lie. A total stranger hadn't done this to her. It was someone who wanted her out of the way, possibly dead. That's what Landy had said, that *he* was going to kill her too. But who? As she asked herself that question, the door opened and Nathan stepped inside. He was on duty, or at least he had been for the better part of the evening. That was why her release had been delayed until evening even though she had been ready to go home first thing this morning.

He still wore his white jacket with his name scribbled in neat red lettering over his left breast pocket. His eyes looked different. They'd looked different since she'd first regained consciousness and seen him standing above her. Did he know something about the accident? When she shook her head in confusion, the pain escalated and she whimpered.

He was at her side in seconds. "Baby, what's the matter? Do you need more pain medication?" He'd been watching her watch him, tension between them building steadily. What was she thinking? What was she remembering? "I'll get a nurse."

Opening her eyes, she grabbed his wrist, effectively stopping his departure. "No." She didn't dare speak too loud. The throbbing in her head would never subside if she did. "I just took something, it'll get better soon."

When she tried to sit up, he put his hands to her shoulders and helped her. She was already dressed in slacks and a T-shirt he'd brought her from home. She'd lost a couple of pounds in the days she'd been in the hospital. Beneath his hands she seemed so frail, so wounded. He sat on the bed beside her. "You ready to go home?"

She hesitated and he held his breath. He'd been prepared to argue her lodgings with Oneil but thankfully had been spared that fight. But if he had to, he'd handcuff Tenile and lock her in his house. He wanted her with him, needed to protect her from whatever else might happen. And he was sure something else would happen. He was getting too close to the truth for it not to.

"Nathan," she spoke in a shaky voice. "We need to talk. There's something I think you should know."

He put a finger to her lips to silence her, then replaced it with a featherlike kiss. "Not now. Let's get you home and settled first."

His touch sent shivers down her entire body, and her fingers itched to reach up and clasp around his neck. Instead, she buried them in the sheet beneath her and nodded. "Okay."

They could talk once they were back at his place. She still wasn't sure she could call that house her home, but she knew without a doubt she wanted to be there with him tonight, despite the warnings she'd received.

Chapter 16

Nathan pulled two long white candles out of the box, praying that tonight some of the tension between them would ebb.

Tenile was here with him physically, but he couldn't help noticing the distance emotionally. She'd wanted to talk to him. Tonight they'd talk. They'd clear the air, and then he'd tell her what he wanted her to do next.

Shrugging those serious thoughts off, he proceeded to place candles in the crystal candleholders his mother had given him as a house-warming gift a few years back. He'd never figured out what she thought he would do with them, but when he was planning for tonight, they'd instantly come to mind, along with the platinum-rimmed Lennox china and the silverware, also a gift from his mother. He smiled to himself at the realization that his mother had been planning this dinner for him long before he'd even known it would take place.

Checking his watch, he noted it was almost six o'clock. Tenile had been taking a bath when he left her upstairs. Taking the steps two at a time, he rid himself of his now stained T-shirt, a victim of sauce he'd splashed while cooking. He used the guest bathroom, taking a quick shower.

Standing in front of the mirror to shave, he wondered at the image he saw. In just a few weeks he'd been transformed. No longer was he the sulking workaholic people knew in New York. Now he was a successful doctor with a woman in his life, a woman who meant more to him than anything else. Even more than bringing a killer to justice.

Tenile was enjoying her bath. Hot water and vanilla-scented bubbles filled the tub, and she lay back against the porcelain. Almost well, she felt only a dull ache in her side if she moved too fast or in the wrong direction. In changing the bandage on her forehead, she'd grimaced at the jagged two-inch mark threaded with black string. The scar it left would always be a reminder of fear. Fear of dying, fear of confronting a killer.

Nathan was so much to her—a savior, a caretaker, a lover. Could she ever believe he was a killer? Nonsense. It was all nonsense. Landy had been their friend. He'd come back to clear his name, to find Landy's killer. She believed that. Needed to believe that.

The rest was simply nonsense, and she wasn't going to give it any more thought. He was cooking her dinner. He'd run her a bath and would no doubt tuck her in tonight. This was the man she loved, the man she trusted with her life. That was her focus now.

She closed her eyes momentarily as her heart grew light. She'd dreamt of him last night, of the future they could have together. In the dream they were married, with two kids and a dog—the perfect family. He still ran the obstetrics wing while she'd received her surgical credits and worked part time during the kids' school hours. She'd redecorated the house to suit them. And they were happy—all of them were happy.

After ten years of living in limbo, she was determined to reach for that happiness, grab it and hold on to it for dear life. Climbing out of the tub, she toweled off and returned to the mirror. Ignoring the wound, she applied a little lip liner and gloss, outlined her eyes until they were sultry slants and coated her already thick lashes. Returning to the bedroom, she slipped on her dress and found a pair of flat mules pushed to the back of the closet Nathan had designated as hers.

Tonight was theirs—for her and Nathan. Everything else would have to take a backseat.

Nathan dressed in the bathroom, donning clean slacks and shirt. He was downstairs in the living room pouring a drink when he heard her on the steps.

She entered the room like a breath of fresh air. No matter how many times he looked at her, he always got the same reaction—a knee jerk sensation to his groin then a simmering warmth cascading throughout his body. For a moment he felt as if all the oxygen had been sucked out of the room. Then she smiled and, with that small reaction, breathed it right back in again. "Hi," he greeted her with a grin.

Her stomach lurched as that smile hit her in all the right places.

Nathan inhaled her sweet vanilla scent as she walked past him. She wore a pale blue dress that fit tightly across her breasts and torso then fanned out from the waist. Her legs were covered, but he easily visualized the slender limbs carrying her across the room.

"Dinner's not quite ready. Let's sit for a minute." Taking her hand, he led her to the couch. "I've been giving some thought to your suggestion."

She sat with eagerness, tingling from the hand he held to her shoulder, spreading throughout her chest. "Which suggestion was that?" Amazingly, her voice didn't betray the friction going on inside her at the moment.

"Furniture and accessories. I think it's time to make my house a home."

Tenile looked around the room with its homely mauve color and dark oak moldings. "I only mentioned you'd need more dishes eventually. But I guess some real furniture and a few paintings for the walls wouldn't hurt." And she knew just which pictures she'd hang and where.

Following her gaze he said, "I'm sure you'll be able to guide my choices."

She shrugged, not liking that he seemed to know what she was thinking. "I guess I could help."

He threaded his fingers through hers, marveling at the contrast, light and dark, big and small. Yet they were the perfect fit—the perfect pair.

"There's a lot I want to do in life, Tenile."

She didn't answer, sensing he wasn't finished.

"I'd like to expand my research and really make a difference in preventing premature births."

"I've read some of your work. You've made some excellent observations. It's a very noble cause." Pride welled up inside her.

"Not noble, just necessary," he corrected. "If I were expecting a baby, I'd want to take every possible precaution there was, and I'd want the doctor to do the same. I'd want him or her to detect any problems as early as possible and deal with them quickly and effectively. Above all else, I'd want my baby to be born healthy and safe."

Tenile nearly sighed. Such compassion and sincerity—he was truly a unique man. "You want children?" she asked with last night's dream in mind.

"Definitely," he answered quickly. "Actually, I'd like a couple of kids. I never liked being an only child, so I'd want my kids to have siblings they could bond with, someone to keep in touch with when they grow up and move away. You know what I mean?"

Having a brother, she understood his need for the family connection. She didn't know what she'd do without her family. "Yeah, I know what you mean."

"What about you? How many do you want?" There was never a doubt in his mind that Tenile would have kids. She'd make a perfect mother.

"Two." She grinned. "At least."

"And a husband? Do you plan on having one of those?"

Because he seemed to turn really serious, really quickly, she giggled to soften the mood. "One. At least."

Nathan cracked a small smile. She was so easy to be with, so easy to talk to. So why was he holding back?

His demeanor was changing, she felt him slipping away and hastily said, "What did you cook? I'm starved."

Snapping out of his momentary lapse, he rose from the couch, pulling her up beside him. "You eat like a pregnant woman already."

She happily followed his lead into the kitchen. "Are you complaining about having to feed me? Because if you are, I'm sure my mother would gladly welcome me home."

Nathan stopped abruptly, turned to face her just inside the kitchen doorway. "I want you here with me. There's no doubt about that. So you can dismiss any thoughts of leaving." He was serious, his eyes raking over her face intently.

Her heart thumped, and her body melded against his as his hands found the small of her back and pulled her close. "I hadn't planned on going anywhere just yet."

"I don't plan on letting you go, ever."

Damn, that sounded good. "Well, I haven't eaten all day, so any minute now, I'm going to fall to the floor from low blood sugar. That may forfeit your not letting me go."

He nipped her bottom lip. "Very funny. C'mon, let's feed you then."

"Mmmmm, that smells good. What is it? Lasagna?" She stood on the opposite side of the island in the center of the kitchen.

Nathan opened the oven and removed a Pyrex dish. "Nope, stuffed shells." He inhaled the glorious scent again himself before placing it on the counter and returning to the oven to retrieve the bread.

"You made this yourself?" Placing both elbows on the counter top, Tenile leaned over to look at the dish more closely. Cheese oozed from inside the shells, and thick red sauce bubbled around them. It looked fantastic, and she was willing to bet that it tasted just as good. A homey feel settled over her, and she pictured herself and Nathan in this kitchen twenty years from now, still enjoying an evening meal. "Yeah, cooking's one of my hobbies." With a long, serrated knife, he sliced the bread so that it fell in perfect slices, steam rising to meet their nostrils. "Ahhhh, I love fresh baked bread." Actually, fresh out of the freezer into the oven, he thought to himself. His hobby hadn't yet carried him into bread baking.

Tenile groaned. "I'd gain at least twenty pounds a year if I were married to you." The words were out before she realized what she'd said. His hand stilled on the knife, his eyes finding hers.

He had no idea how he looked to her; he just knew that his heart had suddenly beat a little faster. Her words touched a part of him he'd been wondering how to let her see.

Tenile chewed her bottom lip. He'd taken her words much more seriously then she'd meant, she could tell. Still, she wondered what exactly was going through his mind. What had been going through hers? Why had that statement slipped so easily from her mouth? That damned dream, that's why. Either way, now was not the time to explore it. "I'll take the bread in," she cheerfully volunteered, leaving him in the kitchen to get his own thoughts together as she continued to berate herself over her own mistake.

She placed the basket of fresh bread on the white linen tablecloth. It covered the old worn oak table with a classy elegance. The china and silverware looked new and expensive. She wondered if he'd just purchased it. She'd been through all his kitchen cabinets, and it hadn't been there the day before.

Two long white candles burned inside crystal candleholders, and a Waterford vase of fresh white roses stood front and center.

She could definitely be his wife, her traitorous mind thought again, despite the inevitable weight gain. Any man who would go through all this for a woman was definitely a keeper.

"Shall we sit?"

She hadn't heard him approach and jumped at the feel of him close behind her as he placed the dish in the middle of the table.

She turned the moment his hands were free, standing on tiptoe to kiss him slowly. Never one to complain when being kissed by a beautiful woman, Nathan opened his mouth to hers, and his hands found her waist.

She spoke to him through that kiss, conveying any apologies needed, confirming her desire for him and promising a night to remember.

He broke the kiss before stuffed shells and French bread were the farthest thing from his mind. "Dessert before dinner? What would your mother say?"

Tenile moved away from him reluctantly. His clean masculine scent permeated her senses, trying to convince her to linger in his arms. Wisely, she sat in the chair he pulled out for her. "She'd say, 'Tee, any man who can kiss like that and cook too is definitely a keeper.'"

Nathan laughed as he took his seat across from her. "I doubt she'd say that. But I'm glad you're thinking it."

They shared a prayer and ate the first few bites in virtual silence. But there were things that needed to be said, and they couldn't be put off any longer.

"So who do you think it is?" He stopped chewing when she spoke and looked at her. She knew he didn't want to share his information. He'd been talking to John, his P.I., several times a day, which confirmed that something was going on.

"I'm not really sure."

She'd seen the hesitation in his eyes and hated it. "Oh come on, you're talking to that P.I. all the time now. Either he knows something or you're wasting your money." She bit into a slice of bread.

He took a drink of his wine and let the liquid linger in his mouth, savoring the bitter fruity taste. "I don't want you to worry about it."

"If there's something I should know—and since I was almost killed—I think you should tell me. Christ, I'm worrying every minute of every day anyhow."

He reached over the table, rubbed the back of her hand. "Don't worry. I'm not going to let anything happen to you."

She sat back in her chair, not removing her hand from his. "That's really nice that you want to protect me, but you can't be with me all the time. I need to know what I'm dealing with."

He knew she was right, knew that the best protection was knowledge. Still, telling her all he knew didn't sit right with him, especially since people close to them weren't above suspicion. He sat back in his chair, dragging his hands down his face.

"I didn't kill Landy," he began.

She didn't respond, wasn't sure how to respond.

"About two years ago, I came across a box that I'd packed when I left. I'd thrown most of my things in storage until I found my own place, and I guess I just forgot to unpack it."

"What was in the box?"

"Just some old papers and photos. There was one photo that caught my eye though." He conjured the memory in his mind as if he held the picture in his hand right now. "It was of Landy and that older guy with a beard she'd been dating. The one we told her was only after her money. What was his name?" He hesitated, testing her memory.

"Kent Regan."

He nodded. "That's right. You remember him."

She was silent again.

"Anyway, the picture got me to thinking. Regan and Landy broke up just a few weeks before the murder. So I called John and asked him to do some research."

Leaning forward now, she watched him carefully, digesting everything he said. "What did he find out?"

"That Regan all but dropped off the face of the earth after leaving Tanner. I figured it was probably a dead end anyway and forgot about it. Then about nine months ago, I got the first letter."

The candles flickered low between them, casting shadows along the wall. "From the same person that sent the one when I was here?"

"I believe so. After it, I had a message on my answering machine at work to meet the author in the park."

"You didn't tell me that," she gasped. "He's here, in Tanner?"

He saw the fear cold and stark across her face and cursed the inevitable. "He wasn't there. I got there as soon as I could, waited a while and nothing. There was no one there."

"You think it's the same guy that tried to run me down?"

"I don't know." He shrugged.

"Nathan, I don't understand. Why am I a threat? Why would someone want to kill me?" She was afraid, but then her fear turned into anger. Adrenaline flowed through her veins, and she jumped up from the chair, pacing the floor with quick strides. "She said he wanted to kill me.

She said he would kill me if I didn't hurry. That you and I were the key."
She was babbling, walking back and forth, remembering everything
Landy had said to her.

Nathan watched her a few seconds, trying to decipher her words.
When he thought she would pass out from hysterics, he stood and
clasped her shoulders, forcing her to look at him. "Who told you this?
Who said we were the key?"

She stopped, her eyes finding his. They were intense, dark and
serious as he stared down at her. Then she realized what she'd been
saying and cringed.

"Tenile, tell me who told you this," he demanded.

She opened her mouth to speak, doubted herself, then closed it
again.

His grip on her tightened. "Tenile!"

She pulled away, sending a bolt of pain through her side. "You're
hurting me," she spat and turned her back to him.

His fists clenched at his sides, and he took a long, steadying breath.
"Tenile, tell me what's going on. This is serious. We're in this together."
She'd turned away from him. He'd overreacted and she'd shut down. "I
didn't mean to shout and I'm sorry if I hurt you."

Gently, he placed his hands on her shoulders again, not to turn her
towards him, just to show that he was still there.

"You won't believe me," she whispered, her arms folded over her
chest as she cradled the pain. "I had a hard time accepting it myself."

Her voice was so small, so fragile in the large room. He moved to
stand in front of her, putting a finger to her chin.

She looked up.

"We have to trust each other. I'm not exactly sure what's going on,
but I know it's getting deadly serious. We have to stick together, and that
means no secrets."

She blinked furiously to keep the tears at bay.

"Whatever it is, we'll deal with it together," he promised.

She wanted desperately to trust him with this. After all, she hadn't
been able to tell anyone else, and the questions were continuously eating

away at her. He'd said she could trust him, that they were in this together. She took a deep breath. "Landy told me."

He didn't speak, didn't even move.

"I've been having these dreams, even though the last two times I've been wide awake." He didn't say anything so she continued. "She talks to me. More like warnings, I guess."

She looked absolutely serious, as if she were telling him an ordinary truth. The candlelit room cast a warm glaze over her caramel-toned skin, and her eyes were wide and serious as she spoke.

A ghost. She was telling him that the ghost of their best friend was warning her. Of all the things he could have imagined, this would have never crossed his mind. Tenile wasn't crazy, nor was she gullible enough to believe in ghosts and goblins...unless she had good reason.

"What did she say?" He couldn't believe he was even asking, yet the words tumbled from his mouth.

"She keeps saying that *he's* out there. That *he's* watching and that you and I are the key. What does that mean?"

He hadn't any idea, but that wasn't what she needed to hear. He smoothed her hair back and closed his eyes as he leaned down and kissed her forehead. "Maybe it is some form of warning. Let's go upstairs. You need some rest."

She moved out of his grip. "You don't believe me. You think I'm imagining it, don't you?"

He couldn't lie to her, at least not outright. "To tell you the truth, Tenile, I don't know what to think. All I know is that we've been through a lot these last few weeks, and maybe things are starting to get the best of you. This whole situation is a lot for anybody to handle, so I can understand if—" He stopped.

"If what? If I'm losing my mind because of the stress from a murderer running loose in my town, a murderer who in all likelihood has his sights set on me now?" She put a hand on her hip and straightened her back. "I am not crazy, Nathan. And whether you believe me or not, Landy is speaking to me. She's warning me."

Because he loved her, because he knew the woman standing across from him very well, he sighed and gave in to what she was saying. If Tenile believed it so desperately, then it had to be true. "Baby, if you say she's talking to you, I believe you. I just don't want you to be so burdened down by all this." He was standing near her again, cupping her face and folding his arm around her waist. "I don't know if I can protect you from a ghost, though." He gave a wan smile.

Despite her skepticism about him really believing her, she smiled. "She's not the one trying to kill me."

"I know and that makes me even angrier. My return brought all this on, and I'm seriously doubting the intelligence of that decision."

Her palms flattened on his chest. "Don't be silly. You're innocent, and it's time this town knew that. It's time we found out who really did this to her and make him pay. I only wish she'd just tell me who it is and be done with it."

"We're getting closer; we have to be. That's why he tried to hurt you." He refused to say *kill*, refused to acknowledge the fact that she could have died in that car. He pulled her closer, hugging her as tightly as he dared, keeping her injuries in mind.

With her head pillowed on his chest, she tried to relax. "At first I thought seeing Landy was just a dream, but then I could still smell her in my room. You remember the fragrance she used to wear?"

Nathan smiled, pressed his lips to her hair. "Something floral."

"Jasmine. She always smelled like jasmine." Tenile lifted her head and looked up at him. "Thank you for believing me."

"Thank you for trusting me." She'd never know how much that meant to him. Then, because he couldn't begin to explain what he was feeling at this very moment, he kissed her. Watching her, keeping his eyes focused on her, his lips brushed lightly over hers.

She didn't pull away, but he knew she was tense, still worried over the situation, over the helplessness they both felt. Slowly and sweetly, her shoulders relaxed and her lips softened, parted, invited. Her heartbeat slowed, thickened. And as she opened for him, he abandoned subtleness and began a passionate assault.

172

The sudden demand rushed over her, alerting her senses and scraping her nerves. He mastered her mouth, and moans sounded deep in her throat as she arched against the heat simmering in her belly.

Nathan didn't want her to think, didn't want her to consider what they were doing or where they were doing it. All he wanted, all he needed, was for all her senses to be tuned to him. His hands moved from her face, pushed through her hair and down her shoulders as the kiss roughened and heightened desire in them both. His hands shook with intensity, and he lowered her to the floor.

"What do you want from me, Nathan?"

How could she not know? How could she not feel everything he had inside for her? He explored her face, raining kisses over the smooth delicate skin. "I want all of you." His hands lightly skimmed her ribs, felt the jolt of reaction as he took her breast in his palm. "Just give me all of you."

He said her name over and over again, whispered it, and she was lost.

He grabbed the hem of her dress and pulled it over her head. Her bra and panties were a lost cause as he tore them from her in his haste.

Her fingers shook as she released his belt, pushing his pants and boxers down over muscled thighs. He finished the job and pulled his shirt savagely over his head.

She reached for him. Her scent, her slender body pressed seductively against his own, invited and insisted.

Her breath quickened as he curved his hand under her breast, letting its weight and softness rest in his palm. He stroked her nipples with slow and easy movements. She felt herself melting beneath him.

When he allowed his tongue to trace the roundness of each breast, need strong and hot whipped through him. With tantalizing slowness, he familiarized himself with each globe, suckling and biting until she writhed beneath him.

She was changing, right before his eyes. She was letting go, giving him everything he'd asked for. She was so responsive to his touch, so passionate in her loving, he sighed even as his lips left her breasts to travel down her belly, lavish her navel. His fingers grasped her thighs and he kneaded the soft, pliant flesh before kissing what he knew would be a bruise in the morning. Even if he'd tried, he wouldn't have been able to resist. The fact that he'd been longing to taste her here only enhanced the pleasure when his tongue finally sank into her moist center, absorbing the sweet essence that was hers.

Afraid this moment would end, afraid if she didn't have him completely she'd shatter into a million pieces, she pulled on his shoulders until his head raised, his eyes searching hers. "More. Take more."

Need leaped into his stomach, and on her breathless demand, Nathan rose over her, sinking into the dewy center he'd just loved with his mouth. Her legs curled around his back, holding him close.

A furious wave of emotion that went well beyond passion floated over him. His teeth grazed her soft skin while his hands groped and touched her everywhere. She moved impatiently, sighing and murmuring his name as if she had been born with it on her lips. He was feeling something, but the feeling had no name. He couldn't give it one, couldn't figure it out. But it didn't matter. Nothing mattered at this moment. Nothing else had ever mattered but her.

The air seemed too thick to breathe. His tongue, his strokes, all smothered her with pleasure. He drove her hard and fast to a peak she hadn't ventured to often. His name stole from her as she fought the panicky excitement that threatened to overtake her.

With each thrust she fell deeper and deeper into the blind oblivion of ecstasy, ripples of pleasure flooding through her, branding her and making her undeniably his. Then he gripped her hands in his, holding fast. He pumped into her, scorching her system, holding her tightly in his fierce grip.

As she matched every powerful thrust of his hips, Nathan realized he was completely inside of her, as deeply planted as the memory of her had been in him all this time.

He mastered her mouth and body until she thought she would weep. She slid her fingers over his cropped hair, needing the leverage as he pushed her deliberately, undeniably, over the brink. When she knew for sure she would explode, he abruptly pulled out of her only to thrust back in again with a fierce intensity.

His head thrown back, he moaned, "Tenile. Tenile!" He plunged into her deeper, harder. Her legs shivered around him; her fingers splayed over his distended nipples.

His eyes opened and he focused on her face. Her eyes were slits of dark brown, her lips swollen, her cheeks flushed. "Look at me, Tenile." His voice was raw and full of need.

Even as his vision began to dim, the woman, the moment, the certainty of their future mattered, and he wanted her to know it. "It's you. It's always been you. Then, now and forever. Only you."

He found her mouth with a kiss as fierce and demanding as the plunging of his body.

In the foggy aftermath, Nathan rolled onto his back, prepared to drop an elbow over his eyes when his movement stilled. He focused his eyes and saw someone outside the window, watching, waiting in the shadows of the evening sky.

"Shit!" He leaped up and across the floor, stopping only to grab his pants and stumble into them.

"What? What's wrong?" Tenile sat up, startled by his quick change of mood.

"Stay here!" he yelled as he wrenched the door open and disappeared into the night.

He's in the dark. Waiting. It's almost time.

Stark naked, Tenile stood in the dim room amidst strewn clothes. But that wasn't what caused her distress. The smell of jasmine wafted through the air, and her eyes scanned the surroundings looking for her friend. "Landy?" she whispered. She wasn't there, but her words hung in the air, filled the room with an unmistakable presence.

Both hands went to her throat as she stared out the window. "He's in the dark," she repeated.

She was still standing there when she heard the door slam. She turned, saw him fill the doorway and swallowed the fear that threatened to surface.

"He was here. God damn it, he was here again!"

Tenile stood stone still. "He'll come back. It's almost time." Her eyes stared into Nathan's. Suddenly she felt cold and shivered.

Her knees wobbled and she rubbed her own arms to spark heat. Nathan was beside her instantly, sweeping her up against her protests. "I'm sorry. I scared you. It's okay." He cradled her in his arms as he moved to the couch and sat.

"He'll come back, Nathan. He will because it's almost time. It'll be the end this time." She didn't know how she knew; she just felt it deep inside.

She looked different, her eyes wild and glazed as she spoke. "Tenile, what are you talking about?"

"It's *him*. Landy said it's him. And he's going to come back. He's going to keep coming back until it's time."

Instinct had him looking around the room, for what he wasn't sure. Landy's ghost? The Peeping Tom? He had no idea. All he knew was that he'd been spending a wonderful evening with Tenile. They'd connected in a way he'd never experienced before, and then he'd seen the shadow, the silhouette of a man at the window, watching.

"Did she say who it was?"

Tenile shook her head, pushing away the tendrils of hair that hung in her face. "She just knows he'll come back. He was here, Nathan." She looked at him then, as if just realizing something. "He watched as we—" She grew silent as nausea claimed her.

He knew her thoughts before she could voice them. "Don't! Don't you dare let him win. That was between you and me, our feelings, our night. Don't let him destroy that."

"We were on display. He watched us, like some...some—"

"Like some sick pervert. That's exactly what he is." He hugged her close to him. "He's going to slip up. It's just a matter of time. He's been coming here too much. Almost like—"

She sighed once, touched the back of his hand with her fingers. "Like he wants us to know he's here, waiting."

Chapter 17

Tenile returned to work the following week. Her stitches had been removed, and with an extra fifteen minutes' dedication, curling strands of hair covered her scar. Myla hadn't mentioned another word about her and Nathan, even though she'd half expected some smart comment, especially since it was common knowledge that they were now living together. Nathan had promised her he'd take care of it. The woman's tight-lipped countenance proved that he had.

She was taking her break alone this evening. Nathan was in surgery, one she hadn't felt up to assisting with him. Besides, with Myla's watchful glare, she thought it better if she stayed out of the OR until she received the proper credits. She'd start accruing them come this September when she enrolled in the college.

The cafeteria was almost empty at this time of night. She went to one of the vending machines and selected some chips and a bottled water. Choosing a table off in a secluded corner, she took a seat and opened her water first, taking a long satisfying gulp. A hand lit on her shoulder, and she choked on the cool liquid. Quickly setting down the bottle, she grabbed a napkin, put it to her mouth, then mopped up the spilled water.

"Sorry. I didn't mean to frighten you."

Her gaze found his as he made his way to the chair across from her and sat down.

"I just thought I'd stop by and see an old friend." He gave her a quick smile and watched as her initial shock ebbed.

"Kareem. This is a surprise. What are you doing at the hospital?" Her thumping heart began to slow. She didn't see Kareem frequently. He worked a lot, or so she'd heard through the gossip mill.

"I wanted to see you. I understand you've moved out of your own place and thought this would be the best time to catch up with you."

Tenile opened her chips, tilted the bag towards Kareem in invitation. He declined. "How are you? How's the business? I hear you're running the whole company now." She casually crunched on her chips.

He shrugged. "Business is good. I've been training for the head office all my life, so it's pretty much what I expected. How are you? I've heard about all the strange things going on."

Briefly, she wondered why he hadn't mentioned Nathan and his return. If he'd been hearing things, and it was likely he had, why act as if they concerned only her? Good grief, this whole situation was making her paranoid. This was Kareem, for goodness sake. "Strange doesn't begin to describe it. I'm looking over my shoulder in my sleep now."

"So what's going on? Did you piss somebody off? An old boyfriend maybe?"

Because she knew this was a sore subject for them all, she took her time before answering. "It's about Landy, Kareem. Nathan and I are trying to find her killer. I guess we're getting close, and somebody doesn't like it."

"That case is closed, Tenile. It's been closed for ten years," he said solemnly.

"Unsolved, not closed. We've got some pretty good information and believe that the killer is still in Tanner." She didn't know why, but something told her not to go into great detail about what they knew and didn't know.

Of all of them, Kareem had taken Landy's death the worst. He'd gone into a deep depression for the year that followed. His parents had been so concerned they'd put him in a hospital on a suicide watch. When he'd returned, he'd thrown himself into his work. He spoke to her whenever they saw each other in town, which wasn't frequently, but all other contact with her or Eli and Nicole was shut off completely.

It was strange how they'd all found a different way to deal with the death of a friend. Nathan ran. Nicole and Eli slept around with anybody they could, including each other. Kareem went crazy, then buried his emotions in work. And she…she convinced herself that it was the past and lived in a pretend world until things finally came full circle and she had no choice but to re-visit the worst time in her life.

"What do you expect to find that the police didn't ten years ago? And why would you want to put us all through that again?"

He watched her closely, his hands still on the table in front of him. He wore the suit he'd most likely had on all day; his gray tie was loosened at his neck.

"Closure. We all need to know what happened so we can move on."

"I've moved on."

"Have you? From what I hear, you have no personal life. You spend all your time working then cage yourself up in that big old house that belonged to your parents and refuse to see anyone. I don't think that's moving on."

"Things would have been different if she'd lived," he said quietly.

Because Tenile knew that Kareem had been in love with Landy, she reached a hand over the table, touching the back of his. "I believe that too. But she didn't live, and as her friend, I feel honor bound to see that the person who killed her pays."

He looked at her then, eyes filled with confusion and pain. Tenile wished there were something she could say, something she could do to take that look away, but knew there was no use. He still loved her, had never gotten over her, after all these years. She instantly thought of herself and Nathan.

"We can't change the past." He looked away, toward the window where the evening sky covered the town in darkness. "Sometimes things are better left alone."

His voice changed, his words going from ripe with emotion to bitter coldness. Tenile pulled her hand away as if she'd just been burned. "We won't stop looking until we find him. I'm sorry if that hurts you." She stood then, grabbing her bag and the water bottle. "I'll see you around."

Before she could make a clean exit, he stood and grabbed her wrist. "Tell Nathan I said hello."

His fingers clenched her wrist tightly, and she had to pull twice to break free of his grip. "I will."

Her legs couldn't move fast enough. What the hell was that all about? Balling her fist, she banged the button for the elevator and tapped her foot as it took its time coming. Once inside and after the electronic doors closed tightly, she let out the breath she'd been holding.

Tenile would be at work another hour or so in a hospital full of people—full of witnesses. He'd left right after the surgery was complete. John had paged him; he had some information, but Nathan didn't want to discuss anything at the hospital. He'd left a message at the desk for Tenile and headed straight out of the hospital. Once home, he would call John and they'd go over the new developments.

Taking the last turn to his house, he noticed a light-colored car parked on the side of the road. No hazard lights were on and there was no other indication that the vehicle had broken down. Nathan slowed his car to a stop and got out. Walking around to the front of the vehicle, he looked for damage to the front bumper. A car similar to this one had rammed Tenile. There was no damage.

Nathan paused, rubbed his temples, then let a hand rest a moment over his goatee and took a deep breath. He was very paranoid, Tenile would say. He called it cautious. There was a killer on the loose, and he was damned close to finding him. Watching his own back was one thing; watching Tenile's back was essential.

Pulling up in his driveway, he looked at his watch. He'd have exactly one hour to follow up with John before heading to the hospital to pick up Tenile. She was not driving alone these days. Yanking the keys from the ignition, he stepped out of the car and took long strides to his front door. He was attempting to put his key in the lock when the door opened before him.

Feeling the natural animal instinct to protect and defend, he reached into his pocket and pulled out the blade he'd carried since childhood. It wasn't large but it was sharp; it would cut and cut deep with the right amount of pressure.

He stepped inside slowly, careful not to make a sound. His head moved from side to side as he tried to take in everything around him. There was no one on the steps, no one behind the door. Flattening his back against the wall, he peeked into the living room but saw nothing.

Something hit the floor and he stilled. The sound had come from his office. He hurried to his office door. It was open, the light inside turned on. More noise. Someone was moving furniture across the floor, swearing when a number of books fell. He moved to stand in the doorway, crouched and gripped the knife in his right hand. "Hold it!" he shouted.

The man stood with his back to the door. He'd been trying to push the credenza back up against the wall beneath the window. He turned at the familiar voice and grinned.

Nathan met eyes that he'd stared into many times before and felt himself straightening, the knife going slack in his hand. "Eli? What the hell are you doing here?"

Eli's hands went to the tie around his neck, and he nervously tightened the knot. "Nathan? I was wondering when you'd get home."

Nathan flicked the handle, pulling the blade back into its casing and moving closer to his friend. His office was a mess, with files strewn over his desk, chairs upturned and all the furniture that had been along the walls pushed almost to the center of the floor. "I see. So you simply let yourself in? What's going on, Eli? What are you looking for?"

Eli came from behind the desk, stepping over the trashcan and a box of books. "Let's go into the other room and talk, Nathan," he said easily, trying to make his way to the door.

Nathan reached out, grabbed his arm. "Let's talk right here, right now. And start with why the hell you broke into my house." Nathan's jaw clenched as fury raced through him. He wasn't sure what was going on, but he was damned sure he wasn't going to like it.

"There's no need to get upset, Nathan." Eli casually pulled his arm from Nathan's grip, taking a few careful steps back. "Really, I was just looking for something that I left here when I moved out. That's all."

"Something you left?" Nathan's eyes narrowed. He looked around the disheveled room again and frowned. "You moved out of this house ten years ago. I'm well aware that nobody has lived here since us, so why wait until now to come back and look? You've had more than enough time to remember leaving something. It would have damn sure been easier to break into an empty house than to wait until somebody moved into it to go snooping around."

Eli shrugged, offered a sheepish grin. "I've been busy. I just got around to looking."

Nathan didn't believe him for one second. "Why not call me and ask me to look for it? Or ask if you could come over to look for it? Why break in?" Nathan moved across the room then, stepping over things, picking up his files and books. He didn't keep anything valuable in his office. His notes on Landy's death and anything pertaining to John were locked in his safe, in his bedroom wall, along with some other valuables. So what was Eli really looking for?

"Listen, man, I know you and Tenile are going through some things. I didn't want to burden you with it. I figured I'd just slip in, find it and get out of here before you even knew I was here."

His research notes were out of order, but he could fix that later. Closing a manila folder, he stared up at Eli. He looked perfectly calm, as if he hadn't been doing something illegal, something distrustful. "What are you looking for?"

Eli stuck his hands in his pockets. "A trunk. I left a trunk here and I need to get it back."

Knowledge dawned on Nathan, and he looked down, saw his leather chair turned on its side and bent to pick it up. Then sat in it, leaning back and eyeing the man he'd thought was a friend—the man he knew was not telling him the complete truth. He brushed his hand over his chin as he contemplated his next move. "We shared a room for four years. I don't recall you ever having a trunk. And if you were looking for a trunk, you certainly didn't need to throw stuff around. Obviously, there's no trunk in this room."

Eli didn't speak.

"I do, however, recall Landy bringing a trunk in here after she returned from her father's funeral."

They both grew silent.

Then Eli spoke. "When I didn't see the trunk, I figured maybe you'd have the stuff that was in the trunk somewhere or at the very least have some documentation showing what you did with it."

Nathan remembered the trunk from the night Landy showed it to him. As to the contents of the trunk, all he knew for a fact was what she'd told him…and what she'd given him. Still, he wondered how much Eli really knew. "What's in the trunk that you want?"

Eli could have lied but figured it was too late for that. It was too late for a lot of things. "Money," he answered simply.

The root of all evil. Nathan sighed. He could be really angry with Eli. He could have him arrested, but what good would that do? Eli had been his best friend for years. He'd kept in touch with him after he'd left Tanner, and Eli had always encouraged him to come back.

Eli believed in Nathan's innocence.

And Nathan didn't take that lightly.

"Why don't you take off your jacket while we get my office back in order. Then we can discuss Landy's trunk and why you think you're entitled to its contents."

Eli had made a fool of himself. He didn't want to have this conversation, and he sure as hell didn't want to tell Nathan about the mess he'd gotten himself into. "Nah, man. Let's just forget it. I'll just get your office together, and then I'll leave."

When Eli would have turned to leave, Nathan picked up the phone, acting as if he were prepared to dial. "I wonder how much time you get nowadays for breaking and entering. You think Sheriff Ross would feel like stopping by to tell us?"

Eli froze, frowned and pulled his jacket off, throwing it across the room before bending to pick up books and put them into a box.

"So why did Nathan send you to pick me up?"

Nicole shrugged, her hand gripping the steering wheel. "I don't know. He just said you needed a ride home. So I came."

Tenile stared out the window, contemplating the matter. Nathan had left a note saying that he was coming back to pick her up, but he hadn't. Something must have happened. He wouldn't not come unless something important came up.

"Anyway, I've been wanting to talk to you about something."

"What? How to stop a man from lusting after you?"

"Hell no. You're the last person I'd ask a question like that. You don't know anything about men and lust."

Tenile laid her head against the headrest. "Yeah, whatever. What do you want to talk about?"

"You remember when Landy's father died?"

That was definitely not what she was expecting. Her eyes shot open, her head turning towards Nicole. "Mr. Connor? Yeah, I remember. Why?"

"I was just wondering. You went back to the house after Landy's funeral. You packed her stuff."

"Yeah. I did. I asked you to go with me, but you were busy." Tenile sat up completely now, her eyes glued to the woman driving.

"She had this trunk, the one her Dad gave her."

Tenile didn't answer. Nicole cast a quick look her way.

"I'd run out of space in my closet. You know, after one of my shopping sprees." Nicole smiled. "Anyway, she let me borrow some of her trunk space, and I put some stuff in there."

"And?" Tenile's mind began to click.

"I was just thinking about that stuff the other day and figured since you were staying with Nathan you'd know if the trunk was still there."

Nicole turned down the road leading to the house.

"I haven't seen a trunk," Tenile said slowly. "But when we get there, you can ask Nathan about it. Maybe he moved it."

Tenile used the next few minutes to rack her brain for any memory of Landy and that trunk.

She remembered it vaguely. When Landy returned from her father's funeral, she'd brought back a lot of her mother's things. Since she and her stepmother had a hate/hate relationship, and Landy had been sure the new Mrs. Connor wouldn't hesitate to throw out her mother's things, Landy had packed up all her mother's stuff and brought it home with the intention of moving it into her own house after graduation.

The trunk used to sit at the end of Landy's bed, she remembered. It was so clunky, dark and ugly as sin that Landy used to put a quilt over it to hide the hideous carvings that she said were links to her Greek heritage.

Tenile never knew what was inside the trunk, just that the trunk and its contents were very important to Landy. The funny thing was, she mused as they pulled into the driveway, she definitely didn't recall shipping the trunk with the rest of Landy's stuff back to the family home. The trunk had already been gone from the room.

Chapter 18

Nathan's car was in the driveway, but Nicole decided not to go in and talk to him. "Just forget about it. That stuff's most likely out of style anyway."

Tenile climbed out of the car, thoroughly confused by the conversation and in even more of a hurry to speak with Nathan about it.

The house was dark when she entered, and she called his name to let him know she was home. When he didn't answer right away, prickles of panic soared through her chest. The faint sound of music coming from the direction of his office had her calming a bit as she dropped her purse and walked through the foyer.

She remembered the song, Nancy Wilson's "Someone To Watch Over Me." It had been one of her favorites, and she had listened to it all the time when they were in school. The small lamp on his desk was lit, and his chair was turned with its back to the door. Her footsteps were muffled due to her rubber soled nursing shoes, so he didn't hear her approach.

Smooth, melodic sounds came from the CD player on the bookshelf as she reached out, turning his chair slightly so she could see his face. When his cold, dark eyes focused on her, she gasped. Never had she seen him look so...so angry. Rage emanated in thick dark rays from him. Her hand went to her chest as the full impact struck her.

He still wore his clothes from work. His shirt was unbuttoned at the neck, his tie undone but hanging on his shoulders. His hands lay clenched on his thick thighs. She inhaled, smelled the stale odor of tension and cringed.

Something had definitely happened.

"Nathan? What's the matter?" Her voice seemed small, even in the quiet of the room. A part of her wanted to touch him; another was too afraid his anger would scorch.

He stared at her then, his pupils adjusting to the petite female form in front of him. He'd been sitting in his office alone for a while. Eli had long since gone. Nathan had learned some things about his friend he hadn't wanted to know.

What he knew now without a doubt was the painful truth of broken trust. And for a man in his position, a man already under the allegation of murder, it was just another brick falling from the already collapsing wall of his life.

Searching the pretty face, the eyes that feared yet held a certain spark of compassion, the lips he'd kissed only hours ago, he wondered. Could he trust her? Was she with him for the same reason Eli had been here? Was she looking for the money as well?

"Nicole brought you home?" His voice was gruff. He'd been silent for a while.

Tenile folded her arms, released them and put her hands behind her back. "She said you called her and said you couldn't come. What happened?" His face was unreadable, his eyes still cold and blank. Hot spikes of fear pummeled her back. She wanted nothing more than to climb onto his lap, have him wrap his strong arms around her and tell her that everything would be alright. She wanted, so desperately, someone to watch over her.

"I saw Eli this evening. He was in the house when I came home." He paused, taking care to watch her for any slip of emotion, any indication that she knew.

Her head jerked, eyes blinking in confusion. "Eli? What was he doing here, and how did he get in?"

Nathan lifted one hand and with his weight pushed his chair back into a reclining position. He contemplated how much he should tell her. "It seems that in addition to his medical skills, Eli is also adept in picking a lock."

"He broke in?" she gasped. "But why?"

She looked genuinely shocked, and his doubt began to weaken. "Do you remember Landy's trunk, the one she brought back with her after her father's death?"

Her gasp was more apparent this time as she took a step back, her hand coming to her mouth. Her conversation with Nicole came rushing back to mind, the questions about the trunk, her bafflement as to why Nicole would want to know about that now.

"What? What do you know?" She knew something; he was sure of that. Just what would tell if all his hope for a future was lost.

"Nicole just asked me the same thing," she whispered. "In the car just now, she asked me about Landy's trunk. She said Landy let her put some things in there and she wanted to get them out."

Nathan's hand stilled on his chin hair, his face tensing again. "Eli said there was money in the trunk."

"Money? Isn't that strange?"

"No, it's convenient. It's fitting more pieces into our puzzle."

Suddenly, her legs began to wobble, and she reached a hand out to grab the corner of the desk for balance.

Nathan didn't miss a beat. He had her in his lap, head against his shoulder before she could speak.

Tenile felt overwhelmed. "I just don't understand," she murmured, loving the feel of his strength surrounding her.

"It's simple. Nicole has always been materialistic. So there's no surprise there. Eli, on the other hand, I'm not real sure about his motives. At any rate, I don't have the trunk, so I can't be of any help in their quest to find it."

He tried to speak flippantly, as if this new development didn't affect him on a personal level. But Tenile knew differently. "You're hurt that he didn't trust you enough to just ask you about the trunk."

Nathan sighed. "Yeah. I am." But he didn't want to think about it anymore. "It's late; let's not think about this any more tonight."

She lifted enough so that they were face-to-face. "How can we not think about it?" Her hands gestured wildly, almost smacking him across the face.

"I was almost killed. Some pervert watches us through the window. Eli and Nicole are acting weird about a trunk neither of us has seen since Landy was alive—"

Nathan grabbed both her hands, bringing them to his lips where he lightly kissed her knuckles. "Shhh, darlin'. I'm going to take care of this. I don't want you to worry."

Because the erotic sensations from his mouth brushing over her skin were blurring her senses, her voice lowered, softened. "What am I supposed to do, Nathan? What am I supposed to think about if not the danger surrounding me?"

"Me." He kissed her hands, turning them over to kiss her palms, all the while watching her closely. "You're supposed to think of me, the way I've thought of you every night since I left you ten years ago." His kisses traced a fiery path up one arm, stopping at her neck where his tongue drew lazy shapes against her skin.

She shifted, giving him more access. "I tried not to think of you."

He grinned, his teeth nipping her earlobe. "I'll bet you did. But it didn't work, did it?" His tongue stroked beneath her ear. "You thought about me." His hand found her breast. "You missed me." He pinched her nipples. "You love me." Dipping his tongue inside her ear, he was rewarded by her deep, throaty sigh.

"Say it, Tenile. Say you love me." He kissed her jaw, her cheeks, her closed eyelids, waiting for her to speak, waiting for her to say the words.

"Nathan." She couldn't think of anything else, had all but forgotten how she came to be in his office, in his lap. She heard his voice, felt his sweet caress, heard his demand and melted beneath him. "I love you, Nathan."

Nicole had been scarce since giving Tenile a ride home a couple of days ago, and so had Eli. No visitors had been lurking around the house, and for a contented minute, Tenile allowed herself the comfort of thinking things were getting back to normal.

But as she walked out of the hospital one cool spring evening to wait for Nathan to pick her up, that changed.

She barely recognized him, he'd changed so with time. The family resemblance was slight, only around the eyes. No longer was he the gangly boy with the nasty attitude. Now he looked more like a rich gigolo eyeing his next prey. With caution, she proceeded to the black Mercedes he leaned against.

"Well, well, well. Look what the season has brought to Tanner." Her words were cordial enough; only her eyes gave away her distaste. Apparently, he picked up on that.

"Now, Tenile, it's been years. I would have thought you'd forgiven and forgot by now." Donovan uncrossed his legs to stand up straight in front of her. She looked good, he'd give her that. Nathan was wise to keep her close.

"I forgive because God says I should. Forgetting is another matter entirely."

Donovan smiled casually, remembering the same night. She'd been soft, her mouth as sweet as the smile she gave to people in her inner circle—not to him. "Need a ride home?" he asked.

"No."

"We need to talk. There's something I think you should know."

"I'm sure you don't know anything that pertains to me." She frowned at him. "But I am curious as to why you're back in town all of a sudden." Gut instinct told her this had something to do with Landy's death, and if she were right, she did need to talk to him.

Donovan leaned closer, his hands never touching her, his mouth not far from her ear. "It's about Nathan."

Her heart lurched and for a brief second she wanted to step back, but that would admit some type of fear or defeat, which she'd never do. "What about him?" she asked in the most nonchalant voice she could conjure up.

"Go for a ride with me." He motioned towards his shiny car.

She looked around him to the fairly new luxury vehicle. "Nice, but I'd rather not. Say what you have to say so I can leave."

"Nathan won't be here to pick you up for another few minutes." He watched the shock register briefly in her eyes. She was very attractive and tried very hard to hide her emotions. "I guess you could say I've been keeping tabs."

That admission didn't sit right with her, but then Donovan Connor had never sat right with her. "Daddy's money must still be supporting your senseless existence," she chirped. He was looking at her in that way again, that way that said he could see right through her clothes. He was a lecherous specimen, nothing short of a…a pervert, she thought with a start.

"Not just Daddy's money. I'm very resourceful. But you wouldn't know that since you never gave me the time of day."

Goosebumps surfaced on her arms, and her discomfort with being near him grew to fear. He could very well be the Peeping Tom and maybe Landy's killer. "Seeing as you're so resourceful, I would think you'd have enough money to buy yourself a watch."

He smiled.

"Look, I have to go. I would say it was nice seeing you, but that would be a lie." She turned to leave, but he grabbed her arm, pulling her back.

"You need to hear this. Maybe then you'll understand what kind of man you're sleeping with, the kind of man you chose over me."

Tenile jerked her hand out of his clutches. "I would choose any man over you, Donovan. And there's nothing you can tell me about Nathan that I don't already know." She walked away this time, got about three steps before his words stopped her.

"He's killed someone else besides my sister."

Try as she might, Tenile couldn't take another step, nor could she turn and look into that smirking face. She heard his footsteps behind her in the quiet parking lot and still did not move.

"You see, when the good Dr. Hamilton went to New York, his urge to kill grew stronger and another innocent woman fell victim to him."

No! Her mind screamed; her heart thumped in her chest. It was suddenly very hot, stifling almost, and she struggled to breathe. "You're lying," she spat when Donovan stood in front of her.

"Now would I come all this way to lie to you, sweetheart?" He stroked her cheek because he knew she was vulnerable at this moment. Tenile was a lot of things, most of them wonderful and alluring, but the most pronounced was that she was no fool. He could see her considering his words, see the pain taking shape in her eyes.

"I don't have time for games, Donovan. If you have something to say, say it so I can leave." She didn't want to hear him out, didn't want to hear the story he was about to tell. She had enough questions as it was.

"Poor Tenile. Always believing in people who don't deserve your trust. I tried to warn you about Hamilton before. I tried to warn you and Landy."

Now both his hands cupped her face as he hovered above her.

"Take your hands off me and say what you came to say," she said through clenched teeth. She was careful to keep her purse tucked right under her armpit, keeping the can of mace she carried in the front flap within reach.

He pulled his hands back, stuffed them in his pockets and shrugged. "Have it your way. It seems Dr. Hamilton was also responsible for the death of a young mother-to-be back in New York."

Tenile felt a certain amount of relief wash over her. "Patients are lost all the time; that's a part of life. Doctors can't save them all."

"That's interesting. Do patients normally die while on their way to dinner in their doctor's car?"

She felt her knees wobbling and gripped the edge of her purse. "I don't understand."

A broad smile spread across Donovan's face. "I see. I'll make it simple. The woman was pregnant and married. Your Dr. Hamilton had been seen with her around town in different places; it was obvious they were having an affair. The assumption was she wouldn't leave her husband for him and he ran her into a tree." He paused for effect. The look on Tenile's face was priceless. "It was probably intended as a murder/suicide. Instead, she died and he didn't."

Tenile took a step back, staggering. Why hadn't Nathan told her about this? It was an accident, right? So why hadn't he told her?

Donovan reached out, grabbed her arms.

"The baby?" She looked up into his face, saw the sheer pleasure he was getting from telling her this.

"Dead as a doornail."

She grimaced and wrenched free of his touch. "You have such a way with words, Donovan."

"Sorry, was that politically incorrect?"

"That was insensitive and cruel." Just as his waiting outside her job to tell her this was.

"Probably, but then the truth's often hard to stomach." He moved closer to her but didn't dare touch her again. The way she was glaring at him right now, he didn't put it past her to slug him. "Listen, why don't you come home with me? It'll give you a minute to straighten things out in your mind. It's not safe staying with him. Just look at what's happened so far."

Her mind was still reeling, and his voice barely registered. Yet some of his words caught her attention. "What?"

"I said look what's happened so far. Your accident. I mean, if it really was an accident. You did crash into a tree."

Oh God, she was going to be sick. The words echoed in her head, and the scene resurfaced in her mind. She hadn't crashed into a tree; she'd been pushed into one—directly in front of Nathan's house. But he said he'd come out to help her, he'd heard the cars. She didn't remember any of that. For all she knew, he could have been the one driving that other car.

No, Nathan wouldn't do that. Nathan loved her, had always loved her.

Could he have killed a woman in New York? She assumed that if Donovan were standing here telling her this there had to be some shred of truth to it. She needed to make sure, confirm the story. "How do you know this?"

"I make it my business to keep tabs on the person responsible for my sister's death. In case he drops any clues, you know. I've got a file at my place. You could go through it and make your own decision."

She knew she shouldn't go with him, knew she shouldn't trust him as far as she could throw his skinny behind. Yet something inside egged her on, pushed her to find out the truth. If Nathan actually had killed the woman in New York, did that mean he'd also killed Landy? She'd been so sure that he was innocent. So sure that all this would blow over once they found the real killer. Could she be wrong?

"I want to see the file."

On the inside Donovan leapt for joy; on the outside he merely nodded, extending his hand to her. "Then come home with me."

Chapter 19

Nathan's mind whirled as he replayed the conversation he'd just had with John. The facts he'd uncovered were disconcerting. Things in Tanner, however, had been quiet. He hadn't received any more letters with veiled references to the killer or his whereabouts. Their Peeping Tom hadn't made an appearance, or rather, they hadn't caught him making an appearance. And as far as he knew, Tenile hadn't heard anything more from the ghost of Landy.

Sighing about the logic of that, he maneuvered his car into the hospital parking lot. Still, Tenile believed she'd seen Landy's ghost, so that gave it some credibility.

However, he couldn't shake the feeling that all of this was about to come to a head. Possibly a violent head.

Ample streetlights posted at regular intervals made the parking lot bright. He drove past the side entrance where Tenile usually met him but didn't see her. Maybe she was near the emergency entrance; sometimes nurses gathered there on their smoke break. She might be there talking to some of her friends.

Not until he passed the emergency entrance, the back entrance and the main entrance a second time without seeing her did he begin to worry. He checked his watch. It was a half hour past the time she normally got off. He pulled into a parking spot near the side entrance, just in case she came out, then reached for his cell phone. Punching the numbers quickly, he waited for Myla to pick up.

"It's Dr. Hamilton. Has Tenile left yet?" His eyes remained fixed on the door, hoping she'd come out at any moment.

"Good evening, Dr. Hamilton," Myla replied in a somewhat snide tone. "Yes, Nurse Barnes ended her shift at exactly eleven this evening. She's already left the floor."

Nathan disconnected. He would not overreact. She probably got a ride with somebody else. Maybe Nicole came to pick her up again.

With that thought, he pulled out of the parking lot, heading for the eastern side of town. If she was with Nicole, she was safe. He believed that Nicole and Eli were only looking for the money. He did not believe they would be so greedy they'd kill their best friend over it. Besides, there was no real proof that the money Eli said was in Landy's trunk actually existed.

He remembered the trunk, remembered one night when Landy had called him into her room and shared its contents with him.

∞

"Can you believe this? My father left it for me." Landy lifted the lid of the trunk and plopped down on the side of her twin-sized bed waiting for Nathan's response.

He knelt on the floor beside the trunk, the sparkling blue gems grabbing his attention. Curious, he put his hand to some of them and felt coolness seep into his skin. Incredulous, he asked, "Are these real?"

"Yup. Remember, I told you he bought this old mine in Africa. It seems these are the fruits of his labor. I'm guessing he didn't want Miranda to know about them. The lawyer said my father left a key in a sealed envelope with my name on it in his office. The key was to a safe deposit box, and when I unlocked it, these were in it."

"Are you sure your stepmother doesn't know about this?" Landy's stepmother was a greedy woman, from what Landy had told him. If she had any idea that Landy had this additional inheritance, she wouldn't be a happy camper.

Landy shook her head. Her silver earrings with the moons and stars dangled at her neck. "The lawyer said he was the only person with my father's safe combination. There was another safe in Daddy's bedroom, and Miranda had the combination to that. She didn't even know about the one in his office."

"He didn't trust his wife much, huh?"

"Would you?"

❧

They'd been in the house alone that night and had talked for hours after she'd showed him the gems. But to his knowledge, there had been no money in the trunk. And Eli had specifically said they were looking for cash.

Turning onto Main Street, he tried to clear his mind of old memories and hoped that Tenile and Nicole were simply having another girls' night out.

❧

Donovan was staying at a house just outside the city limits, in a classic two-story building with white siding and black shutters. Tenile should have been nervous, considering their last encounter, but her mind was too full of questions to be concerned with Donovan and his roaming hands. Besides, she was older and wiser now, and she'd taken self-defense classes at the lodge. Pretty little rich boy didn't stand a chance this time.

He hadn't spoken to her much during the drive, and she was glad. There were a lot of things going through her mind, a lot of emotions she couldn't identify and one she could…doubt.

If what Donovan said was true and could be backed up, she'd let Nathan come into her life only to….Unable to finish the thought, she drummed her fingers against the door, anxiously waiting for Donovan to stop the car so she could get out and read his file.

When he did stop, she grabbed the door handle and flung it open, rushing up the front steps of the house.

"Hold on a second." He grabbed her arm. "You don't have the key."

He was smiling at her, as if he were the happiest man in the world. She felt like smacking him. "Sorry, I just want to hurry up and get this over with."

Donovan fiddled with his keys, then inserted one and pushed the door open. "I understand."

He led her into the dark house, pausing to switch lights on as they went. It was a quaint little setup that she would never have associated with Donovan Connor. "Whose house is this? I know it's not yours," she said when she entered the living room.

"No. It belongs to a friend of mine. Care for a drink?"

"No, thank you. I just want to see the file." She stood near the window noticing the lace curtains and dark drapes that hung from ceiling to floor.

"Then I'll be right back."

He left her alone and she wandered through the room. Her fingers slid over the mantle top, slipped into the holes of a lace doily. Knick-knacks stood on display, and an antique clock chimed midnight in the corner. The house had a homey feel to it, and she turned, hoping to see a picture. Maybe it belonged to someone in town. She had to admit she was curious as to who in Tanner would be friends with Donovan Connor.

He re-entered the room carrying a file. He had replaced his shirt and jacket with a deep purple lounge coat belted with a black sash at his waist. He'd also traded his designer leather loafers for black house shoes.

She frowned. "Since you're obviously in a hurry to get to bed I'll take the file with me."

Donovan smiled. "I'm just making myself comfortable. You're welcome to do the same."

Tenile inhaled deeply to keep calm. The last thing she was up to at this moment was fighting off another one of Donovan's come-ons. And she prayed that all he'd told her wasn't just a ploy to get her to his home. She wondered how he and Landy could be related; they were so different. His creamy, almost ivory complexion shone in the dim lights, and she examined him again for any physical resemblance to Landy.

Landy's skin had been the color of heavily creamed coffee, and her eyes had been bright, revealing her vivacious spirit. Donovan was paler, and his eyes lacked any significant emotion besides lust and greed. Still, he wasn't hard on the eyes, and she suspected he had more than enough females to confirm that fact.

"I'm only here to see the file, Donovan," she said.

He went to the sofa, took a seat and patted the cushion beside him. "C'mon, let's have a look."

She wasn't going to waste time arguing the seating arrangement. She could sit next to him for the time it would take her to go through this stuff and then she would leave. "Fine."

Moving to the couch, she sat down and he placed the manila folder on her lap. She opened it to a newspaper clipping showing Nathan in a trench coat, shielded by two other men as he walked out of the hospital. The headline read, "Doctor Kills Mistress and Unborn Child."

She cringed, her hands shaking as she held the tattered paper, reading the complete article.

While she was looking through the file, Donovan's phone rang.

"Excuse me, I'll get that in the other room so I won't disturb you."

She barely noticed him leaving she was so engrossed in the documentation. The victim's name was Kelly Peterson. She'd been married to Mark Peterson for five years, and they had been expecting their first child. Nathan had been her obstetrician. There were reports that Nathan and Kelly had been seen in restaurants on numerous occasions during her pre-natal care as well as in the park. There was a picture in one of the papers of the two of them sitting on a park bench in deep conversation.

She wanted to cry, but the tears wouldn't come. The beat of her heart had seemed to falter about thirty minutes ago as she began to question everything she'd believed just a few hours earlier. The one truth she'd always held on to was that Nathan loved Landy just as she had and that, because of that love, he could never hurt her. But reading about Kelly Peterson made her ask herself whether she'd ever known Nathan at all.

After the last page, she slammed the folder shut and tossed it on the chair. Standing, she paced the room, trying to figure out her next move. What would happen if she confronted him? Wrenching her hands as she moved, she tried to think of the best approach.

She couldn't see Nathan yet, of that she was positive. She was too emotional right now, too upset. She'd go home, back to her own apartment. Then she'd go see Nicole. No, Nicole and her lover were too busy looking for a missing trunk. That was another mystery waiting to be solved. She couldn't go to her mother because Oneil would freak out, grab her butcher knife, and head for Nathan's house.

No, this time she had to figure out what to do on her own. First, she needed to call herself a cab to take her back into the city. She went to her purse, reached in and retrieved her cell phone. She had to turn it on because she couldn't have it on in the hospital. Most times she forgot she even had it.

The moment she switched it on, it began to ring, the screen lighting up with a number she hadn't seen in weeks. Pressing the 'talk' button, she lifted the phone to her ear. "Hello?"

"Hello, Tenile. It's good to hear your voice."

"Where are you? Where have you been?"

"I had some business in Bar Harbor. I was going to call you, but I got pretty busy."

Too busy to call and say he was alright? She frowned. "So why are you calling now?"

"I missed you. I want to see you."

Tenile let out a deep breath. This was turning into one hell of a night for her. With her free hand she rubbed her eyes. "Where are you now?"

"I'm still in Bar Harbor. I'm staying at this really nice cabin near the hiking trails. You like to hike, don't you? I remember you telling me that once."

Yes, she did like to hike, but she hadn't done it in a while, and truth be told, she wasn't really in the mood for it now. But she did need to get away. She couldn't possibly stay in Tanner without seeing Nathan, without having to face him and his lies. Maybe going to Bar Harbor would clear her mind enough so that she'd know what to do next. "I'm not at home. I'll need to get my car and get some stuff together."

"That's fine. Write down these directions and get on the road tonight. I'll be waiting for you."

His words sounded good, and it was just the retreat she needed. She didn't give any thought to the fact that before he disappeared she'd been thinking of a way to break things off with him. None of that mattered now. She was sick and tired of men and all their lies. No, she was sick and tired of Nathan Hamilton and all his lies.

She grabbed a pen and a pad from her purse and wrote down the directions, told him she'd see him soon and began to dial a number for a cab.

❦

"I've called her cell a million times, and I'm not getting any answer." Nathan paced the floor of Nicole's apartment.

Eli sat on the barstool while Nicole lit what had to be her fifth cigarette in the last hour. While the jury was still out on Eli and Nicole's little scheme to find Landy's trunk, Nathan had no one else in Tanner to turn to. And despite everything that was happening around them, he still believed in their circle of friendship. He'd done a lot to cause them to mistrust him, so pointing the finger of blame wasn't exactly fair. Besides, he didn't have the trunk, and odds were none of them would ever see it or its contents again.

"I don't understand, Nathan. How could she just be gone? You told her to wait for you there. Why wouldn't she have waited?" Nicole questioned and then took a puff.

"She would have waited. Tenile wouldn't have gone with anyone else." Eli paused. "Not by choice."

Stopping, Nathan squeezed the bridge of his nose. Eli's words were exactly what he'd been afraid of.

"What are you saying, Eli?" Nicole's fingers shook as she struggled to hold on to the cigarette.

Eli looked at Nathan. Nathan looked up at Eli, his jaw clenching with fury. "If he hurts her, I'll kill him."

"You don't even know who he is," Eli countered. "You need to let the sheriff know she's missing, then call your P.I. friend and get him up here quick."

"P.I.? Sheriff? What the hell are you two talking about? Who would take Tenile against her will? Is all this about the money?" Nicole was ranting now.

"No." Nathan turned to her slowly. "It's not about the money. It's about Landy's murder and the murderer's plan to kill again." And that was the simple truth of it. He didn't care about Eli and Nicole looking for money or gems or whatever else they would find in that trunk. His only concern was that Tenile was safe.

Nicole gasped, and this time the cigarette tumbled to the floor. Eli moved quickly to grab it and wipe up the ashes. He placed it in the ashtray on the table, then grabbed Nicole by her shoulders and lowered her to the chair.

Silence fell over the room as each of them remembered the scariest night of their lives and prayed they weren't about to relive that time all over again.

Robert watched as Tenile pulled into the driveway. "She just pulled up. I'll check in with you later."

"Don't mess up this time. Get it done," Donovan directed.

"I won't."

"And make it look like an accident."

"I will. She likes hiking, remember."

"Yeah, a nice hiking accident. That's good. Just hurry up. Hamilton's getting too close."

"I'll take care of it." Robert hung up then because she was at the door.

Crossing the wood-planked floor, he reached for the knob and pulled the heavy door open. She looked tired. A duffle bag was on one shoulder, her purse on the other. He reached for her, took her in his arms, then led her into the cabin.

Chapter 20

Her mother hasn't seen or heard from her. The last person to see her was the shift manager and the front desk volunteer of the hospital who said she stood at the side entrance waiting for a ride for a few minutes, and then she was gone." Nathan gave the disturbing report to Sheriff Ross early the next morning.

He'd waited by the phone all night, hoping Tenile would call, but she hadn't. Now, as Nathan talked to Sheriff Ross, Eli sat across the room holding Nicole, who looked frail and disheveled. Nathan had left them only four hours ago, and now they were back, sitting in his living room and waiting for any news. By some small miracle, he'd been able to convince Oneil and Tracy to stay at home in case Tenile tried to call them.

Sheriff Ross looked at him with a disbelieving eye when he finished, but Nathan ignored it. Now was not the time for a confrontation.

"Would she be trying to get away from you for any reason?" he asked Nathan.

Nathan bit back a smart retort. "We hadn't argued, if that's what you mean. There was no reason that I know of for her to leave that hospital without me."

Sheriff Ross turned his attention to Nicole. "When's the last time you talked to her?" "I haven't seen or heard from her in about a week. The last time I brought her home, to this house."

"And you?"

Eli cleared his throat. "I saw her at the hospital the day before yesterday."

Nathan's eye quickly turned to him. "You haven't been on duty for the past week. I thought you were using your vacation time to get things organized for the new practice."

"I wasn't working." Eli looked at Nicole, then back to Nathan. "I was there with an old friend who's thinking about investing in my new practice. We were observing the clinic and how it functions."

Nathan stood, his hands in his jean pockets. "The clinic closes at six. Tenile isn't at work until seven."

Sheriff Ross scribbled quickly in his notebook.

"Oh for Pete's sake, Eli, tell him the truth. This is really serious now. To hell with the money and the practice. What if he hurts her?" Nicole screeched.

All eyes were on Eli, including steely dark brown ones that would surely kill him if anything happened to Tenile as a result of his need.

Eli took a deep breath, stood and walked to the window. "Like I told you before, Nathan, Landy promised to split the money with us. She said she really didn't need all of it because she had a trust fund. Nicole and I just want what we were promised. We need it now. I didn't know he knew about it, didn't know she'd ever told him about it."

With his heart racing, Nathan took one careful, controlled step toward the man he'd once called his best friend. "Who?"

The room was silent. Only the ticking of the grandfather clock Tenile had convinced Nathan to buy to add character to the room reminded them that they were all alive.

Eli turned, faced the eyes staring at him. "Donovan Connor is back in Tanner."

❧

Tenile took a deep breath, pulled the covers up over her head and tried to go back to sleep. She'd been up since the first rays of light began to creep into the cabin. Robert had slept in the living room on the couch, and she'd closed herself into this room, alone.

Thoughts of Nathan and the things she'd learned about him last night had kept going through her mind all night. She felt exhausted and sore from the tension but knew she couldn't hide in the bedroom forever.

Beyond the door she could hear Robert moving about, could smell the coffee he was brewing.

Why had she come here? She didn't feel like dealing with Robert any more than she felt like accepting the fact that she'd been a fool for Nathan Hamilton again. But she was here now, so she'd make the best of it. She had her car. There was no reason she couldn't simply stay here for breakfast then drive to a hotel where she could be alone.

Throwing the covers back, she looked around for a phone. She needed to call her mother to let her know she was alright. Things had happened too fast last night, and it was close to three in the morning by the time she'd arrived at the cabin. No doubt, when Nathan realized she wasn't at the hospital, he'd put out the word that she was missing. Her mother would be nearly hysterical by now. She'd forgotten to pack her slippers, so her bare feet hit the cool wood planks. She looked unsuccessfully for a phone jack. Apparently, people came to this cabin to get away from modern amenities. Moving to her duffle bag, she looked for her purse, which contained her cell phone but didn't see it either. She'd probably left it in the living room where she'd initially dropped her bags last night, well, earlier this morning.

Grabbing some clothes, she headed for the bathroom, deciding to retrieve her purse and call her mother after she was dressed.

A few minutes later, clad in jeans, a white shirt and ankle boots, Tenile made her way into the small kitchen area where Robert stood at the stove frying bacon.

"Mornin' sleepyhead," he called over his shoulder.

"Good morning," she responded just as her stomach rumbled. "That smells good."

"Sit down. I've got pancakes too. Do you like your eggs scrambled or fried?"

Tenile took a seat at the light oak table and lifted the coffee pot, pouring herself a cup. "Hard scrambled."

"A woman after my own tastes." Robert chuckled and cracked four eggs into a bowl.

"So what business did you have up here?" she asked as she scooped sugar into her cup. Coffee was only as good as the amount of sugar and cream used to enhance it.

"You'll never believe this. Apparently, I'm missing some of my teaching credits, so I had to come up here and take a class before I could be re-certified in September."

Robert had his back to her as he worked near the stove. He was tall, not as tall as Nathan, but tall just the same. His frame was not as muscular either, and his skin was a couple tones lighter than...She shook her head quickly, picked up her cup and sipped at the hot coffee. She would not think of Nathan today. That was a promise she'd made to herself while she showered. A promise she intended to keep.

"They pulled you out of school six weeks before classes ended so that you could work on being re-certified? That's weird." Just last week the students of Tanner had celebrated their last day of school before the summer.

"I know, I thought that was crazy too. But what could I do?" He shrugged while placing the plate of bacon and huge pancakes down on the table. "Maple syrup?"

Tenile inhaled again. "Of course." She smiled easily.

She'd always been comfortable with Robert and, at this moment, wondered again why she'd been considering ending things with him. In the back of her mind an insolent voice whispered the name she'd sworn not to think about today. She forked one huge pancake onto her plate and let the smell smother the voice, once and for all.

"Your eggs, madame." With a flourish, he put the bowl of eggs on the table and took a seat across from her. "I rented this cabin just a couple of days ago. I needed a break, and then I thought of you and wanted us to spend some time alone together." Reaching over the table, he took one of her hands in his. "I missed you."

Tenile smiled. She couldn't really say she'd missed him, as her weeks had been spent in another man's arms. "I'm glad you called," she said with a modest amount of truth. Looking into his eyes, she knew she could never love him, could never be with him the way he wanted. She'd make sure he knew this before she left today. But for right now they'd enjoy this breakfast. She slipped her hand from his and finished fixing her plate.

After they'd blessed their food, Robert took a bite and began to speak as she ate. "I've scheduled some time for us to take a hike later this morning. I thought it'd be good for us to see some sights while we're here. The caretaker said if we follow the trail we can get a birds-eye view of the mountains while they're still snow-topped."

Tenile had all but decided she was leaving right after breakfast but admitted to herself she'd like to see the mountains, put all her worries behind her if for just this one day. "That sounds great." She lifted a slice of bacon to her mouth, now looking forward to the outing.

Robert smiled. "Great. We can leave right after breakfast."

"Where do you think you're going?" Sheriff Ross grabbed Nathan's arm as he headed toward the front door.

After one glaring look from Nathan, Albert released his arm and moved to stand in front of the door instead.

"I'm going to question Connor," Nathan replied impatiently.

"Oh, no you don't. You've done enough investigating on your own. I'll be the one questioning Connor. I *am* the law around here."

Ross grabbed his belt and pulled his pants up, puffing out his chest. It was a pitiful sight, but Nathan let the man have his moment. "Fine. We'll question him together."

"You are *not* the law, and you don't call the shots around here. You don't have any business questioning a witness."

"You mean a suspect," Nathan countered. "And I have every right if he's harmed Tenile. Now get out of my way." He moved toward Ross, but Eli was at his side, a hand on his shoulder.

"Neither one of you has to go anywhere. Donovan's on his way over here," he told them.

Nathan turned to face him. His glare must have been questioning because Eli suddenly looked very guilty.

"I'm sorry, man. I guess I didn't realize how serious this thing really was."

"What thing? The money or the murder? When this is over, you and I are going to have a long talk." Nathan brushed past him on his way back into the living room where Nicole sat, still looking a little shaky.

"Are you okay? Do you want some coffee or something?" he offered.

She shook her head. "No, I'll be fine. I just never thought things would go this far. I only wanted to help Eli."

Nathan sat beside her and took her hand in his. "You couldn't have known, Nicole. Anyway, we don't know that Donovan has anything to do with Tenile's disappearance." But he suspected he did.

"It was all for the money," she mumbled quietly.

Eli and the Sheriff had come back into the room, taking seats quietly.

"I never knew there was any money in that trunk. Are you two absolutely sure about the cash?" Nathan looked at Eli then.

"We saw it," Eli replied.

This was the second time Eli had mentioned this money. When Nathan had looked into the trunk, there had been only gems and some of Landy's old baby stuff. He kept that to himself. If Eli and Nicole had seen money in the trunk, it must have been at a different time. He doubted they'd be looking so hard for it if they didn't have some proof that it was there. The fact that Donovan had returned to Tanner proved there was something of importance in that trunk. The only thing was, nobody knew where it was.

In less than a half hour, Donovan Connor walked into Nathan's living room with a smile on his face.

"Gang's all here," he quipped when he entered.

"Not really, we're missing a few key people," Nathan retorted.

"It's good to see you again, Hamilton." Donovan slipped a hand into the pocket of his black slacks, pushed back his matching jacket to reveal a teal dress shirt. "I heard you came back. Can't help wondering why though."

"My comings and goings really aren't any of your business."

"True. Still, I like to keep tabs on people who were once close to my dearly departed sister."

Nathan stood, made a move toward Donovan before being cut off by Sheriff Ross. "Mr. Connor, we'd like to ask you a few questions. When was the last time you saw Tenile Barnes?"

Donovan grinned, his eyes flashing with glee at Nathan. "Oh, Tenile. Yeah, we go way back. Had a thing going for a minute before the good doctor here stepped in."

"That's a lie. Tenile despised you," Nicole stated. "And for good reason. You were a spoiled little rich boy with no personality."

Donovan turned to her, tilted his head slightly, then laughed. "And you're still sleeping with good ole Eli, who doesn't give a damn about making you his wife. I'd say you aren't in a real good position to throw stones."

"Donovan, I told you what's between Nicole and me is none of your business." Eli moved closer to Nicole, but she slid away from him.

"We all know Donovan's delusional. Tenile told him she didn't want anything to do with him, and when he couldn't quite decipher her words, she sent him a pretty decent physical message in the form of a bloody nose," Nathan interrupted. He frowned, not really caring for this little trip down memory lane. "Now I think the question was, when was the last time you saw her?"

Donovan rubbed his chin, his eyes going to the ceiling as if in deep thought. "The last time I saw her was…hmmm…uh, last night. That's it, last night." His eyes lowered, leveled with Nathan's. "We had a drink at my house around midnight."

Nathan's hands fisted at his sides, his vision dimming until only Donovan's smiling face was in sight.

For good measure Sheriff Ross moved between the two men again, then scribbled something in his little book. "How did Ms. Barnes get to your house? It was my impression that she was last seen waiting in front of the hospital for Dr. Hamilton to pick her up."

"Oh yeah, well, I happened to be at the hospital when she came out, and we got to talking about the past, and the next thing I knew, she was in my car and we were on our way home. *My* home."

"What did you do to her? How did you make her go with you?" Nathan asked. He was trying like hell to stay calm, not to lose his head, but Donovan was making it extremely hard. He swallowed the anger, watched Donovan gloat. It was getting damned hard.

"I don't know how you work, but I don't have to *make* a woman go anywhere with me. It's all her choice. And with Tenile, I only had to tell her something she needed to know."

"What did you tell her?" Nathan glowered.

"You know what I told her." Donovan sobered. "I told her about the little incident in New York. You know, the one where you killed another woman."

Sheriff Ross turned quickly to face Nathan as Eli and Nicole's eyes found him as well. Nathan remained still while rage and regret slid through him slowly, fiercely.

"That was an accident. It was investigated and ruled an accident. The press took it to another level, and I see your conniving mind has managed to do so as well." The memories of Kelly Peterson came rushing back, just as they had the night of Tenile's accident when he'd opened his door to see a car being pushed into a tree, the metal wrapping around thick bark just the way it had that fateful night. What had been Tenile's reaction when she heard this? No doubt Donovan had made it seem intentional, murderous. Had she run away because of it?

"Where is she now?" Ignoring everyone else around him, he moved until he was standing face to face with Donovan Connor.

Donovan didn't move, although Nathan's bigger form caused a hitch in his heart rate. "I don't know, man. She's supposed to be your lady. You should keep better tabs on her."

Grabbing him by the collar, Nathan pushed until Connor's back was against the wall. "You tell me where she is or for the first time in my life I *will* commit a murder," he growled.

"I told you, I don't know where she is. She got a call on her cell, and the next thing I knew, a cab pulled up. She left and I haven't seen or heard from her since."

Nathan shoved him again, and Donovan's head rapped violently against the wall. "Don't lie to me, Connor!"

Sheriff Ross and Eli were at Nathan's back, trying to pull him off of Donovan. No one heard the doorbell but Nicole. Now she was re-entering the room with John, Nathan's P.I., in tow.

"Tell me where she went," Nathan roared again.

"Let him go, Nate. I know where she is." John's calm voice had everyone turning to face him, including Nathan, although he still held on to Donovan's jacket.

"What? Where is she?"

"Let him go and we'll talk. He doesn't need to be here."

"That's right, let me go. I don't need to be here with you and the rest of you crazy folk."

Nathan pulled his hands away from Donovan but eyed him suspiciously.

"I'm going home." Donovan moved towards the door. "And I'll expect a call about our private business, Eli."

"Don't expect any calls from me, Connor. It's over. I don't care where the money is, and I don't care what lies you fish up to trash my career. It's all over." Eli stood back, feeling the weight of the world being lifted from his shoulders.

Nicole went to him, taking his hand in hers.

"Oh, it's not over. You're going to find my money, and you're going to do it soon. I don't think you know how much damage I can do," Donovan retorted.

"I don't care anymore. People are getting hurt over money we've only seen once. I don't want to be a part of it anymore." Eli folded his arms around Nicole. "It's time I re-thought my life anyway."

"This is definitely not over." Donovan left the house, slamming the door in the process.

"Alright, I'd like for someone to tell me what the hell is going on." Sheriff Ross faced the men.

Nathan knew they all wanted to hear about New York, and as much as he didn't want to discuss it now, he figured it was best to get it out of the way. "Five years ago in New York, I had a patient, Kelly Peterson. Kelly was married to a very influential yet violent man. When she was three months pregnant, her husband threw her into a concrete wall, almost causing Kelly to miscarry. I treated her and tried to get her counseling, but she wouldn't go. Instead, when things got rough between her and her husband, she would come to me. That's what happened the night she died. Her husband had threatened to kill her and the baby and chased her around the house with a butcher knife until she locked herself in the attic and called me. When I got to the house, her husband was gone. I told her to pack some things, and I was on my way to drop her off at a mission where I'd arranged for her to stay when a car side-swiped us and we ran into a tree." Nathan took a deep breath. "Kelly and the baby died. I was accused of sleeping with and impregnating a married woman. I was cleared of fathering her child when DNA was tested, and then her death was ruled an accident."

"Donovan probably told Tenile about it all, except I'm sure he didn't include that I was cleared of all charges. It probably scared her to death and sent her running. Now I have to explain this to her as well. It seems I'm always trying to prove my innocence to her." Nathan sat down, suddenly very tired.

"I'm gonna have to call the office. Check out a few things in New York. Can I use your phone?" Sheriff Ross asked.

"Whatever." Nathan waved the man away. Right now he didn't give two cents about the sheriff investigating him.

John went to Nathan's side, placed a hand on his shoulder. "Remember you asked me to do some research on Robert Gibson?"

"Yeah," Nathan whispered.

"Robert? Isn't that the guy Tenile was seeing? Why would you research him? He's as boring as a box of stale crackers," Nicole chimed in.

John pulled a folder from his briefcase. "Robert Gibson might be boring, but Kent Regan was anything but."

"Kent Regan?" Nicole whispered.

"That's the guy Landy was seeing before she died," Nathan finished.

"Wait a minute, the guy that we thought was too old for her? He left town after she broke up with him. Why would he come back and start dating Tenile?" Eli was confused and from the looks everybody was throwing at John, he wasn't the only one.

"It seems that Kent Regan has some interesting connections with Miranda Connor, including a steady monthly allowance going into his bank account that paid for his facial reconstruction. Kent Regan has a couple of aliases, one of which is Robert Gibson, gym teacher and resident of Tanner, Maine, for the last two years, according to the DMV."

"None of us ever met the guy. Landy didn't want us upsetting him. Again, why would he come back and date Tenile?"

"You said Eli and Nicole were looking for Landy's trunk of money, right?" John asked.

"Yeah, but I saw the contents of that trunk once. I didn't see any money," Nathan confessed.

"Oh, there was money alright." Nicole moved closer to Nathan and John, Eli in tow. "Stacks and stacks of crisp one hundred dollar bills. Eli and I saw it one night when we were drunk and opened the trunk in search of more booze. Landy was always trying to hide the liquor. Donovan said there was more than a half a million dollars in that trunk. Said his old man left it to her, but she was supposed to split it with him and his mother."

"So Donovan wants his money back," Eli started.

"And Miranda wanted the money back, so she hired Kent to seduce Landy, hoping she'd fall for his marriage proposal and he could get his hands on the money." Nathan sat back in the chair, his hands cupping his head. The pieces to the puzzle were beginning to fall into place now, and he didn't like the picture that was forming.

"When Landy broke things off with Kent…" John paused.

"Oh my God, you think Kent killed her?" she whispered.

Nathan stood quickly. "Where is Gibson or Kent or whatever the hell his name is?"

John stood, eyeing Nathan carefully, picking his words so as to calm the panic he knew would come. "Gibson rented a cabin in the mountains up in Bar Harbor two days ago. Before then he was incommunicado. Probably overseas somewhere; that's where Miranda lives."

"Then you go to the cabin and talk to him, and I'll try to track down Tenile. She probably didn't go far. I'll call her mother to see if she's called her yet. I know she'll call her mother, even if she won't call me." Nathan was going to the phone when John stopped him.

"I traced the calls to Tenile's cell."

Nathan looked at John, waiting for the man to finish.

"She got a call from Gibson around twelve-thirty this morning."

"Donovan said she got a call then left in a cab," Nicole whispered.

The room grew quiet for eerie seconds before Nathan spoke. "I'm going up there to get her."

"I'm going with you," John responded.

"You're not leaving us behind. She's our friend too." Eli grabbed Nicole's hand and pulled her along.

They all loaded into John's SUV and pulled off without thinking to tell Sheriff Ross anything.

Chapter 21

Kareem closed his office door and watched as Sheriff Ross took a seat across from his desk. He wasn't quite sure what this visit was about but assumed he wasn't going to like it.

"What can I do for you, Sheriff?" He moved to sit behind his desk. That was his sanctuary. He didn't feel so small, so insignificant when he was sitting there. Instead, he was in charge and commanded respect.

Sheriff Ross cut right to the chase. "Tenile Barnes is missing." Since the other members of the gang had skipped out while he was on the phone, he figured he'd question the only living member that hadn't been present. He thought it strange that the group that had once been inseparable would leave one of its own out. But then Kareem had always been a strange duck.

"Missing?" Kareem laced his fingers together on top of the desk blotter, trying desperately to keep them still.

Sheriff Ross nodded. "Seems she was supposed to be picked up last night by her boyfriend, and when he got there she was already gone. You know Donovan Connor?"

Kareem's clenched his teeth and nodded. "Yes, I do. He's Landy Connor's brother."

"That's right. And it seems he's made himself at home in Tanner. Said he saw Ms. Barnes last night, gave her some disturbing information. You wouldn't happen to know what that information was, would you?" Kareem looked nervous, Albert noted. But then he'd always looked as if he were about to burst into tears.

"I didn't know Mr. Connor was back in Tanner. You said Tenile was supposed to be picked up by her boyfriend? You mean Nathan Hamilton?"

"Yup, she and Dr. Hamilton are a couple. Pretty hot and heavy as far as I can tell."

Kareem's fingers tightened. "Have you questioned him about her disappearance? I mean, he would be the most likely suspect, wouldn't he?"

"I reckon he would." Albert rose, walked around the room surveying Kareem's degrees and certificates. "You're pretty educated, aren't you?"

"My father thought education was important. I happen to agree with him." Releasing his hands, he drummed his fingers on the desk. "Have you questioned Nathan?"

Albert continued walking around, picking up photos from Kareem's credenza. "This is the Connor girl. Landy was her name, right?" He held up a silver-framed portrait of a pretty face with dancing eyes.

Kareem leapt from his chair, snatching the picture out of the sheriff's hand and placing it back in its place gently. "Yes, it is." He made sure the picture was in its exact spot. "Look, Sheriff, I haven't seen Tenile for a couple of weeks."

Albert watched Kareem's movements carefully. "Last time you saw her, what did you talk about?"

Kareem took a deep breath. "We talked about why she was sleeping with that murderer."

"So you think Hamilton killed Landy Connor?"

"I know he did."

"Seem pretty sure of that, don't you? If you're so sure, why's Hamilton still walking around a free man, ten years later?"

"Proving him guilty is not my job. It's yours. Now if you'll excuse me, I have work to do." Kareem went to the door and wrenched it open. "I hope you find Tenile and that she's safe. But living with a man like Hamilton, I don't see how that can happen."

Albert had all he'd come to get, so he walked toward the door. "I'll be sure to keep you posted. If there's been another murder in Tanner, you can bet I'm going to arrest me a killer this time."

Kareem hastily closed the door behind the rotund officer. His head rested momentarily on the door before he went to his desk and picked up the phone.

⚬⚬⚬

It was still pretty early in the morning and little slivers of sunlight fought their way through the gaps of trees, shimmering on the newly green leaves of maples and ferns. The air was cool as they climbed higher. Tenile let herself get lost in the scenery.

She noted the various patterns of bark on the giant trees, the shape of the leaves, sounds that echoed around her. Robert was silent as he walked ahead of her, and she was glad. She didn't want the pressure of keeping up a conversation as she walked through the rugged terrain. At some point while they were up here, she'd have to tell him there was no future between them. Then when she returned to the cabin, she'd gather her stuff and find a hotel.

He maneuvered them along trails and through brush as if he were very familiar with the area. As she watched him, her footing slipped again on the twigs and moss underfoot. They were pretty high now. She heard a rustling sound and looked to her left. There, about eighty feet down, a stream bubbled placidly, sweeping through a leafy bed of ferns.

"Need a break?" Robert yelled over his shoulder.

Because she was getting a little winded and the sound of the stream had made her thirsty, she nodded.

Robert walked only a bit further until he was standing beneath a thick patch of trees, their branches so full the sun couldn't penetrate. Out of his backpack, he withdrew a blanket and laid it on the ground. "C'mon, take a load off."

She did just that, dropping her own hiking pack to the ground before sitting on the blanket. "It's beautiful out here," she commented when Robert joined her.

"Yeah, it is." He leaned in, put a hand to her cheek. "You're beautiful, Tenile."

His voice was soft, his eyes tender as his fingers rubbed lightly against her skin. She didn't want to tell him now, but he looked as if he were still thinking them a couple, which was partially her fault because she hadn't told him otherwise. "Robert," she began.

His fingers brushed over her lips. "I've been thinking about you so much lately, thinking about our relationship and what the future holds for us."

"About the future, Robert, maybe now's a good time to talk about that."

"I don't want to talk right now." He moved closer to her, until his long legs were lined up with hers. "It's been weeks since I've been near you. I just want to enjoy some time looking at you, touching you."

A hand behind her head moved her face closer to his. Then his lips touched hers. The kiss felt foreign, out of place. His lips were cold, intruding. She tried to pull back, but he wrapped an arm around her waist and pulled her even closer, his tongue dipping into her mouth, which had opened in protest.

She felt as if she were choking as his thick tongue plunged and probed. His head moved insistently, and his hands groped her body. "Robert," she gasped.

"Oh, Tenile, baby, I've missed you so much."

He was lowering her to the ground, climbing on top of her. All the while his tongue was finding her cheeks, her chin, as she moved her head from side to side in avoidance. "Robert, we need to talk." Planting her palms on his chest, she pushed to no avail.

Robert grabbed her right breast, squeezing until she yelped in pain. His other hand went to her jeans, pulling at them until they were open. "Tenile," he murmured as he continued to grind his pelvis against hers.

For the first time in her life, she felt real fear of a man, thought that she might be raped. Briefly, she wondered if this was what Landy had felt the last moments of her life. She would not be a victim! With all the strength she could muster, she bucked beneath him, swinging her arms wildly at the same time. Her nails caught him across the cheek.

Robert reared back, howling in pain.

Balling her fingers into a fist, she rammed it in his groin and waited for him to roll over in predicted pain. When he was off her, she jumped up, scrambling away from the blanket.

Run.

She heard the voice, didn't stop to question it, only obeyed.

Her legs moved faster than they ever had. Low hanging branches and vine maple created havoc for her getaway, slapping against her face and arms at every turn. Still, she kept moving. The problem was, she didn't know where she was running to, and the second she realized that, she stopped to look around, to catch her breath. She had no sense of direction, no clue which way was back to the cabin. She cursed herself for not being more observant. As if on cue, dark clouds moved overhead, covering the sun. Tenile looked frantically one way, then another.

Then she felt a blinding pain at her temple and all went dark.

❦

Nathan was quiet as they rode toward the resort where Robert had rented a cabin. Thoughts of Tenile and her safety ran rampant through his mind. If this Robert person hurt her in any way, he'd kill him, plain and simple. He'd come back after all this time to claim the love he'd been denied, and he wasn't about to let anyone take her from him.

He only hoped he wasn't already too late.

John pulled the truck to a stop. "Wait here; I'll go see what I can find out from the caretaker."

Nathan obliged, only because he was in no shape to talk to anyone rationally at the moment.

"I thought Robert was the dullest guy on earth when Tenile introduced me to him," Nicole said from the backseat. "Never would I have imagined him a killer."

"A killer?" Eli questioned.

"Yes, a killer. If he's working for that bitch Miranda Connor, then he's the one who killed Landy. Miranda never liked Landy. And you said

Donovan and his mother thought that Landy had inherited too much of her father's fortune. That gives them more than enough motive."

Nathan listened. Her logic was right on the nose. Robert or Kent or whoever the hell he was would have had the perfect opportunity to lure Landy away. He'd gotten intimately involved with her for that purpose alone. And if that were true, then the odds were he'd gotten intimately involved with Tenile for the same purpose. But Tenile didn't have any inheritance.

"My only question is, why would he now go after Tenile?" Nicole continued, ignoring Nathan's silence.

"Because he thinks she knows where the money is, just like Donovan did," Eli said solemnly, trying not to feel guilty for the way things were turning out.

"He thinks that she knows where it is or I do." Nathan finally joined in the conversation, his hand rubbing nervously over his beard. "But he can't find the money if we're dead. So he'll keep her alive long enough to question her at least." He reached for the door handle, about to get out of the truck and demand to know where Robert was, when he spotted John exiting the log cabin.

The driver's side door swung open and John hopped in. "Not good news," he frowned.

"Don't tell me that, John. I don't want to hear anything negative."

John shrugged. "Okay, then I'm positive they've gone on the hiking trail towards the mountain."

Nicole looked out the window. In the distance, far in the distance, was a mountaintop. "Oh my God," she whispered.

"We'll never find them," Eli added.

"Drive the truck as far up the trail as you can, John. I'll walk the rest of the way." Nathan pulled his seatbelt across his body and latched it. "I *will* find her," he vowed. "I have to."

❧

She looked so innocent, so quiet and serene. He didn't want to tie her up, didn't want her to look as if he were forcing her to be with him. He'd tried to force someone else to be with him, but that hadn't worked either.

It was just a job, he knew, but somehow these women seemed to grow on him, making him wish—even if just for a moment—that they could be more than just a means to an end. Miranda was paying him well this time, whether or not the money was ever found. She wanted this entire episode wiped from her life. Any and all connections to her stepdaughter and that trunk were to be erased.

Over the course of time, the others would succumb to accidents or be lost without a trace, but Tenile, she had to go now. That would force Hamilton to be more cooperative. Landy had confided in him; she would have told him where the money was hidden. Of that, he was sure.

But first, he deserved some sort of compensation for the here and now. Landy had been difficult. She'd turned him away, betrayed him. This time would be different. He unbuttoned Tenile's shirt and slowly removed it from her limp body. Her bra was sexy, pink lace that barely held the huge globes in place. He licked his dry lips and swallowed. Impatience got the best of him, and he ripped the wisp of a bra from her chest, heaving as her breasts exploded into full view.

He filled both his hands, moaning as the soft skin gave under his ministrations. His penis hardened to the point of distraction, and he quickly undid his pants to set it free. Leaning over, he stroked one nipple with his tongue, grabbing the tiny nub between his teeth and biting down. She didn't move, didn't say a word. She wasn't dead yet; he'd already made sure of that. He hoped she'd regain consciousness just as he entered her. She'd look up and see him atop her, feel him inside her and want more. She'd beg for more.

With one hand he stroked his hardness while the other fondled her right breast, his mouth gorging on the left one. He was in heaven, pleasure sending him into a haze of euphoria. When he felt sure he'd burst with joy, he went to her pants, pulling at them with zeal.

She murmured.

"Not yet, baby." His breathing was hitched as he pulled the denim down her hips, along with her panties. "In a few minutes. Everything will be just fine in a few minutes." Thrusting two fingers into his mouth, he licked them thoroughly, then slipped them into the triangle of brown curls until they were deep inside her. He closed his eyes in sheer bliss.

Get up, Tenile. He'll hurt you.

The words echoed in her head. She tried to clear the fog from her mind, but it was so thick; her eyelids felt so heavy. And pain, somewhere far off she could feel pain pressing its weight against her.

"Tenile."

She heard a voice unlike the previous one. This voice was deeper.

"Tenile."

A man's voice.

"Tenile, can you hear me?"

Nathan. The voice belonged to Nathan.

The terrain was rugged the higher Nathan climbed. He wasn't wearing boots, so he slipped frequently. But that didn't deter him; he needed to find Tenile. The truck had taken them as far as it could; then he, John and Eli had jumped out to search on foot. They were all shouting her name, prayerfully alerting Gibson that they were there, looking for him.

As he tackled a few particularly bothersome vines, Nathan heard water murmuring and moved in that direction. Scanning the area, he spotted a bag and moved to retrieve it.

"What've you got?" John approached.

Nathan opened the bag and pulled out a small black wallet. He almost lost his voice at the discovery. "It's hers. She's been here. Let's go!" Nathan tossed the bag to Eli and kept moving.

She whimpered; that was all she could manage. Somebody was touching her. Was it Nathan? Hands were all over her, in private places, touching, stroking. It couldn't be Nathan. She didn't feel that familiar warmth she did when he touched her. But who?

Get up, Tenile!

Landy's voice yelled at her this time, just as she felt her legs being spread wide. Gathering all her strength, she opened her eyes, tried to focus. Her breath was stolen as she recognized Robert. He was smiling down at her, his eyes dark and traitorous.

"Yeah, that's it. Wake up, baby. It's time," he whispered.

His cold lips touched hers, and his tongue thrust into her mouth, causing an instant gag reflex. She raised her arms then, pushing at his shoulders. "Stop. Stop it."

"Not yet. Not yet. I'm almost there. It'll feel so much better when I'm there." Robert used his hand to guide his erection closer to her opening.

Tenile felt him between her legs, felt him trying to gain entry. She desperately locked her legs together and raised up on her elbows. "Robert! Stop it! Get off of me!"

Damn it! He couldn't get inside of her; she was moving too much. "Keep still. Keep still and it'll all be better."

She ignored his words and began swinging her arms in wild circles, hitting him in the face, chest, everywhere. "Get off of me! Get away from me!"

Robert cursed himself for not having been smart enough to tie her up. He grabbed both her wrists and pinned her down. "It'll be good, baby. I promise." He dragged his tongue down her cheek and tried to enter her again.

Tenile screamed for her life. She'd rather die than be raped. She wouldn't go down without a fight. Taking a deep breath, she screamed again.

"Shhh, I'm almost there," Robert groaned before the collar of his shirt tightened around his neck and he felt himself being lifted into the air.

Nicole, who was supposed to be in the truck, came from behind the men she'd been following and ran to Tenile's side. "Oh my God. Oh my God. Did he hurt you?" she was asking as she found Tenile's clothes and tried to help her up.

Nathan didn't notice Nicole. He was too busy pummeling Robert. Emerging from the trees, he'd heard her scream a second time. When he saw Robert on top of her, his vision had gone red.

"Nate! Let him up! That's enough." John tried to grab Nathan, but the man was swinging wildly, and if he wasn't careful, he'd be the recipient of one of those vicious blows himself.

Eli approached the men and motioned to John. On the count of three, they both grabbed one of Nathan's muscled arms and pulled him away from Robert, who now lay in a pitiful heap, his genitals exposed, his face bloodied.

"Nathan." Tenile's voice cracked as she called out to him. She'd seen him beating Robert, seen the rage flowing through each punch as he beat Robert.

He heard her voice, turned to see her staring at him, felt his heart thumping wildly. John and Eli still held his arms, and he tried to break free to get to her. "Tenile."

When John and Eli let him go, he moved quickly to where she stood but stopped cold when she stepped behind Nicole. "No. Stay away from me. I don't want you near me ever again."

Chapter 22

Nathan, Eli and John sat on the hard bench of the Bar Harbor Police Department watching as Robert Gibson, a.k.a. Kent Regan, was arrested for the murder of Landy Connor and the abduction and sexual assault of Tenile Barnes. As was to be expected, Regan was denying the murder of Landy since he hadn't been caught in the act. However, no one gave any credence to his denial.

The joy Nathan had thought he'd feel at uncovering the real murderer was dulled by Tenile's refusal to see or talk to him. She'd allowed Nicole and Eli to help her down the mountainside, never once looking his way. Taking John's advice, he'd left her alone, giving her time to get herself together. She'd just been through a really traumatic ordeal and didn't need him pressuring her.

Still, he hated not being able to touch her, to hold her, to assure her that everything would be fine now. The distance between them now felt further than it had when he was in New York. He knew this stemmed from what Donovan had so carelessly told her. He wanted the chance to explain, but she wasn't giving him one. This time Tenile was the one leaving.

"She'll come around," Eli told him when they'd all piled into John's SUV again.

Nathan let his head fall back on the seat. His hands were bruised and swollen, and his head and his chest hurt with an indescribable pain. "I guess."

"I can tell her what you told us. That might make it better," Eli offered.

"No. When the explanation comes, it should come from me," Nathan said. "I'll just give her some time."

"You want to go back to Tanner now, or do you want to stop by the cabin to see if she's still there?" John asked.

"They're already gone. Nicole called me a half hour ago saying that Tenile wanted to go home." Eli looked over at Nathan. "To her mother's house."

Nathan's lips set in a firm line as he tried not to frown. That act alone caused his head more pain. "We'll go back to Tanner now. I want to sleep in my own bed tonight." Tomorrow he'd go and talk to Tenile. He'd give her tonight to get herself together, and tomorrow he'd go to her and make her listen to what he had to say. From there, the ball would be in her court.

After a long soak in the tub, Tenile sat in her mother's living room with a cup of hot tea. Nicole was still there, sitting on the sofa with Tracy while Oneil hovered, fussing with a quilt over Tenile's legs.

"Mama, I'm fine," she complained.

"I know you are now that the crazy fool that tried to hurt you is behind bars." She fluffed the pillows behind Tenile's head before she gently guided her cup to her lips. "Drink this; it'll help you relax."

Tenile gave a bleak smile. "Then maybe *you* should have two cups."

"That's for sure," Tracy laughed.

"Hush up, the both of you." Oneil moved across the room to pull Nicole's hair from her face. "You alright, baby? You've been through something too. Climbing mountains and approaching murderers."

Nicole sighed. "I'm fine, Mrs. Barnes. Actually, I think I'm going to head home now." She tried to stand.

"Nonsense." Oneil clapped both hands on the young woman's shoulders and pushed her back into the chair. "You don't need to be alone. You'll stay here tonight. In the mornin' I'll fix us all a good breakfast, and then we can move on."

"That's not necessary—" Nicole began.

"For goodness sake." Oneil put her hands up in the air. "You are the mouthiest girls I've ever seen. Don't know how to hush and do as you're told."

"Don't argue with her, Nicole. Just get your cup of tea and relax for the night," Tracy added.

Nicole looked at Tenile when Oneil left to get her the cup of hot tea. "How're you doing?"

Tenile sighed. She didn't really know the answer to that question. "I don't know. I don't really think it's all had a chance to hit me yet."

"You must have been terrified when you came to and he was on top of you." Tracy frowned.

"I was." Tenile held her cup tightly in both hands. "I was actually more afraid when I saw Nathan beating him. He could have killed him."

Nicole sensed where Tenile was going with this and interceded. "He wouldn't have killed him. Nathan was angry, but he's no murderer."

Tenile rolled her eyes. "Says who?"

"Oh, come on, Tee. You don't believe he's a murderer any more than I do."

"After the last two days, I don't know what I believe anymore."

"I know one thing for sure," Tracy spoke up.

"What's that?"

"He's crazy about you. He was frantic when he couldn't find you."

"I know. You should have seen him jumping all over Donovan and Sheriff Ross," Nicole added.

"That's just because he likes to be in control. He came back to Tanner, said he wasn't a killer, and maneuvered me into his bed. When he couldn't find me, he was simply afraid I was finally thinking for myself."

"You know damned well he didn't maneuver you," Nicole snapped. "You were in his bed because that's where you wanted to be. Where you've wanted to be ever since you first met him"

"That's vulgar," Tenile sighed.

Nicole rolled her eyes. "That's the truth."

"He left me," she said quietly.

"He came back," Tracy offered.

"Only to prove his innocence."

"And to get you back." Nicole stood. "If you're too stupid or too blind to see how much he loves you, then that's your problem. But I was there when we found out who Robert Gibson really was. When we made the connection to the Connors and Landy's death, I've never seen a man so afraid."

"I don't want his fear," Tenile confessed.

"You don't know what the hell you want. That's your problem." Nicole said those last words then joined Oneil in the kitchen.

Tenile contemplated Nicole's words and realized with a start that the pain-in-the-ass chick was right.

She lay awake that night in her childhood bed feeling the worries of an adult. She was in love with Nathan, of that she had no doubt. But could she trust him? He'd come back into her life, taking her on that same roller coaster ride of emotions he had ten years ago. And instead of leaving her, this time he'd lied to her. He'd looked in her eyes, made love to her and lied to her face.

Anger simmered in the pit of her stomach as she remembered their late night talks, when she'd told him about her life in the last ten years and she'd thought he was doing the same. How could he not have told her about this? How could he have kept something like this a secret? And could she ever forgive him for doing so?

Things aren't always what they seem.

The voice echoed through the room. Tenile moaned, pulled the sheets up over her head. "Go away. I've had enough of you too."

Keep your eyes open. The truth has yet to be revealed.

"Go away!" Tenile yelled one last time. She didn't venture from beneath the sheets, but the voice didn't speak again.

Oneil watched her daughter pick at the Cream of Wheat she'd sat in front of her almost twenty minutes ago. If she hadn't looked so distressed, Oneil would have hounded her for wasting food. But she knew what the problem was. She knew that in matters of the heart people often lost their appetite.

Grabbing her cup of coffee, she pulled out the chair next to Tenile and took a seat. "You know you always did blow things out of proportion."

Tenile groaned. "Mama, please." She'd already had this discussion with Nicole again before she'd gone home this morning.

Oneil took a sip. "Since you're begging for my advice, I'll give it to you."

Tenile sighed. She should have skipped breakfast; besides, she wasn't eating it anyway.

"Men are peculiar creatures. Their natural instinct is to protect. And sometimes when they're trying to protect the women they love, they make foolish decisions."

"Then we agree. Nathan was a fool for lying to me, and I was a fool for trusting him again. Case closed." She got up, emptying her bowl into the garbage before carrying it to the sink.

"There was a song like that. You remember it?"

Tenile ignored her.

"'Why Do Fools Fall in Love?' That's what it was called."

"Mama, I've accepted that I was a fool. I don't need you rubbing it in."

"No, you need me to slap some sense into you. And if you keep giving me that sass, that's exactly what I'm going to do," Oneil snapped. "Now take a seat. I'm not finished."

Grudgingly, Tenile went back to the table but cautiously took a seat across from her mother instead of beside her. Her mother's urge to slap her might prove too powerful, and Tenile was in no mood for that. "Sorry, Mama."

"I don't need your apology." Oneil watched her daughter carefully. "But Nathan does."

"What?" Slamming her palms onto the table, Tenile felt her temper rising. She'd been wise to sit across the table. "Why should I apologize to him? He's the one who lied."

"I wouldn't say he lied. He kept something from you. Something he should have told you when he first came back. But that's not lying, and you're not giving him a chance to explain why he didn't tell you in the first place."

"What can he say? How can he explain keeping something like that from me?"

"Baby, sometimes there are things you don't want people you love to know."

"That's ridiculous. You and Daddy didn't keep secrets."

Oneil raised a brow. "Don't be so sure."

"What's that supposed to mean?"

"When your daddy died, I found out some things about him I never knew in all the years we were together."

"Like?" Tenile questioned.

"Like none of your business. All I'm saying is that when I found out, I was angry at first. But then I thought about it, and I began to understand that he didn't tell me because he wanted to protect me. Knowing would have put a lot of stress on me. Stress, he decided as the man of this house, to carry himself." Oneil reached for her child's hand. "I respect that because I loved him. If you love Nathan, you have to at least give him the chance to explain, to tell you that he was only trying to protect you. I can say it, but you won't believe it until you hear it from him."

"Mama, he killed a woman. I mean, Nicole says it was an accident, but still, he was with her and she died. She and her baby died, and he didn't think to share that with me."

"So? You ran off with another man, a man Nathan had to rescue you from."

The women were silent.

"You keep that in mind. He loves you and he came to save you. You owe him the chance to explain."

One part of her mind hadn't let go of that incident either. The thought of Robert and what he'd tried to do to her still made her nauseous. But it didn't change anything with her and Nathan. "And then what?" she pouted. "What do I do after he explains and I still feel I can't trust him? What do I do then?"

Oneil shook her head. "I can't answer that for you, baby. All I can tell you is that if you love him, you'll find a way to forgive him."

There was a knock at the door.

"It's not even eleven in the morning and people are at my door. Probably those damned newspaper salesmen." Oneil got up from her chair, mumbling as she went into the foyer. "I don't want no damned newspaper. Don't know how many times I have to tell them that."

Tenile dropped her head to the kitchen table. She did love Nathan, but right now she had no clue if she could trust him. A part of her didn't even want to try. It had been so much easier those years without him. Her heart wasn't constantly exposed, her mind so frazzled.

Yet she was lonely. Ten years of loneliness had begun to take its toll on her as well.

"Hello, Tenile." His voice was calm and deep, echoing through the quiet room.

Chapter 23

Was she shaking? Of course not.

She'd known Nathan way too long to be affected by him this way. To prove to herself that she could and to show him that she was in control, she stood.

"What are you doing here?"

She looked fragile. Dark circles lay like tattoos beneath her eyes. Her T-shirt was big and hung loosely on her body, yet he still felt a stirring deep in the pit of his stomach. He wanted to take her in his arms, to convince himself that she was safe and the nightmare they'd experienced yesterday was over.

That spark of anger in her eyes held him back. "There's something I need to clear up. Something I need to say to you."

"Why say it now? You haven't felt the need to purge yourself in all this time." Needing to get away from him, she walked out of the kitchen.

Nathan followed her into the living room.

"Okay, you can pout while I talk."

"I don't want to hear anything you think you need to say." *And I'm not pouting.*

Her attitude was making this harder than he had anticipated, but he wasn't giving up. "Kelly Peterson was my patient. Her husband abused her. When I tried to help her, we were run off the road. I crashed into a tree, and she and her unborn baby died." He moved to the window, looking out at the overcast sky, the children playing across the street.

"I don't blame myself for her death. I blame the person responsible, the person who hit my car. Her husband."

Tenile listened although she'd sworn she didn't want to hear it.

"I should have told you." He turned to face her then.

She watched him, her eyes asking the question she refused to speak.

"I didn't want you to wonder about me. For years I've lived with the belief that you considered me a murderer, just like everyone else in this town. I could deal with what they thought because they didn't matter. You mattered, your opinion of me mattered." He brushed a hand over his goatee and sighed heavily. "When I came back, I wanted to prove to you that I wasn't a murderer. Telling you about Kelly Peterson to start with seemed like a big complication."

"So you lied."

"I didn't lie. I just kept it from you."

He moved closer to the chair where she sat. "I was wrong. I should have trusted you—trusted us—enough to tell you. And for that I apologize."

Tenile stood, outraged that he thought his soft-spoken apology was all she needed. "I don't want or need your apology, Nathan. You made a choice, and now it's time I do the same."

"So my apology is useless?" Slipping a hand into his pocket, he looked grim. "Tell me, Tenile, what can I do to make it up to you?"

She hesitated.

"There's nothing you can do." Wringing her hands in an effort to keep from touching him, she tried to remain focused. "This whole thing is stupid. We're two different people now. We should have never tried to rekindle something that went so wrong before."

He took a step closer, reached for her.

"We didn't go wrong. Circumstances got in the way. We were fine."

They had been more than fine. On their way to New York, to a new life together.

"We were young, idealistic and immature." She took a step back. "Things are different now."

He continued to close in on her. "I love you more now than I did before. I am so sure that you are the woman for me."

His words pierced her heart, leaving a tingling in her chest even as her head tried to shake it away. "I'm not sure I feel the same way."

"What are you afraid of, Tee?" He had her backed against the wall now, trapped.

"I...I'm not afraid of anything." She licked her dry lips. "I just don't think this is going to work."

He grabbed her at the waist, locking them together. "I think you're wrong."

She closed her eyes, trying to find the strength to pull away.

Dipping his head, he kissed her ear. "Tell me this doesn't feel right." He dared her to deny that the same heat that was seeping through him was invading her body as well. He traced a path along her jaw with his tongue.

Tenile sucked in her breath. "This is chemistry, plain and simple," she breathed.

He took her lips then. In a fierce swoop his tongue was in her mouth, stroking and caressing hers with heated passion.

She couldn't push him away, couldn't stop herself from joining in the tumultuous dance he choreographed.

Nathan held her close, his hands moving over the curves of her body, remembering the feel of her bare skin.

She said this was chemistry. He knew it was fate.

"I love you, Tenile," he breathed into her hair when he finally tore his mouth from hers. "I love you."

His words echoed in her head. But they were just words. He hadn't trusted that she'd understand about Kelly Peterson, hadn't trusted that she'd believe in him. That's what hurt her the most. With pain prevailing over lust, she placed her palms on his chest and pushed him away. "That's not enough." She moved away quickly. "You should have trusted me. You should have trusted what we had together."

He was pissed now. What else did she want? He'd apologized, he'd admitted he was wrong—not to mention he'd saved her from being raped, a thought that still had his blood boiling.

His emotions were running high, as he was sure hers were, but he wasn't going to stand there and grovel when she was hell-bent on shooting him down. "Look Tenile, I don't know what else you want from me." He remained where he stood because if he moved any closer to her he couldn't trust what he might do.

"I don't want anything from you. I just want to put this whole nightmare behind me."

"And I'm a part of that nightmare?"

She didn't answer. She didn't need to.

He moved toward the door; there was nothing else he could do. Then he stopped, wanting—no, needing—to say one last thing. "I was stupid to leave you ten years ago. I came back for you, for our future. But I can't make you want me. And I won't beg you to accept my feelings for you." He chanced one last look at her. His eyes held hers captive. "I will always love you, Tenile. When you're mature enough to accept that, you know where to find me."

With that he left her standing there and closed the door between them, cursing the events that had again torn them apart.

"So you let her go just like that?" Eli asked when he and Nathan sat across from each other in the hospital cafeteria.

Nathan sprinkled salt on his french fries. "I can't keep a woman who doesn't want to be kept."

"You aren't even going to fight for her?"

Nathan threw Eli an irritated look. "I've been fighting for her for the last ten years. My twelve rounds are up."

"The ten years were your fault," Eli added as he took a bite of his burger. "You backed yourself into a corner with that one."

"I know it's my fault." He stuffed a fry into his mouth. "Everything's my fault, but at least I'm man enough to admit my mistakes and try to make amends. She's content to sit in her corner crying about trust and love not being enough."

"Nothing's ever enough for women."

Nathan almost agreed with him. "Did you fix things with Nicole?"

Eli chewed, shaking his head.

"Then don't give your advice about me and Tenile. All Nicole wants is a commitment. Tenile wants my heart on a stake."

"I don't know about a commitment. Nicole is just gonna have to get over that. You, on the other hand, need to keep at Tenile. If you two aren't together, I'll lose all faith in relationships."

Nathan paused, another french fry half way to his mouth. "You don't have any faith in them now. That's why you won't commit to Nicole."

Eli took another bite then drank some soda. "You and Tenile give me inspiration."

Nathan smirked. "Then you'd better find religion or something because it doesn't look like I'll be able to help you."

❧

It was June 18.

Ten years to the date that had changed his life.

Tonight the circle would be complete.

The betrayal would come to an end.

❧

Tenile stepped out of the car wondering why she'd allowed her mother and Nicole to talk her into coming out.

"You need some air, you're starting to look sickly," Oneil had crooned.

It had been almost a week since she'd been out of her mother's house. She'd taken sick leave from work, stating that she was emotionally ill after her traumatic experience.

Only she, her mother and Nicole knew she was really just avoiding Nathan. But she didn't have many sick days left, so she would either have to find another job or get over Nathan really quickly.

From the vivid dreams she had nightly, wherein he was the main attraction, she doubted the latter was going to happen anytime soon.

The park always looked so festive at the annual picnic. White lights twinkled in the young trees lining the entrance, and tables topped with linen cloths and citronella candles were everywhere. Kids ran free, some with sparklers in hand. Grills were fired up and the DJ the mayor had hired—instead of the huge band he usually commissioned that everybody hated—was playing some funky tracks.

Everybody looked to be having a wonderful time. Tenile vowed she was going to put forth the effort to do the same. And she was on her way to doing just that when dark eyes seemed to search through the crowd and land on her.

"He should be the spokesman for the local gym or the poster child for sexy ass black attire. Look at those arms." Nicole ogled him.

Tenile didn't have to ask who she meant. She wasn't blind and Nathan did look good in all black, his muscled legs showing from beneath his shorts, his defined chest wearing that shirt like no other man could.

"There are a lot of handsome men out tonight," Oneil added.

"The one I was talking about is headed this way." Nicole elbowed Tenile with a grin. "I could just drink him up, like a tall glass of fine wine," she moaned.

"Put a cork in it, hot pants. Your entrée's on the left," Tenile told her. She and Nicole were friends, which meant that even though Tenile didn't want Nathan, he was off limits to Nicole.

"How do you know I wasn't talking about him?"

"Because you don't want to see Eli any more than I want to see Nathan."

"Yeah, but that's totally different." Nicole smoothed down her blouse, licking her lips as the men approached.

Tenile looked at her, shaking her head. Nicole would never change. In just a matter of time, she'd be sleeping with Eli again. She couldn't resist. Turning her gaze back to the fine brother in black, Tenile vowed she wouldn't give in so easily.

"Ladies, it's a pleasure to see you here." Eli stepped up first, kissing Oneil on her cheek, then pulling Tenile close for a hug. He didn't touch Nicole but looked at her longingly.

"It looks like a good turnout this year," Oneil said just before Nathan gave her a hug.

"Hello, Mrs. Barnes." Nathan embraced the woman he'd always thought would be his mother-in-law.

"Don't give up," Oneil whispered in his ear before he released her.

"Everybody always shows up for good food," Tenile was saying just as Nathan's gaze fell on her. For a moment she feared he would touch her, possibly hug her. She knew she couldn't stand that, wouldn't be able to keep her resolve if he did. So she did the only thing she thought possible. "I see Mrs. Finley over there. I'm going to go speak to her." She was walking away from the little group before anybody could say a word.

All the way across the park, she cursed herself for being a coward. Then, as soon as Mrs. Finley stepped up to give her a hug, asking how she felt after her dilemma on the mountain, she changed that curse to *stupid coward*.

"She'll come around, son." Oneil clapped Nathan on the back as he watched her daughter walk briskly to the other side of the park.

He shook his head. "That may be true, but I don't know if I'm going to wait around for that to happen."

"I tried to tell him he's giving up too soon," Eli responded.

Nicole crossed her arms beneath her chest, giving her breasts and her oil-coated cleavage a lift. "That must be why the two of you are thick as thieves. Neither one of you can stand the heat."

Nathan looked at Nicole and grinned. "I only wish my problem were as simple as yours. As it stands now, I'm about to look for an air conditioner."

Across the grass he watched as Mrs. Finley and Tenile were joined by another familiar face. Kareem, dressed in slacks and a button-down shirt, had appeared, smiling and talking merrily with the two women. Nathan's gut tightened. He'd known Kareem a long time, known what type of guy he was and known that Landy was the love of his life, yet he didn't like seeing him so close to Tenile.

"Mmmmm, I haven't seen Kareem in a while," Nicole said, following Nathan's gaze. "Maybe I'll go on over and get reacquainted." She tossed Eli a seductive look and let her swaying hips carry her over to where Kareem and the women stood.

"I'll tell you what. You two keep standing over here acting like schoolboys, you're not gonna have nobody warming your bed at night." Oneil huffed and left the two men alone.

Nathan looked at Eli. Eli looked at Nathan. They both frowned and turned to walk in the opposite direction, deciding simultaneously that those two women were too much of a hassle.

"I'm glad you're okay, Tenile. I was worried when the sheriff told me what was going on." Kareem looked at her, enjoying the feel of Nathan's eyes on them as they spoke.

"Yes, I'm fine. It was a terrible ordeal and I'm glad it's over."

"Why, Kareem, you're looking really good today," Nicole purred, coming up to stand beside Tenile.

"Hmph, some things shouldn't come from a woman's mouth in public," Mrs. Finley snorted.

"Oh, Mrs. Finley, you'd be surprised what comes out of my mouth." Nicole tossed an appealing grin at the older woman.

"It's a shame. That's all I know. It's a terrible shame." Mrs. Finely couldn't get away from them fast enough.

Nicole thought that was really funny. She laughed and her hands went into the air, only to fall, in a well-orchestrated gesture, on Kareem's chest.

Kareem smiled down at her, remembering a time when she'd barely noticed him. While they'd all been roommates, Nicole had spent most of her time in Eli's bed or following Landy around trying to tell her what kind of man she should be seeing. He resisted the urge to peel the conniving hands from his clothes. Instead, he stroked her cheek. "You've always been attractive, Nicole. It's good to see that hasn't changed."

Nicole leaned in closer to him. "Good things never change. Don't you know that?"

Tenile wanted to laugh. Nicole was so obviously toying with Kareem. She wondered if Kareem knew, wondered if he'd ever known how women toyed with him. Kareem had had a crush on Landy, and Landy had known it. While she was never hurtful to him, she didn't care for him in that way. Sometimes Tenile had sensed that Kareem wasn't all too happy about that. Yet right now, he seemed pleased enough to have Nicole fawning over him.

"I think I'll find the lemonade stand," Tenile said, tired of being the third wheel.

"Go ahead and bring me one too." Nicole continued to wrap herself around Kareem while out of the corner of her eye she looked for Eli.

"Why don't all three of us go? I could use something to drink. Suddenly my throat is very dry." Kareem looked down at Nicole, licking his lips.

Nicole ate that right up. Tossing her head back she giggled. "Sure, a threesome sounds good."

Tenile thought she was going to gag. Instead, she walked along ahead of them, convincing herself that she was looking for the lemonade stand and not Nathan.

As they grew closer to the stand, Tenile turned to make sure they were still following her. They were. As a matter of fact, they'd gotten quite close to her, and when she turned, she bumped into Kareem. He smiled and put an arm around her waist, similar to the way he was holding Nicole, and directed them in the direction opposite from the lemonade stand.

"You know, girls, I was thinking that maybe we could take a walk. You know, find some privacy to catch up on old times."

"That sounds like a good idea," Nicole said cheerfully.

242

Tenile didn't feel comfortable. Kareem was holding her pretty tight. "I'd really like something to drink." She tried to move in the other direction, but Kareem held her firmly at his side.

"We can get some later, after we catch up."

"Come on, Tenile, let's catch up." Nicole wasn't even looking at them. She was searching the crowd.

"I know the perfect spot." Kareem led them to the farthest end of the park, away from the picnic.

"We're leaving the picnic?" Tenile questioned, hoping Nicole would hear the urgency in her voice.

"There're benches over there where we can sit and talk."

Nicole finally got a clue and looked at Tenile in question. "There were plenty of seats back at the picnic."

They were clear of the festivities now, and Tenile was truly panicked. It might have just been remnants of her ordeal with Robert, but she felt something wasn't quite right about this little reunion. "Yeah, I think we should go back and find us a table. That way we can grab something to eat while we reminisce."

"That sounds like a good idea," Nicole added.

With a quick shove, she and Nicole were thrown together. Kareem lifted the hem of his shirt and pulled out a gun. "I have an even better idea," he said, pointing the gun at them.

"What are you doing?" Nicole screeched.

Tenile gasped. "Kareem?"

"Turn around and keep walking into the trees until you reach the clearing," he instructed.

"What? Why are we going into the trees?" Nicole asked stupidly.

"So we can have a tea party," Tenile responded snidely. "Why the hell do you think we're going into the trees?" She cursed Nicole and her flirtatious ways that had brought them this far with Kareem. She would have simply spoken to him and kept on going, but no, Nicole had to show off for Eli, who hadn't been paying a bit of attention.

"Just shut up and go!" Kareem directed.

The women turned and walked towards the trees.

"Oh my God! He's serious, isn't he?" Nicole asked when they were huddled together and headed for the stand of trees under a darkening sky.

"What gave you that idea? The gun perhaps?"

"Look, don't snap at me. I was just talking to him. How was I supposed to know he was a lunatic?"

"You shouldn't have been flirting. Eli didn't even see you."

Nicole pushed her. "I wasn't doing it for him."

Tenile resisted the urge to shove her back. It was pointless, especially with a man holding a gun on them. "Yeah, right. Whatever. We're here now."

"Shut up and keep walking!" Kareem ordered from behind.

"What the hell happened to him? I used to think he was such a geek."

Tenile resumed her spot next to Nicole. Like it or not, they were in this together. "So did everybody else. I'm suspecting that's why he's ticked off."

So much was starting to make sense to her now. But the answers seemed too late.

Chapter 24

The fireworks had begun. Flashes of blue, red, white and green lit up Tanner's night sky. Onlookers ooohed and ahhhed as each new burst offered a kaleidoscope of colors, forging a new memory for each mind.

Nathan remembered the last time he'd watched fireworks in Tanner. Tenile had been by his side, smiling and clapping. Their contest to see who could anticipate the biggest and brightest explosion had been in high gear.

This year he stood beside Eli, who, with a half cup of flat soda and what had been for the last hour a permanent frown on his face, was not his choice of fireworks company. They'd walked around the park, speaking to people they'd known for years, smiling and pretending to be as happy as the rest of the townfolk. Both were too manly and ego-sensitive to admit that inside they were falling apart.

Kareem had cheerfully stood talking to their women while they were left on the outside. That was an awesome twist of fate in and of itself. The norm had been Kareem tagging along behind them, while they—Landy, Eli, Nicole, Tenile and Nathan—stuck together like glue. While Kareem had lived with them, he hadn't really shared the bond. His quiet, distant personality had prevented him from getting closer to the others and had allowed the group to pretty much ignore his existence.

Nathan and Landy had been the only two to put forth any effort to get to know Kareem better, but sometimes even those attempts had proven futile. Nathan remembered the night Kareem's feelings for Landy became apparent to him. It was about a year before Landy's death, when Landy had just returned from a date. She was late coming home, and Kareem was pacing the floor like an angry father waiting for her to slip her key into the lock.

Nathan had been studying for a test but heard Kareem wearing a hole in the foyer floor as he waited. When Landy came in, she and Kareem argued, Kareem yelling that she was irresponsible and inconsiderate of the feelings of others; Landy telling him to mind his own business and to stay away from her because he was creeping her out.

As the peacemaker, Nathan entered the room. Kareem looked embarrassed, Landy infuriated. He offered Kareem a drink and bid Landy goodnight. Kareem didn't instantly admit that he was in love with Landy, but after talking with him for the next hour and loosening him up with shots of tequila, Nathan pretty much got the point.

To his knowledge though, Landy had never returned Kareem's feelings, no matter how hard he'd tried. Landy had confided in Nathan some of the times when Kareem came on to her, even once asking Nathan to tell him to back off. That hadn't gone too well, and from that point on, Nathan and Kareem hadn't been overly close.

Even now with Nathan's return, there seemed to be tension between them. Nathan rubbed his jaw as he remembered Kareem's surprise visit to his house.

But Kareem was the least of his worries. His concern now, tonight, was Tenile. She looked a lot better than she had a week ago when he'd left her standing in her mother's living room. Her eyes had that light of life back in them. She'd seemed happy with her mother and Nicole at her side, until she'd seen him. She'd looked at him with what he'd first mistaken for longing. But it had been distaste.

The man in him wanted to grab her, throw her over his shoulder and carry her away, keep her locked in his bedroom until she melted in his arms. The gentleman, the distinguished doctor, wanted to afford her the space she seemed to beg for. Even with Oneil's encouragement, he hadn't pressed the issue, hadn't even spoken to her.

Now he wondered where she was, wondered if she was thinking about him, remembering the last time they'd been at this picnic together. Another loud burst of color transformed the sky and everyone clapped. Everyone except Nathan. He wanted her, needed her. If he could just find her, he'd try to talk to her one more time—try to reach her, to make her see how much he loved her. If she rejected him, then he'd leave her alone forever.

People crowded around the gazebo, but he was taller than most of the townfolk, so his visual search for her was a little easier. However, he didn't see her. Nor did he see Nicole.

There was another explosive sound, but this time it wasn't from the fireworks. Judging from the thunder and lightening, they were about to be treated to a summer storm.

"You ready to go?" Eli asked, chucking his cup into a nearby trashcan. "It's about to rain anyway."

Nathan still scanned the crowd. He wanted to see Tenile before he left. He spotted her mother and motioned for Eli to follow. "I just want to say goodnight first."

Eli followed, sensing that there was more to it than that.

"Mrs. Barnes," Nathan said as he approached the table where Oneil sat with a few of her lady friends. "I'm going to call it a night."

Oneil stood. "Yeah, I think I'm about ready to go too. Rain's coming." She looked up at the dark, angry sky.

"Are Nicole and Tenile riding with you?" He thought he sounded casual enough even though his stomach had begun to lurch with an unnamed emotion.

"We all came together, so I suspect we'll be leaving together." Oneil eyed Nathan and Eli hopefully. "Unless you fellas have something else in mind for the young ladies tonight."

Eli shook his head negatively. Nathan shrugged.

"Would you like me to find them and tell them you're ready?" Nathan asked.

Oneil saw the expression in his eyes and felt sorry for him. Why on earth her daughter was being so bullheaded, she didn't know. She wanted to help them along as much as possible, remembering her own true love. "Yes, could you do that please. There are a few folks I'd like to say goodnight to. So if you could gather them and tell them to meet me at the entrance, I'd appreciate it."

Nathan smiled. "No problem."

Hurrying away from the table, he grabbed Eli's arm and walked briskly.

"What are you up to?"

"I'm saving both our asses a lot of heartache. We're going to find those women," he said as they threaded their way through people going in the opposite direction. "And we're going to shake some sense into them." Then he looked over at Eli. "I'm going to stand by and watch Nicole shake some sense into you."

"Very funny." Eli pulled his arm from Nathan's grip. "It just so happens I've been thinking things over, and I figure she might have a point."

Nathan grinned.

"A small point," he added. "I'm not hearing wedding bells, but I'm considering a bit of exclusivity."

Nathan continued moving. "That's just grand. Now if we could just find them."

Eli began looking around too. Neither one of them saw Mrs. Finley approach.

"Gentlemen, it was a pleasure seeing you both this evening. I sure hope you don't make yourselves scarce around town now in light of all the talk." She smiled at both of them.

Nathan, a bit agitated by the interruption, searched himself for a genuine smile but came up empty. "Of course not, Mrs. Finley. This is our town and we plan to make that known."

"Nathan's right," Eli chimed in. "The hospital's planning a lot of events in the next few months, and we're going to be heavily involved in the community. So you'll definitely be seeing us around."

Mrs. Finley grinned. "That's just grand. Are you in a hurry?" she asked Nathan, who was still looking around.

"Actually, Mrs. Barnes asked us to locate Tenile and Nicole. She's ready to leave. So if you'll excuse us—"

"Oh, well, you're going in the wrong direction. I saw them headed towards the outskirts of the park with that lovely young Kareem." Mrs. Finley pointed towards the trees at the south end of the park.

Nathan's stomach did one wild lurch, and he found the name for that emotion—fear. He hadn't a clue why he should be afraid but didn't intend to ignore it. "Are you sure?" he asked.

"Sure as I'm standing here. I watched the three of them oh, about fifteen minutes ago. I was wondering where they were going. You know, all three of them. But then I said to myself—"

Eli frowned. "Thank you, Mrs. Finley. Nathan, let's go." He didn't like the implication any more than he suspected Nathan did.

The two men left Mrs. Finley standing right there, staring after them with her mouth agape. "Young people are so fickle."

It had begun to rain, a steady pattering sifting through the trees. Tenile and Nicole stood close, their backs against a huge tree. It was dark here in the midst of all these trees—dark and eerie. There were sounds all around them, crickets, owls, and in the distance rumbling and flashes of lights from the fireworks.

Tenile looked around, trying to ignore the man standing a few feet from them holding a gun. He watched them both in deadly silence. In the growing dark, his features were becoming hard to make out, but what she saw she identified instantly. His eyes were glazed, trance-like, and his mouth occasionally moved as if he were mumbling something to himself. The rest of his body was still, rigid.

He's in the dark.

Landy's words from weeks ago echoed in her head. Pressure built inside her, a hot gush of fear and knowledge.

Twigs rustled beneath his feet as Kareem moved, coming closer to them.

Nicole shifted, pushing closer to Tenile's side. Tenile reached down and grabbed her hand, silently relaying that she too was afraid.

"They will come; I know they will." Kareem spoke slowly, in a calm whisper. "They're the protectors, the saviors. They always were."

He was close enough now that she could see his face more clearly though his tall, long frame was shadowed by the trees and the night. Tenile was afraid, yet curious. She wanted to know the truth. After all this time, she just wanted to know the truth.

"Who will come?" she asked.

"You know," he snarled. "You both know. Nathan and Eli, the ones who always got exactly what they wanted. Money, prestige, women."

"They're your friends," Tenile whispered. "We all are."

He threw back his head and laughed, sending a chill right down her spine.

"I never had any friends. People kept me around because I had money. It was my money that paid the security deposit on that house, and most months, it was my money that kept food on the table and the utilities on."

"We paid our share," Nicole spoke up.

"You," he glanced menacingly at her, "never did a damned thing. Except flaunt your body in front of whoever wanted it. But I didn't want it; I knew better."

Tenile felt Nicole's fear being replaced by anger and silently begged her to stay calm.

"You don't know anything!" Nicole yelled.

Kareem moved to stand directly in front of Nicole, holding the gun to her temple. "You were a slut then, and you're an even bigger slut now. Just look how you were all over me just a few minutes ago. No wonder Eli doesn't want to marry you. You're all used up."

Nicole spat in his face.

Tenile gasped, for she wasn't sure what Kareem would do in response. On impulse, she moved in front of Nicole, shielding her. "Calm down. Let's all of us just calm down."

Kareem wiped his face but still stood close enough so that he had only to lean in to place his lips near Tenile's ear and poke the gun into her side. "You were always the peacekeeper. Your words kept her from loving me while you and Nathan screwed yourselves silly. I wonder. If I'd slept with you, would I have stopped loving her?"

He thrust his tongue into her ear, and Tenile gasped. She didn't move but felt bile swirling in the pit of her stomach.

"It doesn't matter now. None of it matters now," Kareem roared.

Before either of them could utter another word, Kareem pushed them both to the ground, instructing them to lie on their stomachs. "Now we'll all wait, wait until your rescuers come and I can finally end it all. Tonight is the night. The circle will be complete, and we'll all be together once again."

❧

White-hot fear burned through Nathan's gut. His mind circled back to a conversation he'd had with John just this morning. John was a bit concerned that Robert was still adamantly denying any involvement in Landy's murder. He'd confessed that Miranda and Donovan Connor had paid him to seduce Landy in an effort to get closer to her money, but when that failed and Landy turned up dead, he claimed he'd simply joined Miranda in Greece for a vacation. He'd come back to Tanner a little over a year ago at Miranda's request because she felt Tenile might know where the trunk was since she had been the one to pack up Landy's things. Tenile was to be his next target, and he had been ordered by Donovan to kill her if she didn't cooperate. That's what he'd been planning to do on their hike, before his lust got in the way.

Nathan had dismissed it as a lie. The man would much rather face a sexual assault charge than murder one. But since arriving at the park today, since seeing Tenile, something hadn't set right with him. And now he was headed towards the woods to find her. Why would Kareem take them into the woods?

"If she's getting it on with him, I swear I'll—" Eli said as they walked.

"She's not getting it on with him," Nathan answered, positive that they weren't having a threesome in the woods. They passed the first few trees and were thrust into the murky darkness of wooded night.

"You don't know that," Eli whined.

"Look." Nathan turned to him quickly. "I've got a really bad feeling about this." He reached into his pocket, pulled out his knife. "I want you to stay alert. Stop thinking about her messing with Kareem and start thinking about saving her life."

Eli stared for a moment, realization of danger sinking in. "What aren't you telling me?"

Nathan sighed. He hadn't wanted to tell Eli about Robert's statement because he hadn't wanted to believe it himself. But now it looked as if he had no choice. "John said that Gibson's denying Landy's murder, and they don't really have any evidence to support the charge."

"So he's a liar. He's a pervert and a liar."

"And what if he's not?"

"Let's go."

Eli passed him and Nathan followed, secure in the belief that they were both thinking the same thing, both aiming for the same mark.

Nathan had to rely on his senses, straining to catch any sound. To the right? To the left? Straight ahead? He tapped Eli's shoulder and led him in the direction he felt most comfortable with. As he moved deeper, the trees grew thicker, more humanlike with their branches and vines reaching out like arms to snatch the unsuspecting wanderer.

He moved swiftly. The clouds overhead rumbled louder, and rain pelted his face. The storm was coming, in more ways than one.

"We're here, Kareem. It's finally time to end this." Nathan's voice echoed through the night. Instinct had him heading towards the center of the forest, to where there was a clearing—a clearing like the one in the wooded area behind his house, a clearing like the one where they'd found Landy's body.

Kareem heard a voice, then a rustling in the brush, just to his left.

They were here. Excitement and anticipation began to spread through him, and his lips curved into a smile.

With a foot planted firmly in Nicole's back, he applied just enough pressure to make her yell.

"Good girl," he whispered.

And as if on cue, Nathan and Eli appeared through the trees, stepping into the clearing, making the circle of friends complete.

In an instant Eli took in the situation and made a move towards Kareem. Nathan held him back. Kareem laughed.

"C'mon, Doc. Try me." He pointed the gun to Nicole's head as she squirmed beneath his foot.

Nathan found Tenile's eyes. He could tell she was afraid, but she wouldn't show it, wouldn't give Kareem the satisfaction of seeing her fear. She lay perfectly still, watching him, waiting for his next move. Without a word, he assured her that he would save her, that they would make it out of this alive.

Tenile felt a surge of relief as she met Nathan's gaze. He held a knife; not much competition for Kareem's gun, it was still something. She willed herself to remain calm. Nathan would need her calmness. Nicole would jump up and try to scratch Kareem's eyes out the moment she had a chance, so Tenile needed to remain cool. Irrational thinking would make things end badly for them all. She scooted a little closer to Nicole, urging her to keep quiet. The ground was wet beneath her thin T-shirt, and the rain pummeled her back as it grew more intense.

"Now what, Kareem? Where do we go from here?" Nathan asked, taking one cautious step forward.

"To hell, where you belong."

"If I go, I won't be going alone." With his legs spread slightly Nathan gripped the hilt of the knife, waiting for the opportunity to strike. He didn't dismiss the gun in Kareem's hand, nor the fact that in all likelihood Kareem would get one shot off before he could sink the blade into his gut. Nevertheless, that's exactly what he planned to do.

Kareem stared at him. The rain was coming faster now, making him blink away the moisture fiercely. "I've hated you for so long I'm not sure how to react now that the end is finally here." He was soaked, but the gun remained steady in his hand as he glared at Nathan. "I never did anything but try to be your friend. But that was never what you wanted, was it?" Nathan moved a little closer, Eli following right behind him.

"I didn't need your friendship. I had everything: money, a promising future. All I needed was a wife to share that with." Kareem's voice rose over the rumbling thunder and steady patter.

"And you wanted that to be Landy." Nathan stated what he'd already known.

"I loved her more than any of you ever could," he said softly. "I would have given her the world. We were so compatible." A parody of a smile turned quickly into a snarl. "But all of you stopped that! You stood in our way. You never left her alone to figure out that I was best for her."

"Oh my God," Nicole whispered. "You killed her because she didn't want you."

Tenile reached for her hand, squeezing it as they both realized the truth.

"I loved her!" Kareem's voice hitched just as a bolt of lighting stretched above and beyond the trees.

"But she didn't love you," Eli added.

Kareem shook his head, water slinging from his forehead to the ground. "She could have. If you hadn't been constantly telling her what to do, what to be, she would have realized that I was the only one there for her, the only one who truly cared for her." Tears slipped from his eyes now.

"So you killed her because you couldn't have her?" Nathan asked.

"No!" he screamed, aiming the gun at Nathan's head. "I killed her so that you wouldn't have her. I saw how close the two of you were." The gun shook in his hand as he neared Nathan, inching away from the women. "I saw how she came to you with all her problems. It wasn't enough that Tenile worshipped the ground you walked on; you had to pull Landy in too." He shifted the gun to Eli then. "And you and Nicole were selfish and greedy. You wanted her money, her inheritance. I heard you talking about it, plotting how you would get her to invest in your business ideas. None of you really loved her. Not even you!" In a flash he moved near Tenile again, kicking her viciously in the side.

She gasped with the pain but quickly looked to Nathan to assure him she was okay. Nathan gulped. Rage threatened to erupt at any moment. She'd nodded that she was okay—no, she wasn't but she wouldn't ever say that.

"And killing her somehow showed how much you loved her?" Eli probed.

"I wanted to protect her! To keep you all from hurting her the way I knew you eventually would." His head dropped for a moment. "If she'd only listened to me." His voice lowered to a whisper, the gun shaking in his hand. "If she'd just let me touch her, let me make it better."

Nathan saw the gun waver and moved in. He was about two steps away when Kareem yelled, raised his arm and pointed the gun directly at Nathan's head, stopping him cold. "I told her I loved her, that I was the one she was supposed to be with, not you. She tried to say that you were just friends, but I knew the truth. I knew it. I saw you two together. You killed her! All of you killed her!" Kareem was openly crying now, his salty tears mixing with the evening storm, distorting his face and breaking him down.

Nathan stood perfectly still. A sound to the left caught their attention. Kareem turned and squeezed the trigger.

There was a flash of lightening and the distinct popping of a gun, and then a tree splintered. Nathan lunged, his right arm raised to strike. Just as the knife sank into Kareem's shoulder, the gun went off again.

Eli moved quickly, dragging both women across the soggy ground by their arms, shielding them from Kareem.

Tenile jumped when she heard the second shot and turned in that direction.

Nicole screamed, grabbed hold of Eli and wouldn't let go.

Both Nathan and Kareem fell to the ground, the force from the fall knocking the gun out of Kareem's hand. With the knife still lodged in his shoulder, Kareem grabbed Nathan's throat and squeezed. "She would have loved me if it weren't for you!" he wailed.

Nathan struggled to breathe as Kareem's fingers tightened unmercifully. Kareem was on top of him, and he felt the wet earth beneath him, seeping through his shirt and into his skin, heard a rumbling in the sky even as the outside world faded.

Then Tenile screamed his name, and an overwhelming urge to fight built in his gut, rose throughout his body, granting movement to his arms, fitting his hand around the hilt of the blade protruding from Kareem's shoulder. He pulled, feeling the flesh tear from his savage action.

His head felt as if it would explode, his eyes as if they would burst from their sockets, yet he repositioned his hand and thrust the knife into the center of Kareem's chest.

Kareem felt the searing pain but didn't release his hold. This was not how tonight was supposed to end. They were all supposed to die. But if he could just take Nathan to hell with him, all would be well. For years he'd carried so much pain, harbored so much hatred, a release of it all was welcome now. But Nathan still moved beneath him, so he squeezed harder.

Nathan couldn't hold on any longer.

Tenile watched in horror as Nathan ceased movement. Before she could think about her actions, she was standing and moving across the sopping ground, ignoring the chill of drenched clothes against her skin. The smell of blood was thick in the air, turning her stomach as she grew nearer. She saw the gun, bent to retrieve it, held it in shaky hands and aimed.

Pulling the trigger knocked her off her feet, and she landed flat on her back with rain pouring over her and lightning streaking the indigo sky. She didn't know if she'd hit him or not, didn't know if Kareem's terror would continue, spilling onto Nicole and Eli, and truth be told, she didn't care. Nathan was no longer moving, most likely dead because he'd been a good friend.

She lay on the ground with her mind empty of all thoughts except him, his hands on her body, his voice in her ear. He'd said he loved her, that he had come back for her. And now he was gone and with him her will to survive.

Chapter 25

Two weeks had passed, and Tenile still hadn't heard from Nathan, hadn't seen him. Nicole gave steady updates, and Eli had even stopped by once or twice to check on her. Nathan was doing well, recuperating from his gunshot wound and near strangulation, taking a much needed vacation from the hospital.

She had returned to work only last night but had immediately felt the difference with Nathan not around. The town was still abuzz about Kareem's betrayal and death. It would serve as Tanner's main conversation piece for months to come. And would haunt her for much longer. Her job was to save lives not to take them. Still, she knew she hadn't had a choice. But she didn't want to hear anymore about it. Didn't want to think of it another minute. It was over now, finally.

And it was time for her to get on with her life.

But how could she do that? How could she move on when a place in her heart still felt vacant?

"When are you going to give up on this little pity party and get your ass over to his house?" Nicole asked after she'd shared another meal at the Barnes residence. She and Eli were taking things very slowly, so slowly she refused to see him every night. They would maybe have lunch or take in an early movie, but then she'd end her evenings with the Barneses, reveling in the feel of belonging to a family.

Tenile shrank into the corners of the sofa, not really wanting to discuss this with Nicole for the billionth time. "It's over. I wish you would let it be."

"It's not over. Only a moron like you would try on a daily basis to convince herself that she's not madly in love."

Tenile sighed. "Why should I be madly in love? He's not."

"Bull. He's boarded himself up in that big ole house licking his wounds too. I swear, I used to think the two of you were the smartest of the bunch. Now I'm second-guessing that assumption."

Tenile threw a pillow at her. "Shut up."

Nicole blocked the pillow with ease. "Nope, I'm going to say my piece, and this time," she moved closer to Tenile, pulling her by the arm until she sat straight up on the sofa, "you're going to listen."

Tenile tossed her an annoyed glare that Nicole promptly ignored. "You love him and he loves you. Being apart makes no sense. And since you're the one who told him it was over, you have to be the one to go and tell him what a big fat lie that was. Now I want you to go upstairs, get a shower and for God's sake, do something to your hair, then get your body over to his house and seduce him into forgiveness."

Tenile grimaced. "You're out of your everlasting mind."

Nicole stood, hauling Tenile to her feet right along with her. "No, dear, I'm the only one in my right mind nowadays. Get upstairs and get yourself together. I'll drive you over because if you do what I tell you, you won't need a ride home."

Tenile started to protest again.

"Tee, I've never hit you, but you're coming dangerously close to being 'bitch' slapped."

Tenile looked her up and down. She wore black Versace pumps, skintight black pants and a red wraparound top that shimmered like a candy apple. Her nails were painted and designed, her makeup flawless. Who the hell was she kidding? She didn't have a fighting bone in her body. With a chuckle she pushed past her. "Yeah, right. I'm shaking in my pants."

Nicole smirked. "I see you're going upstairs though."

Tenile paused at the bottom of the steps. "Only because the thought of spending another evening with you and your delusions of grandeur makes me want to puke."

"Whatever." Nicole waved a hand and plopped back down onto the couch. "Hurry up, I've got other things to do besides cart you around all night."

"Sure you do," Tenile hollered from the top of the stairs.

❧

Nathan had thought of nothing else except Tenile. Try as he might—all the sports channels, all the medical journals, all the evenings spent talking to Eli and John—Nathan couldn't get Tenile out of his mind.

The incessant pain in his chest could not be treated. No medication could ease his discomfort. Lying in the bed at night was worse. He could still smell her in the room and could still hear her laughter as he tickled her bare feet, her soft moans as he touched her in the right place.

He missed her.

He still loved her.

He wondered if he'd ever stop. If by some small miracle he'd wake up one morning and not feel at a total loss because she wasn't with him. If he'd ever love again.

Moving to the CD player, he absently pushed the play button, not really caring what came on, just wanting some sound in the house. The smooth cords of instrumental jazz filled the air as he poured himself a drink. Sipping it he had to grin. Drinking alone was the first sign of loneliness.

Then lifting the glass, he offered a toast to the empty room. "To loneliness, may it welcome me with open arms." He emptied his glass and was just about to pour another when there was a knock at the door. He might not have heard the faint sound, except for the momentary break in music.

Assuming it was Eli, he put the glass down and took slow strides to the door. He really wasn't in the mood for company tonight. Tonight he just wanted to bask in his own misery.

He opened the door.

"Hello, Nathan."

"Mrs. Winston," he said unable to mask his surprise. He hadn't seen Kareem's mother since Landy's funeral. "Ah, come in."

Betty Winston walked past him hesitantly. Dressed in a pale yellow suit with diamonds in her ears and on her fingers, her silver-streaked hair neatly coiffed, she turned to him. "I won't be long. I just wanted to say something."

Nathan tensed as he closed the door. Kareem was dead. He was a murderer, but he was her son and now he was gone. Nathan couldn't bring himself to be sorry for it, but he could respect the woman's pain. "Let's go into the living room where you can have a seat."

Mrs. Winston held up a hand. "That's not necessary. I just need to explain something."

"I don't understand."

She nodded. "I was the one who sent you the letters and called you. I knew Kareem had killed the Connor girl."

If munchkins had come through the walls singing about a wicked witch, Nathan could not have been more surprised. "What exactly did you know?"

Mrs. Winston took a deep breath and squared her shoulders. "I knew he was in love with Landy Connor and I knew that he killed her. His father and I tried to get him help. Putting him in a mental hospital was the best we could come up with. We tried to keep him in that hospital, but the doctors said he was fine. I knew he wasn't. He was fixated on you."

Nathan could not believe what he was hearing. "So you sent me those letters so I could find out he killed her. Why didn't you just tell the police?"

"The scandal. Stanford was dead set against anything smearing the Winston name. I wanted to go to the police, but my husband forbade it." Tears welled in her eyes. "Kareem was a good boy until he fell in love with that Connor girl. He hurt people and he was ready to do it again. I wanted to stop him this time."

"You just wanted him sent to jail," Nathan said solemnly. Betty Winston had loved her son but had known that he was a danger to others. She hadn't wanted him dead, just shut away as much for his protection as theirs.

She nodded. "I don't blame you or Tenile for what happened. You did what you had to do to protect yourselves. If I had been stronger ten years ago, Kareem would still be alive. He'd be in jail, but he'd be alive. I'll have to live with that guilt for the rest of my life."

She reached for the door and opened it. Turning to Nathan one last time, she said in an emotion-filled voice, "But it was right for you to come back to clear your name, even though it ended the way it did."

Nathan moved to her, impulsively pulling her into a hug. "Thank you, Mrs. Winston, for everything you did to help. Try not to let guilt eat away at you. We all have to learn to live with our mistakes. It's a part of life." He kissed her wet cheek and watched as she walked to her car.

With a deep breath and an even heavier heart, Nathan closed the door again and rested his head against it, wondering when all the surprises would end. Before he could come up with an answer, he heard another knock at the door. He turned and wrenched it open, not sure who he would see this time, but certain he was not in the mood for any more company.

She gave a weak smile. "Hello."

But then again, misery loves company.

He smiled back. "Hi."

"Were you busy?" Tenile held her hands behind her back, her fingers twisting together as her stomach did massive flip-flops.

"No, just relaxing." She looked really good. She'd cut her hair so that it just brushed against her jawbone, framing her face like a dark halo. She didn't wear any makeup, yet her bright eyes and full lips looked absolutely glamorous.

"Oh. How's your arm?" She leaned a little, looking at the spot where he'd taken the bullet. His T-shirt fit him perfectly, outlining his tight pectorals and toned abs. His basketball shorts brushed past his knees, hiding what she knew to be muscular thighs.

He rotated his shoulder, flexing the limb. "It still gets a little stiff, but otherwise it's okay."

They both jumped at the blare of a car horn. At the curb Nicole slammed her palm against the center of the steering wheel. "I don't have all night," she yelled. "Kiss and make up why don'tcha."

Tenile sighed with embarrassment. "Sorry, she's a little antsy. She and Eli still haven't sealed their new deal."

Nathan grinned. "I know. I'm tired of spending my evenings with him. I wish they'd get on with it." He motioned at Nicole. "Why don't you come on in so she'll feel it's okay to leave you?" He stepped to the side so she could enter.

"That's probably a good idea." Tenile turned to wave Nicole off, then made her way through the door, being extra careful not to touch him.

She caught a whiff of him, not cologne, but something all male and all satisfying. Maybe coming in wasn't such a good idea.

Nathan closed the door after he watched Nicole pull off. He turned to see that Tenile hadn't moved past the foyer. She looked about as nervous as he felt. Just a few weeks ago, they'd made love in this foyer. Now they couldn't seem to take a step near each other without second-guessing.

"You look good," he said when he couldn't hold it in any longer.

Her fingers automatically went to her short hair. "I wanted to try something different."

He reached out, hoping she didn't mind, but not caring because he needed to touch her. Soft strands ran through his fingers, and he gave a half smile. "I like it long, but this is cute."

She swatted his hand away. "I'm thirty-one, Nathan. Cute is not an attribute I wish to possess."

He laughed. "Okay. Well, it's appealing."

Her lips turned up at the corners, and she narrowed her eyes at him. "That's better."

"Can I get you a drink?"

She needed a clear mind. Alcohol, combined with the music she could hear clearly and the close proximity of this man she loved, would divert her attention. "No, thanks. But I'd like to sit down."

"Sure, come on in." He led the way into the living room. He went to the bar while she took a seat on the couch. He needed a drink. She wore beige capris, hip huggers that fit her curvaceous form. Her white top was strapless, held up by the heavy globes his hands missed massaging. She smelled fantastic, of soap and summer breeze. Her skin looked sun-kissed, alluring, touchable. The warm liquid slid down his throat, coated his stomach and did nothing to abate the growing desire in his groin.

"I was thinking that we should probably talk," she began. He hadn't looked at her since she'd sat down. He drank his brandy and carefully kept his gaze straight ahead. She wondered if she were too late, if Nicole had been wrong and he was actually over her.

Taking extra care to put the glass down on the counter gently, he cleared his throat. "Talk about what? I thought you'd said all you needed to say."

She rubbed her hands up and down her thighs. This was really hard. She remembered their last conversation, her last foolish words to him. Licking her lips, she decided to simply jump in. Worst case scenario, he'd tell her she'd lost her chance and call her a cab home. Best case scenario…well, she'd just have to see about that.

"A lot has changed since then."

Finally looking over at her, he arched a brow. "And some things haven't."

Tenile expelled a deep breath. "Look, Nathan, the last few months have been really tumultuous for the both of us. I mean, after ten years you came waltzing back into my life, and from there things went out of control."

He grimaced. "Yeah, like a runaway roller coaster."

"I never liked roller coasters." She frowned. "Couldn't stomach them."

"So what now?"

She shrugged. "I don't know really."

He looked at her with impatience.

"I mean, we know who killed Landy now and we know why. We also know that her family is greedy and insane. But besides all that—" She hesitated, took a steadying breath. "Besides all that, I think we both know that there's still something between us that needs to be resolved."

Standing behind the bar was his saving grace. In the loose fitting shorts the sight of his erection would probably send her running. Each breath she'd inhaled and exhaled had sliced him with razor sharp pangs of lust. Her words would have been lost to him but for the fact that he sensed they did need to talk things through before going any further. And he planned to go much further with her. Despite what she said, the moment he saw her he knew. He knew it wasn't over between them, that he'd never be complete without her. Within seconds of their conversation at the door, he'd decided that if he had to, he'd hold her hostage in this house until she accepted the inevitable—that they were meant to be together.

"So are you here to resolve it?"

Was that desire in his eyes? She wasn't sure but he was looking at her strangely, so strangely her breasts began to ache. "I'm here to find out where we stand."

His palms flattened on the bar. "Do you trust my answer to that question?"

"What's that supposed to mean?"

"It means that we can't begin to discuss where we stand until we know if there's basic trust between us. Like you said, a lot has happened in the past few months. A lot of things have come to light. I need to know if you trust me."

His statement didn't really surprise her. She'd accepted that she'd been wrong. She'd been busy whining that he hadn't trusted her or her feelings enough to tell her the truth about Kelly Peterson when she'd been doubting him all along. "I trust you not to intentionally hurt me."

Those words, though they meant a lot to him, were not enough. "Do you trust me to love you?"

She wavered, not sure what to say.

"Tenile?"

Her eyes began to water, and she swallowed, fighting to hold back the useless tears. "I don't know how to answer you, Nathan."

Nancy Wilson crooned "Someone to Watch Over Me" from the speakers.

She shook her head, determined to speak her mind. "All I know is that when we were in that forest, when I thought Kareem had killed you," she paused, her throat clogging with emotion, "I didn't want to go on. I didn't want to live without you."

He moved from behind the bar, slowly.

"These last two weeks have been hell." Her chest heaved as she sighed. "To tell you the truth, I don't know how I lasted for ten years."

He was standing in front of her now, not speaking, just looking down at her with those piercing brown eyes.

"But I know I can't go another day, another minute, without telling you how much I need you." Encouraged by his closeness she continued. "How much I love you," she whispered.

Nathan reached for her hands and pulled her up until her breasts brushed against his chest. "You don't have to, baby." His lips brushed her forehead. "You don't ever have to feel that way again." He hugged her to him.

Her arms wrapped around his waist, and she sighed loudly with relief. "Oh, Nathan."

Leaning back, still cradling her in his arms, he looked into her eyes. "I told you I came back for you. And now that I've got you again, I'm never letting you go."

"I've loved you for so long," she whispered, blinking away tears, though a few escaped.

Nathan kissed each eyelid as it closed and, with the pads of his thumbs, wiped the dampness away before it could stain her face. "About as long as I've been loving you."

He lowered his head, brushed her lips lightly with his own, pulled her bottom lip between his teeth and sucked. Tenile moaned, leaning into him for support. His tongue traced the inside of her mouth, along her teeth. Her legs wobbled. His tongue urged hers to join in. Pulling her closer, he deepened the kiss, loving the way she felt in his arms.

Tenile was completely absorbed, locked in his embrace and enthralled by his kiss.

Then he pulled back, steadied her and let her go.

She stared at him in confusion.

"I'll be right back." Surely he was not going to get her all riled up then casually mosey into another room. Her hands on her hips, she stared after him. That was exactly what he was doing. And she couldn't leave even if she wanted to; she didn't have a car. But it was okay because within a few seconds he was back, a ratty piece of cloth in hand.

He approached her, put his hands on her bare shoulders, then, because he couldn't resist, bent down and kissed one succulent shoulder bone, dragging his tongue across the smooth skin.

Tenile closed her eyes to the sensuous sensations.

He pushed her down onto the chair.

"Look, I'm starting to have second thoughts," she complained when she plopped down unceremoniously.

"Shhh," he advised as he lowered himself to the floor beside her. "I've waited a really long time to do this."

Tenile sucked in a breath as she realized he was on bended knee.

He unfolded the cloth in his hand, revealing a silver band with a sparkling sapphire in its center.

"The night before she died, Landy and I had a long talk about our future. She was really happy for you and me."

Damn! Those pesky tears were forming again. Her bottom lip quivered.

"In that trunk were some gems her father had left her from a mine he bought—"

"—in Africa," she finished for him. "She showed me some of the gems when she first came back from settling his estate. Among the gems was a single ring, this one."

With his free hand, Nathan wiped the falling tears from her cheeks. "She wanted us to always have a piece of her, so she gave it to me. She told me that when I was ready to make it official I'd better do it with this ring."

Trembling fingers came to her lips as she nodded in agreement. "I must have held this ring for over an hour. Just gazing at it, feeling it in the palm of my hand. I loved it."

Taking her left hand in his, he slid the ring onto her third finger. "She wanted you to have it." He kissed the ring atop her finger. "I want you to be my wife."

Her entire body began to tremble, tears flowing freely, blurring her vision. The emotion welling up choked her into silence, so she nodded in agreement. The words simply would not come.

But they didn't need to. He knew. Pulling her into his arms, he cradled her, thanking the heavens and whoever else would listen that they'd been given another chance.

Epilogue

I see you finally had the guts to give her the ring.

Nathan was lying in bed, Tenile by his side when he heard the voice. The bedroom was dark and he'd been awake since he and Tenile had showered and turned in for the night, more than an hour ago. His mind was full of all the things that had happened since his return to Tanner.

He sat straight up, feeling a strange mixture of alarm and familiarity.

I know you didn't believe what Tenile told you. But it's true. I'm still here. Landy.

"Why?" he whispered quietly so as not to wake Tenile who was sleeping soundly beside him.

It's not over.

"What's not over? Kareem is gone. Donovan and Kent are in jail. I don't understand."

My trunk. Nathan, you have to find my trunk.

With both hands Nathan covered his face. He was so tired of hearing about that trunk he wanted to scream. "I don't even know where to look," he said, still not really believing he was talking to a ghost.

Athens. Landy whispered, her voice echoing throughout the room.

"Nathan?" Tenile stirred beside him. "Who are you talking to?"

Not wanting to have her upset and asking a bunch of questions at two in the morning, Nathan lay back down, pulling Tenile close and kissing the top of her head. "Nobody. I was just thinking aloud." His thoughts continuing, he asked, "Baby, what do you think about going to Greece for our honeymoon?"

Tenile cuddled closer, loving the warmth he exuded, and smiled. "That sounds wonderful."

Group Discussion Questions:

1. Tenile and Nicole were totally different and made no qualms about not liking each other. Why do you think they remained friends even after the group had broken up?

2. After Nathan left, Tenile adjusted her career goals. Why do you think she only switched her medical focus instead of choosing a totally different career?

3. Nathan stayed in New York for ten years and was never charged with Landy's murder. If you were Nathan would you have come back to Tanner?

4. What do you believe Kareem's real problem was?

5. Nicole and Eli had a relationship for years and they both understood the rules of that relationship. Was it fair of Nicole to suddenly change the rules and expect Eli to follow suit?

6. After the murder, Tenile wouldn't speak to Nathan then Nathan left town. When Nathan returned do you feel he owed Tenile an explanation and if so, do you think he needed to constantly prove himself to her?

7. What, if any, part in the breakup of their first relationship do you think Tenile played?

About the Author

Artist C. Arthur was born and raised in Baltimore, Maryland where she currently resides with her husband and three children. An active imagination and a love for reading encouraged her to begin writing in high school and she hasn't stopped since.

Determined to bring a new edge to romance, she continues to develop intriguing plots, racy characters and fresh dialogue—thus keeping the readers on their toes! Visit her website at **www.acarthur.net.**

Parker Publishing, LLC

Celebrating Black
Love Life Literature

Mail or fax orders to:
12523 Limonite Avenue
Suite #220-438
Mira Loma, CA 91752
(866) 205-7902
(951) 685-8036 fax

or order from our Web site:
www.parker-publishing.com
orders@parker-publishing.com

Ship to:
Name: _____
Address: _____
_____
_____
City: _____
State: _____ Zip: _____
Phone: _____

Qty	Title	Price	Total

Shipping and handling is $3.50, Priority Mail shipping is $6.00
FREE standard shipping for orders over $30

Alaska, Hawaii, and international orders – call for rates

See Website for special discounts and promotions

Add S&H	
CA residents add 7.75% sales tax	
Total	

Payment methods: We accept Visa, MasterCard, Discovery, or money orders. NO PERSONAL CHECKS.

Payment Method: (circle one):   VISA   MC   DISC   Money Order

Name on Card: _____
Card Number: _____ Exp Date: _____
Billing Address: _____
_____
City: _____
State: _____ Zip: _____